MY BROTHER'S *Billionaire* BEST FRIEND

xoxo, Max Munroe

max monroe

My Brother's Billionaire Best Friend
Published by Max Monroe LLC © 2019, Max Monroe

Editing by Silently Correcting Your Grammar
Formatting by Champagne Book Design
Cover Design by Peter Alderweireld

Author's Note:

My Brother's Billionaire Best Friend is a full-length, stand-alone romantic comedy novel that is part of our **Billionaire Collection**.

Due to the hilarious nature of this book's content, reading in public is not recommended. And we strongly suggest that you reconsider (aka: don't do it) eating and/or drinking and/or operating heavy machinery while reading.

Sidenote: If you're the type of gal who can successfully operate heavy machinery while reading romantic comedies, please email us at authormaxmonroe@gmail.com. We'd like to meet a badass woman like that with those kinds of multitasking skills.

Happy Reading!
All our love,
Max & Monroe

Dedication

To anyone who has ever hit send on an embarrassing text message they wish they could take back: this book is for you.

To Nina, Monroe's former (and very conservative) boss from that German restaurant she worked at for, like, a year in college: Remember that time you received a picture message with cleavage in a bathing suit top and the words
Look at how much fun my boobs are having?

That was crazy, right? You never responded or even brought it up, but just so you're aware, that actually never happened. You might think it happened, but it didn't. It was just your imagination that a tipsy twenty-one-year-old Monroe accidentally texted you instead of her college boyfriend while on a spring break cruise with her friends. Yeah. That definitely did *not* happen.

To *anyone who's ever texted their dad "Hey, Daddy" and gotten something like "You know I love it when you call me that" in response. We're so sorry for the trauma this case of mistaken text identity has caused.
*We've never received this, thank all that is holy and our fathers, amen.

Intro

Maybe

Here I rest, you guys.

R. I. Mother-flapjacking P. to me.

And now, I'm coming to you live from what I believe is the afterlife.

Just think of this as that morning show with Kelly Ripa and Ryan Seacrest, *Live with Kelly and Ryan*.

Only, change the name to *DEAD with Maybe*, take away the celebrity guests, and fill the audience with people who don't mind witnessing a full-on embarrassment-fueled emotional breakdown.

Good God, if I would've known I was going to kick the bucket right before I reached twenty-five, I sure as shit wouldn't have spent the last six years of my life slaving away at Stanford for a bachelor's and master's degree in English Lit.

I would've partied in college rather than studying until my eyeballs bled.

I would've danced on bars. Flashed some nip for beads at Mardi Gras. Actually *gone* to Mardi Gras.

I would have indulged in unlimited pasta night at the Olive Garden instead of counting carbs, and I wouldn't have stopped binge-watching *Game of Thrones* on season flipping six.

I would have tongue-kissed loads of guys and spread my legs like a contortionist for any of them who seemed reasonably adept.

You know, a little bam-bam in my ham-ham.

Some not-too-big, but not-too-small P in my V.

A good old-fashioned pants-off dance-off…

Sex, you guys. I'm talking about *sex*. And if you haven't picked up what I'm putting down from my delirious ramble, I'll lay it out for you.

I've yet to be sexed up by anyone.

That's right. I have officially bought myself a one-way ticket to the afterlife *as a virgin for-freaking-eternity.*

And now, I guess I'll never know how it feels to have an actual penis rub up against my G-spot because, you know, I'm dead. And I'm pretty certain God probably frowns upon people flashing their boobs at the angels and public displays of leg-spreading and *definitely* the unchaste actions of a desperate-to-bone but unwed woman. No way. Heaven's strictly G-rated.

I put it all off. I figured I had time. I mean, I thought I'd at least get to see *The Office* do a reunion special before I went lights out for good.

Although, my parents' flower shop feels more like purgatory than heaven, and I thought for sure I'd be wearing something other than jean shorts and Converse when I headed to meet the Big Guy upstairs.

Honestly, the afterlife feels eerily like real life, and I'm not one to be dramatic, but I *have* to be dead, you guys. Seriously. Because no one could live through what I did.

I'm talking a 10.0 on the Richter Scale of embarrassing and awkward.

A Category 5 hurricane of humiliation.

A twisting, catastrophic EF5 tornado of comedic disaster.

No freaking way I survived that…*right?*

Okay. Fine. So, I *can* be a little dramatic sometimes…

And maybe, just maybe, I'm exaggerating things a bit here, but I'm doing it in the name of self-preservation.

Because, trust me, if you did what I did, you'd let yourself mentally pretend to be dead for a little bit too.

Because if I'm not dead, I'm going to have to face the consequences of my awful, humiliating, cringeworthy actions.

I'm going to have to face *him*.

Milo Ives—a tall, handsome, unbelievably sexy drink of water.

A man I've known since I was a prepubescent girl.

A man I've basically been crushing on my whole damn life.

A billion-dollar-empire kind of successful man who just so happens to be my brother's best friend.

I'll say it again for the folks in the back.

Milo Ives is my brother's billionaire best friend.

And I'm in *way* over my head.

Chapter ONE

Maybe

"Yoo-hoo, Betty! Where is Maybe? I thought she was going to man the front for a few hours?" my dad shouts, his voice filtering with ease into the back room of the floral shop.

Just the sound of it makes a deep, cavernous sigh escape my lungs.

And the fact that he's asking about my whereabouts? Now that's worthy of a tight chest.

"I think she just needed a minute to—" my mom starts to reply, but she's cut off before she can convey any real information. Bruce the super-sniffing shark only needs a trace of blood in the water to attack.

"Needed a minute?" He guffaws. "I've needed a minute for the past thirty years, but you don't see me dillydallying around."

"*Bruce*," my mom chastises. "Stop being such a grumpy bastard."

My dad's been on the warpath since he found out our shipment of Gerbera daisies is running behind schedule, but his behavior really isn't the slow delivery's fault. Today, when it comes to Bruce, isn't any different from any other day.

He always has zany criticism for me and my mother—what we call Bruce-isms—and an overabundance of dad jokes locked and loaded and ready for use.

Deep breaths, I coach myself as I finish up an email to a potential publishing house. *This is only temporary.*

Too bad it doesn't feel that way.

I've only been back in New York for two weeks, but it may as well have been an eternity.

I just completed graduate school on the West Coast and moved back here to find a career in publishing, and all in all, I felt like I was making the right moves. While I had friends in school, I never found the core group of people that would be mine for life, and in New York, I have an emergency support system.

Plus, New York has far more options for a career in publishing than California and over eight and a half million people who could be potential friends.

Honestly, before turning in my final thesis, it all sounded pretty simple.

Find a job—preferably as an editor at a prominent New York publishing house.

Get an apartment.

Find new friends.

Find a man etc, etc.

Alas, things in real life are never as easy as they are on paper, and as a result, I'm currently spending forty hours of my week working side by side with my parents and living out of my brother Evan's old bachelor pad in Chelsea.

As I'm the blood sister of the former resident, the single-guy paraphernalia littering the place is an actual nightmare. But hey, I guess I can thank the stars, the sun, and the moon that I'm not living in my childhood bedroom.

Still, my New York friend count is at a staggering zero, and I'm not even going to address the reality that when it comes to the whole find-a-man task, I'm *woefully* behind the curve.

I just kind of forgot to make it a priority.

I was too busy reading Stephen King novels, studying hard to keep a perfect GPA, and chasing a level of perfection high enough to trigger unmistakable pride from my hard-to-please father.

Bruce Willis—aka my dad—is a man of too many words and

most of them are stubborn, cantankerous, and filled with enough sarcasm to make Amy Schumer's new Netflix special look watered down.

For as long as I can remember, his life has revolved around two things: his family and his business—Bruce Willis & Sons Floral. Established in 1980, my family's florist shop has become one of Chelsea's pride and joys.

Ironically, my dad only has *one* son, my brother Evan, who lives in Austin, Texas.

So, really, it's just Bruce Willis & Wife & *"Temporarily Back Home from Graduate School but Not Planning on Working Here Forever"* Daughter Floral.

But that's too long to fit on the storefront marquee, so I'm stuck dealing with all the looks I get, wondering if I've undergone gender reassignment surgery.

And now I, Mabel Frances Willis, am a twenty-four-year-old, college-educated, sexually stunted woman, who's barely held a penis in her hands.

Prospects on penis-encounters aren't looking great with that old-lady moniker, but thankfully, everyone calls me Maybe. A nickname that was created because my parents realized about two years into my life that the name Mabel wouldn't suit me until I reached an age where senior citizen discounts and Melba toast became a constant in my daily routine.

Although, maybe Maybe isn't the world's greatest nickname.

The utter definition of the word revolves around indecisiveness.

Do I want to meet a man? *Maybe.*

Do I want to have sex? *Maybe.*

Do I want to live the rest of my life as some virginal literary spinster with more cats than chairs in my house? *Maybe.*

See what I mean?

"Maybe!" My dad's voice fills my ears again. "Where are you?"

With the way he shouts, you'd think the shop was a ginormous warehouse, but it's barely 1500 square feet.

"I'll be there in a sec!" I call back, but he doesn't wait. He never waits. Waiting is nowhere in Bruce's vocabulary.

"Okay! But I need to know one thing! Did Phil follow up on the Carmichael wedding?"

"Yes!" I shout back and add my resume to the email in progress.

"And what's the status?"

"The bride is still convinced she wants tiger lilies and cascading orchids in her bouquet!"

My dad's Dr. Evil-inspired chuckles echo off the walls of the shop. "Sounds like that bride is about to take her dear old dad for an expensive ride!"

Oh my God, get me out of here.

I hit send on my email and cross my fingers that this publishing house—*Windstone Press*—will actually call me for an interview. Once the little whooshing sound that signifies my message was sent fills my ears, I shut my laptop, step back out into the main shop, and prepare to face the Bruce-themed music.

"Where in the hemp oil have ya been?" he asks, crossing his beefy arms over his chest. "I thought you were going to man the front."

"I had a few resumes I needed to send out."

"To who?"

"Publishing houses."

"Which ones?"

I sigh. "New York ones, Dad."

"Pretty sure I had that one figured out." He grins at my sarcasm. "So, that's what you do with a degree in books? You work in publishing?"

A degree in books. Jesus, Mary, and Joseph.

I majored in *English Literature* and got my master's degree at Stanford University, one of the most prestigious English Lit programs in the country. With the way he talks, you'd think I went to some back-alley online university and obtained a degree in dog walking, but it's not worth the explanation. I've said all of these things no fewer than a thousand times, and this is still how the conversation always goes.

"Yeah, Dad, that's what you do when you get a degree in books," I respond blandly. "You work in publishing, preferably as an editor somewhere."

"You think you'll be able to find a job in the city?"

"That's the plan."

"Not to stress you out, but it'd be a real kick in the gonads if you can't put that expensive degree to good use. Me and your mom could'a had a tropical love nest somewhere."

Love nest? Jesus. Now I'm stressed and skeeved.

"I've been back home for two weeks, Pops," I say as much to myself as I do to him. "These things take time."

"Well..." He pauses and gives me a good hearty pat to my shoulder. "I guess I should just be thankful I get to see your smiling face here at the shop for a little while, huh?"

My chest eases a little, and I'm reminded of why my mom and I haven't arranged to have him meet an early grave. "I guess so."

"You certainly brighten the place up," he adds with a secret smile that reminds me so much of Evan it's not even funny.

Whereas I am nearly the spitting image of our mom—*long brown hair and big brown eyes*—my brother could be our father's twin.

Which, surprisingly, isn't a bad thing.

With hazel eyes, now salt-and-pepper hair, and a strong jaw, my dad has always been a handsome guy.

"Not to mention," he adds a little too loudly. "You're a real nice change of pace from cranky Betty."

"I can hear you!" my mom chimes in, and my dad chuckles through a big ole, full-teeth smile.

"I know you can!"

"And like you should talk!" she adds. "You've been on a rampage since you found out that daisy shipment was running one day behind schedule!"

"Now, listen here, Betty." Bruce turns away from me to shout in her direction. "It's the end of May, and everyone and their mother wants fresh bouquets! Which means, unless someone wants trouble, no one should get in the way of a florist man and his godspamming Gerbera daisies!"

My mom cackles. "Yeah, so we've all heard!"

My always-bickering, but still somehow in love parents, ladies and gentlemen.

If I added a white horse and shoved my dad in knight's armor, they might as well be a Disney flick.

"Sheesh." Bruce just smirks at me. "What's stuck in her craw today?"

I grin and jerk my chin toward him. "Pretty sure you should recognize a thorn when you see one, Mr. Florist Man."

Thankfully, Bruce takes jabs almost as well as he hands them out, and he leaves me with a smirk as he heads to the back to do whatever it is he does back there.

"He's a real pain in my ass today," my mother says as she sidles up next to me at the cash register.

I laugh and roll my eyes. "He's always a pain in your ass."

"Yeah." She snorts. "You're right. Every day for thirty years, he does something that makes my kettle steam."

I bite my lip to stop myself from laughing at my mom's metaphor and shrug. "It's safe to say there's no hope for change, then."

"No. I guess not." Her smile turns soft. "If there's one thing to be said about Bruce, it's that he always keeps me on my toes."

"Oh yeah. Lifelong toe-walking is great for you. Just ask a podiatrist," I mutter, and my mom doesn't hesitate to defend her husband.

"He means well, Maybe. You know he only wants the best for you." Her wise brown eyes crinkle at the corners. "Just try to remember his intentions come from the heart. And when it comes to his little girl, that sometimes-grumpy heart of his is enormous."

"But that's the thing, Mom," I retort. "I'm not a little girl anymore. I'm a grown-ass, twenty-four-year-old woman."

Her responding smile is far too knowing and sage. "Oh, honey. Twenty-four is so young. You have so much life to live and learn. You'll see."

All I can do is sigh. Because what can I say to that?

I don't know that my mom will ever think I'm grown up, and Bruce does mean well. He wants me to be happy. I know that.

It's just hard to remember during a bout of criticism.

The bell above the front door chimes, and a man wearing khaki shorts and an "I Heart New York" T-shirt steps inside. He has a camera strapped around his neck and a petite, gray-haired wife by his side.

"Hello. How can I help you today?" my mother greets, and the man glances around the front of the shop.

His eyes scan across the floral displays and sample bouquets of lilies and daisies and roses. "This is Bruce Willis's shop, right?"

My mom nods. "It is."

"Holy shit," he mutters to himself more than anyone else. "I can't believe Bruce Willis owns a floral shop."

Oh, here we go...

"Is he...uh...is he here?" he asks, and my mom tilts her head to the side.

"Is who here?"

"Bruce Willis." The man stutters over his words. "I'd...I'd love to get a picture with him."

Most people might think it's funny, entertaining, even, that my dad shares a name with *the* Bruce Willis, famous Hollywood action star. And truthfully, they'd be right. It gets quite confusing for the tourists, but it's been a serious bright spot for me in the past two weeks.

Especially when they stop in, trying to get autographs and roses from the man who kicked ass in *Die Hard,* only to find my sixty-year-old father in a golf polo, khaki shorts, and loafers.

"He's not here." I busy myself filling the cash register with fresh paper. "He's in LA. Shooting *Die Hard 9.*"

"Maybe." My mom nudges me with her elbow, but I ignore her.

The man's eyes light up with equal parts confusion and excitement. "There's going to be a *Die Hard 9?*"

"Yep. *Die…Hardest.*"

Sure, it could be misconstrued as a little cruel, but I can't help myself. This is a daily conversation in the shop. I have to spice things up every once in a while.

He scrunches his brow. "But I thought there were only five *Die Hard* movies…"

"I guess you're four *Die Hards* short, then." I shrug. "But can we interest you in a fresh bouquet of roses by Bruce Willis for your pretty wife?"

His wife smiles at me and then turns a "you better buy me some damn flowers" look toward her husband.

"Uh…" He pauses, but when his eyes meet the stare of doom, he quickly agrees, "Y-yes. Of course."

"And Bruce doesn't think I do anything around here," I whisper toward my mom as the man proceeds to pick his main squeeze a fresh bouquet of pink roses from one of the displays.

She rolls her eyes and grins at the same time. "You're incorrigible."

"And a fantastic saleswoman."

She pinches my side with a firm grip, and I laugh.

My mom handles the money exchange with Bruce Willis's number one fan, and I walk toward one of the front displays and take inventory.

"We're running low on the wild flower bouquets," I call over my shoulder just as the bell chimes the couple's exit. "Do you want me to cut some fresh ones, or do you want to?"

"I'll do it," she responds, and I hand her one of the empty water buckets before she heads to the back.

With my mom otherwise occupied in the back room and my dad likely taking a secret cigar break, I connect my phone to the Bluetooth speakers of the shop to play some music.

While Bruce is adamant he doesn't smoke stogies anymore, we all know the truth. One whiff of him when he strides back into the shop after four o'clock says otherwise.

I scroll through my playlists and click on the fourth one from the top. Today feels like a Billie Eilish kind of day.

In the name of keeping busy and making this day go by as fast as possible, I drag a trash can over to the DIY-bouquet section and start picking through each bushel of flowers, throwing away the ones that are dead, have lost too many petals, or managed to get a little too smashed for my liking.

But I only get halfway into my task when the bell above the front door chimes another customer's entrance.

Crouched down and riffling through the sunflower section, I call over my shoulder, "Just a minute!"

"Take your time," a man's voice responds, which I've always felt is like the Southern use of *Bless your heart,* so I quickly finish what I'm doing.

I toss three sad-looking sunflowers into the trash and rearrange the ones left in the bin so the proudest and prettiest are in the front and then push myself to standing. My apron is covered in petals and flower debris, so I dust off swiftly before spinning around.

But all of my hustling comes to a screeching stop, feet freezing securely to their exact location on the tile floor, when I see who the customer is.

Holy Godfather Cannolis.

Dark hair, cobalt-blue eyes, broad shoulders, and a sinfully firm body, he is the epitome of tall, dark, and handsome.

He's also, it takes me almost zero time to realize, my brother's best friend, my first real crush, and a guy I haven't seen in nearly a decade.

Milo Ives.

He's sporting a pressed, smart suit, and it's apparent he's forgone his old Converse and vintage band T-shirts and jeans preferences and adopted the wardrobe of a suave man.

I stare a little harder, and my breath catches in my throat. Dear God, if anything, he's only gotten more attractive since I last saw him.

Pounding heart, nervous flutter inside my belly, and an embarrassingly ogling gaze, I've apparently left my current body behind and inhabited my thirteen-year-old self.

Briefly, I open and close my eyes just to verify what I'm seeing is real.

But it is real. *He* is real.

Six years older than me, and my brother Evan's best friend since elementary school, Milo Ives was the unattainable apple of my girlish eye for as long as I can remember, and now, he's standing right in front of me.

As he looks up from his phone, he flashes a handsome and oh-so-familiar smile my way, and my chest tightens like a damn vise.

When I was eleven, for six straight months, after his parents relocated to Florida for his dad's job, Milo lived with us to finish out his senior year in high school.

He was busy galivanting with Evan and countless girls, and I... well, I was counting his smiles.

Sleepy, morning smiles. Excited smiles. Amused smiles. Annoyed smiles. You name it, and I memorized it like a swoony-eyed little psycho.

"Hello," he greets, and his voice is deeper, raspier, *sexier* than I remember.

Probably because the last time you saw him, you were thirteen years old...

"H-hi," I stutter through one simple fucking word.

Sheesh, it's going to be a long encounter if I don't get my shit together.

It takes an insane amount of work, but I finally get my feet to move me over behind the counter.

Jesus. How can he still have this effect on me?

One would think, a decade later, I'd be impervious to his good looks and natural charm.

I clear my throat once, twice, three times, and still, awkward misery fully engaged, I'm unable to find my voice.

His gorgeous smile deepens, and I have to put a hand to the counter to counteract the gravitational effect it has on my knees.

Just say something, Maybe. Ask him how things have been. Ask him how he's been.

My cheeks heat and my stomach feels heavy, and I'm now painfully conscious of the coffee stain on my white shirt from this morning.

Just do something besides standing here like a moron.

I tuck a lock of hair behind my ear with a shaky hand and force out three simple words. "H-how are you?"

"I guess I'm doing pretty good for a Monday," he responds, and that smile turns soft on his lips. "Are you new here?"

"New here?" I repeat his words, and he nods.

"I've known the Willis family for a long time. Did you just start working for them?"

He's known the Willis family? Just start working for them?

"I come in here every month or so," he adds with a smirk that quite literally could drop panties. "It's possible I missed you, but I'm pretty sure I'd remember seeing you here."

Instantly, my underwear stops dissolving, and my pride takes a hike instead.

Milo Ives, the star of *all* of my teenage fantasies, has *no* idea who I am.

My pits are sweating so hard they're testing the strength of my deodorant while I try to come up with the perfect thing to say to his strong-jawed, plush-lipped face, and He. Doesn't. Even. Remember. Me.

Oh my God.

"I…uh…just started working here two weeks ago," I push out impulsively, and I have to clear the awkward cobwebs that have developed inside my throat.

Seriously, Maybe? Instead of righting this awkward situation and say-ing, "Hey, Milo. It's Maybe, Evan's sister. Remember?", you're just going to go with the whole "we don't know each other" vibe?!

"You'll love it here," he says, and genuine affection highlights the deep, raspy tones of his too-sexy voice. "The Willises are good people."

Yeah. Sigh. I know.

"Uh-huh."

Path of least resistance solidified, it becomes apparent Willises can be idiots too.

"Well, I just need to put in an order for a bouquet." Too busy berating myself in my head, I just stare at him, and after the silence stretches on for ten seconds too long, he evidently feels the pressure to add, "It's for my mom's birthday next week..."

"Oh...oh...okay... You want to order something..."

"Yes. I would like to order something. Well, flowers, to be spe-cific." He grins. "The order will be under Milo Ives. I should already have a profile in the system."

Yeah, ha. I nod. *I'm painfully aware of your name.*

It takes a good thirty seconds for me to realize this is the part where I use the computer to take his order, and after fumbling with the mouse and the keyboard like some kind of technology reject for an *additional* thirty seconds, I've officially done my part in giving millennials a bad name. Eventually, though, somehow, some-magi-cal-way, I manage to pull up the order screen.

"Do you have any recommendations?" he asks, and I tilt my head to the side in confusion.

"Recommendations?"

"For a birthday bouquet."

Oh, right. The whole reason he's here. *Ha. Ha-ha-ha. My God, someone help me.*

"Uh...well...we...uh... We have a white lily bouquet that a lot of people love..."

"Does that white lily bouquet also encourage forgiveness from a mother to her son because he often forgets to call and check in with her?"

He's being all teasing and joking and charming, but I'm still too damn busy trying to recover from the initial shock of his presence *and* apparent amnesia of my existence to speak my given language effectively.

Bruce was right. It's a good thing I spent all that money to major in books.

"Well…" I shrug and force a smile to my face that probably looks like I'm suffering from an ugly bout of constipation. "I guess it's worth a shot, huh?"

"Definitely worth a shot." He chuckles, and I swear to God, his laugh vibrates all the way from his throat, across the counter, and hits me like a bullet, square in the chest.

It's so unfair. Your childhood crush isn't supposed to get *more* handsome. He's supposed to grow a beer gut and get wrinkles and just… *not look like this.*

I, on the other hand, am apparently too bland to even trigger a memory.

Thankfully, I manage to place his order without making the computer explode, and once the delivery is set and scheduled, I give him the cost. "The total is $52.30, and the bouquet will be delivered to your mom's Florida address next Monday."

"Perfect," Milo responds with a soft smile as he pulls his wallet out of the back pocket of his trousers. "So, are you new to the area or just the shop?"

"Uh…yeah…sort of… I just moved to Chelsea."

He hands me his credit card—a shiny, black, rich-person's credit card.

And, from what I know of Milo, he *is* a rich person. A billion-dollar kind of rich person for whom my brother now works, in fact.

Evan is the CFO of Milo's company Fuse, and he currently runs their Austin office.

And I am simply his best friend's twenty-four-year-old sister, with no great career, friend, or dating prospects, whom he doesn't even fucking recognize...

The comparison is rock-bottom depressing.

Jesus. My track record of bumbling and awkward is unparalleled. Seriously. Guinness World Records should be calling me any day now.

The transaction goes through without any issues, *obviously*, and I hand him back his shiny card.

"Thank you for your help," he says and slips the card back into his wallet. "Please let Bruce and Betty know that Milo says hello."

All I can do is nod at this point. It's gone too far. There's no fix for my foolish blundering now.

With a simple wave, he turns on his heels and heads toward the door.

As soon as I'm sure he's gone, I do what anyone would do in my situation.

I lean forward and bang my head against the counter.

What in the hell just happened?

Milo fucking Ives and a hideous display of no confidence, that's what happened.

Ugh.

Just like that, my brain is off to the races, taking me way back when, to the good old days when I was thirteen years old and doodling *Mrs. Maybe Ives* all over my Lisa Frank notebooks.

The damn memories burst out like a geyser.

The way I used to spend the majority of my days trying to find excuses to go into my brother's room just to talk to Milo.

The way I was convinced I would marry him when I got older. How I was certain he would be the man to take my virginity. And how I'd even named our future kids.

Jesus.

I distract my mind with getting rid of dead flowers and rearranging the fresh flower bins, and by the time I step back behind the counter, I've nearly forgotten all about the fact that Milo was in the shop and didn't recognize me.

Hah. *Right.*

Frustrated, I slam my hand on the counter next to the computer mouse, and the small jump is apparently enough to bring the screen back to life.

A screen that holds all kinds of interesting things.

His name.

His order.

And his *phone number.*

On impulse, I slide my phone out of my pocket and input the digits into my contacts.

My earlier behavior is evidence enough that I'll never use it, but it couldn't hurt to have it just in case.

Right?

Chapter TWO

Maybe

After putting in eight hours with grumpy Bruce, I finish my day by stopping at the coffee shop up the street from my apartment. Aptly named Jovial Grinds, it has become the bright spot at the end of nearly all of my days.

With stainless-steel countertops, checkerboard black-and-white tiled floors, and walls cluttered with abstract art, this hip spot has the best damn coffee in Chelsea and a much better atmosphere for me to focus on my ongoing job search than the flower shop and Evan's apartment.

Believe me, if Goldilocks had been on the hunt for a career in publishing, she'd say the same.

Although, while I'd love to say I'm all business when I'm here, I have to admit it's more accurately a combination of working a little, acting like I'm working when I'm not, people watching, and eavesdropping on the barista's conversations.

But it's the last that's stolen most of my attention. From what I've gathered, her name is Lena and she's worked here for a little over a year.

I know this because her boss reminds her of this fact often, mostly when she's complaining about some item on her to-do list and suggesting it should be a part of someone else's job description.

In two weeks' time, I've overheard her break up with two boyfriends, get swoony-eyes from nearly every male customer that's walked through the door, and have been inundated with her moody music selections—mostly revolving around BØRNS and Lykke Li and Jeff Buckley—anytime her manager goes on break.

With long curly blond hair, tattoos, and a style that revolves around hippie-chic, it's like Penny Lane from *Almost Famous* just came to life and got a job in Chelsea.

But seeing as we've never actually had a conversation, I don't know anything more about her than her outward appearance.

Nevertheless, I get the feeling she's living the kind of life I want for myself—happy, confident, and filled with enough drama to keep it interesting. Not to mention, given her obvious gift for flirtation, it's probably safe to say she's held more than two penises in her hands and knows what it feels like to have one in other places too.

I take a sip of my coffee and try to focus on the task at hand—sending out more job applications and interview requests, but fuck, it's hard to focus.

Graduating from school and moving into the real world has been a big adjustment.

With classes, I always had something to focus on. A task at hand, an assignment to turn in.

The uncertainty I feel now is a stark contrast. In fact, with more than a hundred resumes floating out in the wild, and only a limited number of publishers to pursue, I feel like I'm sitting idle, just waiting for something to happen.

What that something is, I have no idea.

I mean, who says I'll even get up the courage to pounce on an opportunity when the time is right?

Seeing Milo Ives at the shop today has been the most exciting, adrenaline-inducing thing that's happened over the last two weeks, and I couldn't even muster the courage to tell him who I was.

What is wrong with me?

I take a sip from my cup and swallow the cooling coffee along with my sigh. Barista Lena is two tables over, chatting with a handsome, tatted customer in a beanie, and I'm...doing nothing.

Aggravated, I swipe my phone off the table and start scrolling through apps to occupy my mind. When none of the useless drivel satisfies me, I go back to the beginning and stare at the little phone icon where I know my list of contacts is.

Where I *know* Milo's illegally procured number is.

What could it hurt? I mean, who knows? I might be able to right my awkward wrong and have a conversation with him where I don't have to pretend I'm a complete stranger?

Stranger things have happened…*right?*

I squeeze my eyes tight and my fist closed, but when I open both of those, I also open a new text message.

Okay. First of all, just be cool, Maybe.

Just be cool and say hello. It's literally that simple.

Hi, Milo! It's Maybe! I actually saw you at the shop today and you didn't exactly recognize me, but the girl who took your order was me! Hahahahaha! CRAZY, RIGHT?

Cheese and rice. Why am I shouting at him?

Delete.

Hey, Milo. It's Maybe. Maybe Willis. Evan's sister. Do you remember me?

Considering I was standing right in front of him today and he thought I was a complete stranger, this seems moot.

Delete.

Yo yo yo, Milo.

Son of a weirdo. **Delete.**

So…just out of curiosity…you didn't happen to suffer some sort of brain injury that makes you forget people, did you? Oh, ha. It's Maybe Willis, by the way.

Valid question, but *ugh*. **Delete.**

I start to type out what will be my thirtieth failed text message, but an actual human interrupts me. "Hey there."

It's Lena the barista, and she's talking to me. Not to be dramatic or anything, but I've been coming in here for two weeks, and I don't think this has ever happened before.

"How's it going?" she asks while I glance over my shoulder to make sure there's not another customer behind me.

When all I find behind me is wall, I shrug, look side to side almost comically, and then answer. "Pretty good, I guess."

Her keen blue eyes search mine. "Do you know that you have the prettiest aura I think I've ever seen?"

Uh...what?

"Aura?" I ask with an awkward titter in my throat.

"Yes, girl." Her smile is bright and beaming. "Your vibe. Your spirit. Your *aura*. It's the prettiest shade of pink I've ever seen in my life."

"Well...thanks, I think?" I respond with a tilt of my head. "I mean, I'm not quite sure what all that means, but it sounds pretty good."

"Trust me, it's good," she says through a small laugh. "Your name is Maybe, right?"

At first, I'm surprised she knows who I am. Like, maybe she has the ability to read minds or something in addition to auras. But a quick glance down at the table—and my coffee cup—reminds me that she's been writing it for the last two weeks.

"It is. Maybe Willis. Well, Mabel Willis, but everyone calls me Maybe."

"That's a cool nickname," she says, holding out a hand for me to shake and then turning the chair opposite me around so she can straddle it backward. "I'm Lena Hawkins."

I look around the shop, actually nervous *for her* that she's being so lax about working, but she pulls my focus back to our conversation pretty easily.

"So, I've noticed you're starting to turn into a bit of a regular around here. Do you live close by?"

"Just around the corner," I say hesitantly as Bruce's warnings about stranger danger play uninvited in my head. I never really thought of skin glistening with glitter as something associated with a serial killer, but I guess you never know. "I just moved back to the city two weeks ago."

"Really? You don't seem like a transplant."

I smile at that, wondering if maybe Lena's been watching me a little bit too. The thought is exhilarating for a disenchanted introvert like me. "I'm an original New Yorker," I say with a smirk. "I was in California finishing my master's degree, and now I'm back, trying to survive the pits of hell that is job hunting."

Lena smiles, but it's a little forlorn. "At least you're looking. I'm twenty-seven, and I'm still trying to figure out *what* I want to do with my life."

I let out a relieved sigh. "I may know the job I'm looking for, but I'm hella far from having it all figured out," I assure her.

"Oh, you have no idea," she responds, leaning into the table with her chest. "I'm about the most indecisive person you'll ever meet. Career. Apartments. Boyfriends. I never seem to be able to find exactly what I want."

"Your name should be Maybe," I say with a smirk, and she laughs.

"Okay," she says. "I've decided. We're going to be friends."

Wait...*what?*

"We're going to be friends?"

"Uh-huh. It's officially settled. You and I are going to be friends," she answers without hesitation, like this is a completely normal way to start a friendship.

"And you say you're indecisive," I tease.

A soft laugh escapes her lips. "No time to change like the present, right?" She starts to open her mouth to say more, but two customers walk in the door and head toward the counter. "Shit," she mutters and jumps up. "I better get back to it."

"Oh, okay." I glance to the now-busy counter and back at her. "Well, it was great chatting with you."

"*Girl.*" Lena laughs and nudges my shoulder with her hand. "We are friends now. This isn't a one-time thing."

She pulls her phone out of the back pocket of her skinny jeans, and before she heads back to the counter, we exchange numbers and she pretty much demands that we hang out—*outside of Jovial Grinds*—soon.

By the time I leave the shop about twenty minutes later, I can barely even believe the interaction happened, but a text message from her a short while later confirms it.

Lena: Keep next Tuesday free. I'm off work, have a little extra cash that NEEDS to be spent, and you're going to have lunch and go shopping with me.

Apparently, when Lena decides you're going to be friends, she fucking means it. I guess there's a chance she'll turn out to be the first mass murderer to have a smiling cartoon butterfly tattooed on her shoulder, but I'm lonely enough—and she's fun enough—that I'm willing to take my chances.

Honestly, the mere idea of it makes me smile, but just before I can shoot her a message back, my phone vibrates in my hands and the screen flashes with *Incoming Call Evan.*

I answer it on the second ring.

"What are you doing?" he asks by way of greeting, and instantly, his voice reminds me of seeing Milo in the shop this afternoon.

But it takes exactly one second for me to squash it down and lock the embarrassing details of that interaction in a vault only I can open.

My smartass of a brother would probably have a field day with his best friend not remembering me.

Lord knows, if the situation were reversed, I sure as hell would.

"Uh...not too much," I answer on a sigh. "Just walking home so I can sit on my sofa and try to contemplate the meaning of life."

"Pretty sure you mean sit on *my* sofa."

"Shut up, asshole," I mutter. "I know it's your apartment. Trust me. Every time I turn around, there's another poster just waiting to grace my nightmares. Your Suzanne Somers obsession is frightening. She's older than Mom, you know?"

His laughter is obnoxiously good-natured.

Annoyed, I push it further. "Does Sadie know about your creepy grandma fantasies?"

"Easy, sis. As your landlord, I could kick you right out of that apartment, you know?" He snorts. "And it's not my fault you chose my apartment in Chelsea over the one on the Upper East Side."

"I wanted to be close to the floral shop, *and* we both know you and Sadie use your other place a hell of a lot more, *Mr. Moneybags*. My willingness to be your burden does have limits."

"It does?"

"Funny *ha-ha*, Ev." I roll my eyes. "And I know you kept your Chelsea apartment as an investment, but that doesn't mean you couldn't consider a little redecoration."

He sighs. "Drop it, Maybe."

"Fine," I grumble.

"So, tell me, how are things in the big, bad city?"

"Well...let's see..." I start and smack my lips together pointedly. "I have no friends. I'm living in your apartment, working with our parents every day, and Bruce has to chauffeur me to my wisdom teeth surgery tomorrow morning. How do you think things are?"

He snorts. "It can't be that bad."

"I know it's been like a decade since you've stepped foot in Bruce & Sons, but shall I remind you what it's like to be stuck in the same building with our father for eight hours in a single day?"

"Okay. Yeah. I get it." A chuckle escapes his throat. "But it's only temporary. Plus, you can't deny you have it pretty easy compared to most college grads. You don't have to pay rent, and even though working with our parents sucks ass, it's still a job to tide you over until you find what you're looking for."

"If you're about to give me some kind of Bruce-inspired lecture, I'm hanging up on you."

"Ah, I take that to mean you know I'm right." He laughs again. The know-it-all bastard is just whooping it up at my expense.

"I know you're *annoying*."

"And right."

"*Evan.*"

"Just chill out, little sis," he says, and I can hear the amusement in his voice. "Everything is going to be fine. You'll find a job that doesn't include our parents, and things *will* get better."

"Pfft." I snort and unlock the front lobby door to my building. "I hope you're right."

"I am. I mean, I can't deny I'm secretly laughing at your current situation, but I know it will all work out for you. You're crazy-smart. A publishing house would be lucky to have you."

"Secretly laughing?" I question. "You literally just said that *while* laughing. Hell, I'm pretty sure you haven't stopped laughing since I answered your stupid call."

Of course, he laughs *again*. "Minor details, sis."

I'm so forlorn today that I don't even have the strength to respond with a sarcastic rebuttal. Instead, I just sigh and walk up the three flights of stairs to my apartment.

"So…wisdom teeth surgery? Tomorrow?" he asks.

"Yep. I'm just living the dream," I mutter. "Found out last week that the one and only wisdom tooth they didn't think would have to be removed…now has to be removed."

Seriously. Tooth pain is no joke, and I curse the man who removed the first three wisdom teeth six years ago for not removing this one. *Fucking Dr. Wendell, you bastard.*

"Are you in pain now?"

"Besides the daily pain of hearing Bruce freak out over his flowers? No, I'm fine. They gave me some meds that eased up the tooth discomfort until the surgery."

"God." He chuckles. "You sound miserable."

"And you sound like you're enjoying my misery a little too much."

"I'm not enjoying it…that much."

"You really suck as a brother, you know that?"

"Says the girl who is currently living in my apartment rent-free."

"A sucky brother who is into old women *and* annoying. Does Sadie know what a winner she's with?" I ask and use my shoulder to keep the phone pressed to my ear as I juggle my keys out of my purse.

"Well, she accepted my proposal, so I'm guessing probably not."

"Try to keep it under wraps until the wedding, yeah?" I tease. "I'd prefer to keep things as they are. It's nice knowing you're mostly her problem and not mine."

"Ha. That's cute, you little smart aleck… And, speaking of the wedding, that's actually why I was calling you."

"What's going on?"

"We've set a date and location."

"Really?"

"July 13th of this year."

I count the weeks in my head as I slide my key into the lock. "Holy hell, that's less than two months away, bro…"

"Yeah, but we're keeping it small and intimate."

Small and intimate. I cackle and step inside my apartment. "Hearing you describe your wedding as small and intimate is nearly too much. If you start talking about lilac boutonnieres and table settings, I swear to God, I might die from shock."

"Let me rephrase, smartass," he says. "*Sadie said* we're keeping it small and intimate."

"Sure, sure, blame it all on your fiancée." I grin. "Is it going to be in Austin?"

"Nope. New York."

"Oh shit. Have you told Mom?"

"Unfortunately, she's my next call."

I laugh and toss my purse onto the kitchen counter. "Man oh man, you're going to have a hell of a time keeping her from going nutso with the flowers."

"Fuck, I know." He sighs. "All right, well, I have to head into a meeting. Talk soon?"

"I hope not."

"Yeah. Yeah." His deep chuckle fills my ear. "Love you too, sis."

We hang up a few seconds later, and I waste zero time getting down to business.

Comfy pajama pants? Check.

TV remote? Check.

My ass on the couch? Check.

But just before I can completely lose myself to a few hours of mindless TV, my phone pings from the cushion beside me.

Lena: Also, the next time you come into JG, you need to tell me who you were texting today.

My failed text attempts to Milo? Oh, *hell no*. That is not something I want to share with any-fucking-one.

Not to mention, how in the hell would she know that? Maybe she *is* a psychic.

I respond by pleading the fifth.

Me: I have no idea what you're talking about.

Lena: Girl, I know what that kind of focused means. That wasn't the look of a girl mindlessly browsing Instagram. You were texting... someone. But I'll let you off the hook as long as you promise to go shopping with me next week.

Me: Not going to lie…being friends with you is kind of weird…

Lena: When you say weird, I'm pretty sure you mean FUN. And I'm also taking that last text as a blood-oath-promise that our lunch and shopping date for Tuesday is a go.

Either Lena is batshit crazy or the exact kind of friend I need in New York.

Honestly, at this point, it's a toss-up.

But for some unknown reason, despite her apparent proclivity for demands and threats, I'm amused by her.

Me: LOL. Fine. Count me in.

Lena: FANTASTIC. And PS… My motto when it comes to texting a guy I like is Just Do It.

Me: Who says it was a guy I like?

Lena: HA! So you WERE texting someone…

Avoid. Avoid. Avoid.

Me: I'm pretty sure Just Do It is owned by Nike.

Lena: And look at how far it's taken them…

Yeah, despite my momentary lapse in judgment at Jovial Grinds, hell will freeze over, JK Rowling will give me a call to edit her next book, and Bruce will stop nearly shitting himself whenever his ship-ment of Gerbera daisies is running behind schedule before I'd actually think about hitting send on a text message to Milo Ives.

THREE

Milo

The warm, late-spring air hits my face as I step out of the back seat of my driver Sam's Escalade, and I button the front of my suit jacket and take a breath.

I've lived here nearly my entire life, and still, the city's sounds are almost overwhelming. Taxi cabs honk as they try to race through red lights, pedestrians clamor for their place on busy sidewalks, and a fire truck's siren blares somewhere in the distance.

It's just a little after six thirty on a weekday evening, but instead of going home, I'm heading to dinner at Motel Morris with a woman by the name of Rosemary Cook.

Ever since I landed on *Forbes* Richest List *and* was apparently named one of New York's Most Eligible Bachelors on Page Six, my assistant Clara has more than earned her salary fielding calls from hungry media sources.

It's all a bunch of bullshit if you ask me.

My drive and success have never been and will never be motivated by accolades or attention. And truthfully, if Page Six never mentions me again, it'll be too fucking soon.

But nonetheless, here I am, ready to have dinner with the tenacious Rosemary Cook of the *Times*.

If that woman called my office one hundred times, she called it a thousand.

Not to mention, she managed to snag my personal email address and inundate my inbox with messages. All sort of nice. All kind of friendly. All *pushy as hell*.

Somehow, I found myself admiring her stubborn tenacity, and I agreed to do this interview—something I almost never do.

It only takes one instance of getting stuck in an interview with a woman named Tina who tosses out questions about your cock size and sexual preferences like she's making it rain with dollar bills at a strip club to become prudent with journalist requests.

When I check in with the hostess, she leads me toward a private, white-cloth and candle-lit table at the back of the restaurant where my redheaded dinner companion is seated and ready to dive right in.

I stop on my side of the table and glance down to find a wrinkled legal pad, and the first page is absolutely filled to the brim with questions.

God help me. This woman came real-fucking-prepared.

Internally, I sigh.

"Mr. Ives," she greets with a bright, megawatt smile, jumping up to stand and shake my hand. "Thank you so much for meeting with me this evening."

"You're lucky. I don't normally negotiate with terrorists, Ms. Cook," I say, offering a little smirk, and she blushes.

"I can be persistent," she admits, and my respect for her blossoms a little more. It's always refreshing to come across someone who doesn't falter or apologize when called out for actions they're proud of. "And, please, call me Rosemary."

I gesture for her to take a seat and do the same for myself.

"So, Mr. Ives, what brought you to Chelsea this afternoon?" she asks after I order a scotch on the rocks from the server.

While I might've agreed to the interview, I didn't necessarily make it easy on her. This afternoon, I officially tossed the ball in her court—giving her barely three-hours' notice for an interview over dinner.

An asshole move? Possibly.

But it made her prove just how much she wanted this interview.

I didn't create a thriving business without understanding how to test people's drive and willingness to follow through.

"I had a few errands to run on this side of town."

"Errands?" she asks, and amusement flashes within her gray eyes. "What kinds of errands does a successful man like you still run for himself?"

"I'll have you know, I prefer to run most of my own errands when I have time. And when I don't, I pay people to pretend I did them," I tease. She laughs, thankfully. I've had more than one interview in the past where the journalist didn't understand my sense of humor, and it made the resulting article pretty interesting. "Today, though, I was ordering flowers to be delivered for my mother's birthday next week."

Instantly, a visual of the beautiful woman at the Willises' floral shop filters unbidden into my brain.

Gorgeous brown eyes. Long brown hair. Full, intensely pink lips, and the kind of body that could get a man in trouble.

It took every ounce of strength I had to fight my grin as she nearly broke the damn computer while she placed my order, but her fumbling only added to her charm.

Honestly, I'll be pleasantly surprised if the bouquet actually makes it to my mom next week.

Maybe I should head back in tomorrow and order another...just in case.

The pure thought of another encounter with the awkward goddess with the big, brown doe eyes nearly makes me laugh out loud, but I swallow it back and revert my focus to the interview.

"Flowers for your mother, huh?" A soft laugh leaves Rosemary's red-painted lips. "That's really sweet."

"There's a reason she tells me I'm her favorite son."

She quirks a brow. "You have brothers?"

"Only child."

"Successful and funny." Rosemary's lips crest up into a grin as she taps the end of her pen on her notepad of questions. "Shall we get started?"

Oh, here we go...

I gesture a nonchalant hand toward her and mentally brace myself for the inquisitive onslaught.

Rosemary doesn't disappoint.

Before I know it, she's balls deep in her journalist spiel. "With a net worth just over one billion dollars, you were just named one of *Forbes* richest men in the world," she states. "How does it feel to have amassed such wealth by the age of thirty?"

"That's a fairly ambiguous question and not the easiest to answer."

She quirks one perfectly shaped brow. "And why's that?"

"Because the wealth isn't my priority. I mean, sure, it's great to have such financial stability, but the money has never been the focus."

"What's the focus?"

"The advancement of technology," I answer without hesitation. "Fuse was developed from a passion for creating secure software platforms and collaboration tools for companies all over the world."

Rosemary nods and jots down a few notes. When she eventually meets my eyes again, a sly smile spreads across her lips. "From what I hear, NASA is one of those *companies* Fuse has collaborated with..."

"It appears you've done your research." I grin and take a sip of the fresh glass of scotch the server sets down in front of me.

"How long has NASA been a client of Fuse?"

I smirk at her very forward question. "When it comes to my alleged clients, I never kiss and tell."

She furrows her brow. "So, it's possible they're not a client and it's all just hearsay?"

"Like I said, I never kiss and tell."

NASA *is* one of our clients. But Rosemary doesn't need to know that information.

A small laugh leaves her lips. "You make interviews incredibly difficult."

I shrug. "So I've been told."

"Do you mind telling me a little bit about how you went from a college student at Yale to the CEO of a company that grosses enough money to get your name on *Forbes'* list?"

"Three credit cards. Ten thousand dollars in debt. And a three-year diet of ramen noodles and Kraft Mac & Cheese."

The space between her bright-red lips grows exponentially. "You're not serious." My bluntness has clearly surprised her, but this isn't a question I've ever avoided. I want other people to know it's possible to be where I am. That it's possible to be a regular guy with a vision and seemingly no means to make it happen and to *make it happen anyway.*

"Oh, but I am," I retort. "The company you now know as Fuse was founded on credit card debt and sweat equity. I worked seven days a week, eighteen-hour days for the first year and a half, just to get cash-flow positive." I grin. "Though, the change in the bottom line probably had more to do with the ramen noodles than anything else."

She ignores my lame joke. "That's quite impressive, Mr. Ives."

"That's what it takes to build a company like mine, Rosemary. It's not a secret formula or a political connection or a trust fund. All of those things are helpful," I say with a laugh, "if you're fortunate enough to have access. But they're not necessary."

"You're obviously passionate about this topic," she states, and I nod. But before she can continue, my phone rings from inside my pocket.

"Sorry," I apologize and pull it out to see Evan Willis's name flashing across the screen. "Actually, I need to take this. Excuse me for a minute."

"Of course. No problem." Rosemary nods, and I get up from the table to walk toward the front of the restaurant and out the entrance door.

The front sidewalk is crowded and loud, even more so than inside Motel Morris, so I let the call ring to voice mail as I find a quiet alleyway about fifty feet up the block and step inside.

I dial Evan back, and I don't even wait for him to say hello before jumping in.

"How goes it in Austin?"

"It's so good, I'm not sure you're ready to hear it."

I grin and lean back against the warm bricks on the east side of the alley. It's amazing how well they hold the heat of the summer sun even after the light is gone. "Is that so?"

"You bet your ass."

Evan Willis has been one of my best friends since I was a precocious kid growing up in Brooklyn. We went to elementary, middle, and high school together, hung out on the weekends, and did every organized sport known to man as a duo. Hell, when my dad was relocated to Tampa during high school, I lived with Evan's family for six months so I could finish my senior year without having to switch schools.

We attended college together at Yale, and, while I was building Fuse from the ground up, he was in my corner as my biggest supporter. He's officially the CFO of my company and runs the secondary headquarters in Austin, but if you asked me to tell you about Evan Willis, I'd tell you he's my chosen brother.

"So…" he starts. "You know a company by the name of TechLete Industries?"

"Does a bear shit in the woods?"

"I've never seen it, but I have to assume, given the parameters of a bear's habits and habitat, that, yes, a bear shits in the woods."

"God, Evan. You're such a dork."

"You asked. I answered."

I roll my eyes. Evan is so funny, so smart, so likable. He also has the brain of an accountant, built to focus on the most minute of details. Sure, it comes in handy in his role as my CFO, but it also makes conversations with him sometimes go like this.

"Back to TechLete. Why'd you bring them up?"

"Because they're one of Fuse's newest clients."

I don't even have to look at a financial report to know that client alone will bring in seven-figure numbers. No doubt, Evan just snagged a big, fat, successful fish from the potential client sea.

"I think you're right," I retort on a laugh. "I wasn't prepared for that news."

Evan chuckles too. "The additions they want to our security and collaboration software are arduous, but I'm confident we can have them up and running in about three months."

Three months? Not even I would have promised to have them running in three months with changes to the structure of the software, and I'm a lunatic who's willing to work nights and weekends. Evan's got a fiancée to answer to.

"You do realize that's a lofty goal, right?"

"Yeah, well, I'm a lofty kind of guy," he says cockily, obviously high on the achievement of landing such a big company. "A lofty kind of guy who can make big things happen."

An annoyed laugh escapes my lips. "Yeah, yeah. Now put your dick away and tell me what team you're putting on this job."

"Matt Franks, Lee King, and Sara Miyagawa."

Our best Austin team, without question.

"It sounds like you have everything under control, then."

"Aw…you sound disappointed," he teases. "Are you sad I'm not asking you to hop on a plane and head to Austin to help me figure this out?"

Always the fucking smartass.

I chuckle. "I'm just thankful the junior varsity hasn't bitten off more than they can chew."

"Oh, come on, Milo. Junior varsity? Pretty sure we lowly folks in Austin brought in a higher figure than you professionals in New York did last year."

I bite my lip and shake my head. Giving shit to each other is one of our favorite pastimes. "Austin is a burgeoning market. In New York, we actually have to set the ball before we spike it."

Evan laughs. "Don't worry. You're the face of the company, buddy. We'll keep you even if we don't really need you anymore."

"That's cute, sweetheart. Should I start checking financial records for new life insurance policies that have been taken out on me? Keep an eye over my shoulder for potential hitmen?"

Evan snorts. "I'd never leave such a ridiculously obvious paper trail." I roll my eyes as he laughs. "So, what are you up to? Still slaving away at the office?"

"Nah," I respond. "I'm at a restaurant being interviewed by a shark. What about you?"

"A shark, huh? As in doo doo doo doo doo doo?"

"Shark as in a crimson-lipped woman from the *Times*."

"Ahh. I'm heading home to sit on exactly one hundred conference calls with Sadie to talk to all sorts of fucking people for the wedding."

It's my turn to laugh. "I think you might have it worse than me."

"Tell me about it," he mutters. "I love my future wife, but a man can only talk wedding venues and caterers and party favors so much before his ears start to bleed."

"Does this mean you guys finally set a date?"

"Yep," he says. "The wedding is July 13th. In New York. And oh, by the way, you're my best man."

I smirk. "Pretty sure you're supposed to *ask* me if I want to be your best man..."

"Yeah, but I don't care what you want in this scenario. It's my wedding day, goddammit, and if I have to wear a penguin suit in eighty-degree heat, then so the fuck do you."

I laugh. "Thanks for updating me on my future plans, bridezilla."

"No problem."

"I'm guessing Bruce Willis & Sons will be handling the floral arrangements?"

"Betty officially started losing her mind after I got off the phone with her a few hours ago," he says through a sigh. "No doubt Maybe is getting quite the laugh right now at my expense."

The mention of his kid sister's name makes me smile. It's been ages since I've seen the pip-squeak. She was several years younger than us, cutely awkward, and followed us around with a notebook, a book, and a soda in hand at all times. The thought of her takes me back to the nostalgia of our childhood—a time in my life I enjoyed immensely. "How is Maybe, by the way? Is she going to be in town for the wedding?"

"She's already in town, dude. Finished up her master's at Stanford and moved back to New York earlier this month."

"She already finished her master's degree? What is she, eighteen?"

Evan chuckles. "She's twenty-four, man."

Twenty-four? Maybe is twenty-fucking-four? Jesus.

"Damn. Time flies."

"Tell me about it," he says. "Speaking of which, I was hoping you could do me a favor."

"Honestly, after not firing you during our earlier conversation and agreeing to your demands to be your best man, I'm already in the middle of a couple," I tease. "Not sure I have time for any more."

"Fuck you, dude," he retorts back on a raspy chuckle. "And the favor is more for Maybe than for me."

"Ah, well. I guess I can free up some time for the kid, then. What's she need?"

"She's trying like hell to get her foot in the door at a New York publishing house. She has the skills, but you know how shit is in that industry."

I hum. "You're a nobody until you know somebody."

"Exactly," he agrees. "I was hoping you could call in a few favors with some of your connections. Possibly find her some interview opportunities. Once she has a foot in the door, she'll be able to seal the deal, I'm positive."

"Of course," I respond without hesitation. "I'll definitely see what I can do."

"Thanks, man. I really appreciate it." His tone is equal parts grateful and relieved. I haven't seen their dynamic in person in years, but it's apparent Evan still comes from a positive place in fulfilling his brotherly role. "Anyway," he continues. "I gotta go. I need a minute to prepare myself for the hell that is wedding planning the instant I walk through the door. I'll send you Maybe's number so you can give her a call."

I chuckle. "Good luck, man."

"Same to you. And I hope you're not on your period. I hear sharks can smell blood."

"Fuck you very much for your concern."

He ends the call mid-laugh, and I've barely hung up the phone when it pings with a text.

Evan: Here's her number: 555-150-0200

Maybe Willis's number.

Good God, it feels like it's been forever since I saw Evan's little sister.

Surely, she's not the same knobby-kneed, braces-afflicted, ac-ne-faced, starry-eyed adolescent I remember, but hell if I can picture what she might look like at twenty-four.

Quickly, I add her to my contacts, but right before I can slip my phone back into my pocket, the damn thing vibrates in my hand *again*. I feel like a bartender at fucking happy hour.

Mom: Emory is officially in labor! She's at St. Luke's Hospital and is supposed to have the baby soon!

Emory Black is my cousin on my mom's side, the daughter of my aunt Eileen. Aunt Eileen married a rich Southerner of Creole descent and ended up in New Orleans, so Emory and I didn't grow up right around the corner from each other, but it's safe to say we're close despite the distance.

Our mothers made it a priority to spend holidays together even after the passing of their parents, and as only children, Emory and I had no choice but to be friends.

All of this to say, I'm absolutely certain if I don't show up to meet her bundle of joy at the hospital, my feisty cousin *and* my mother just might kick me in the balls.

I mentally pencil in a trip to the maternity ward in the next couple of days.

Mom: Also, stop acting like you're the bastard son of a negligent mother and call me.

Only she could get away with calling me a bastard *and* make me grin at the same time.

Me: I don't know, Mom. I recall a couple of uncovered outlets making an appearance in my childhood, and I don't really look like you OR dad. What's a boy to think?

Mom: !!!

It amazes me how well I understand her punctuation-only message.

Me: Relax, Mambo. I'm kidding. Things have been busy, but I'll call you tonight when I get home.

With my parents settled in Florida and my very busy business in New York, it's not easy keeping in touch with my folks. Hell, sometimes, weeks go by before I remember to check in with them.

Hence the whole bastard son thing.

Mom: Okay. And I'm not sure if you realize this, but there is a very important day next week...

Me: Lol. I'm very aware that your birthday is next week, but I appreciate the subtle hint.

Mom: Well, you know…just in case. What good is a rich son if not for getting presents?

I laugh out loud just as another text comes in.

Mom: ☺ Love you, Milo.

Me: Love you too.

Mom: Oh, and your father says hello.

Me: Tell him I say hello and that he should finally give in to technology and get a damn cell phone so I can actually reach him.

Where Lydia Ives is all about the technology, Kerry Ives refuses to take part.
The man still watches VHS tapes, for fuck's sake.
The day he gets a cell phone might actually be the apocalypse.

Mom: He says you can always call the landline.

I laugh to myself. *Jesus.* This conversation would go on forever if I'd let it.

Me: All right, well, I have to finish up an interview, but I'll call you tonight.

Mom: What kind of interview?

Me: You can ask me all about it later.

Mom: Do you know what time you're going to call? Your dad and I like to watch **The Bachelorette** *at nine.*

God forbid I interrupt Chris Harrison announcing the final rose of the night.

I shake my head on a laugh and type out what will be my final text of this chat.

Me: I'll make sure it's before then.

I slip my phone into my jacket pocket, and when it vibrates another three times against my chest, I can't not laugh. That woman would keep me in a text message conversation for twelve hours straight if I'd let her.

As I head back into the restaurant, I make a mental note to call two people.

Obviously, when I get home tonight, my mom.

And hopefully, sometime later this week, Maybe Willis. I don't know much about her these days, but I know for sure it'll be good to catch up.

Chapter
FOUR

Maybe

The clock in my dad's SUV clicks to eight in the morning, and I groan as he pulls into the parking lot of my oral surgeon's office in New Jersey for surgery day.

Of course, when I say *my* oral surgeon, I mean the oral surgeon for which Bruce found a coupon on Groupon, so who knows how in the hell this is going to go. And, while I wish it were something fun like a pair of new boobs or a bionic arm, I'm disappointed to say I will just be the owner of one fewer tooth.

A tooth I don't need, obviously, but still.

I feel like any type of surgery shouldn't come with a twenty-percent-off discount, but I'm currently too tired to decide if it's a bad omen or not.

It's too early to be without coffee, and thanks to the mandatory twelve-hour fast, I can't stop thinking about Dunkin' Donuts.

And I have my dad sitting beside me in the driver's seat, belting out the lyrics to "Isn't She Lovely" as if he's Stevie Wonder himself.

Basically, this morning is shit, and I'm grumpier than Bruce on a late-Gerbera-daisy-shipment day.

God help me.

"And everyone laughs over my need to have a car in New York," Bruce says after he finishes singing the chorus. "Looks like it came in pretty handy today."

He's so proud of himself. The man who spends an insane amount of money just to park this fucking car in the city has driven it one day in the last two months to bring me to a discount surgeon, and he's *bragging* about it.

Bruce pulls in front of the office, puts the car in park, and turns toward me before I can get out of the passenger seat to head toward my dismal fate of anesthesia and blood loss.

"Break a leg, Maybe!"

I groan. "Pretty sure that doesn't apply in this scenario."

"Knock their socks off!"

"Not that either."

He grins. "Good luck, honey. I'll be in the waiting room."

"Thanks," I mutter, climbing out of the relic that is his 2010 Hyundai Elantra, and head through the sliding glass doors at the entrance.

In no time at all, I'm standing in front of the receptionist's desk giving a woman named Harriet my information.

She goes through her medical spiel, hands me a stack of forms to sign verifying my insurance information, and then gives me a look that, lack of caffeine or not, demands I dutifully listen to her instructions. I blink three times and steady myself by locking a clamp-like hand on to the counter.

"No cell phones, no headphones, no tablets, no food, no drinks, no loitering, no yelling, no nudity—"

No nudity? During oral surgery? What in the hell happened to make that one end up on the list?

She continues the insane list without even taking a breath. Clearly, she's run through it hundreds of times. "No unauthorized medications, no drugs, no jewelry, no weapons, and absolutely no gum."

It's ironic that on a list with weapons, nudity, and drugs, chewing gum seems to be the biggest offender.

"The only other thing I need is the name and number of the person who will be taking you home from surgery."

"Bruce Willis," I answer, and her fingers stop suddenly on the keyboard. She looks above her wire-rimmed glasses and her eyes meet mine, and there is some serious annoyance behind them.

"And Frank Sinatra is coming back from the dead to take me to dinner after work," she retorts sharply. "Who is picking you up today?"

"I'm actually serious," I respond quickly, timidly offering a shrug and smile while silently cursing my dad for having the same name as a Hollywood action hero. "My dad's name is Bruce Willis."

She furrows her brow. "Your dad's name is Bruce Willis?"

"It is."

Harriet stares at me so hard, I actually consider breaking and telling her my dad's name is something else. But, like...it *is* Bruce Willis. *What am I supposed to do here?!*

Sweat dots my brow, and the clock strikes noon and I put my hand to my pistol.

Okay, not really, but it does get really intense for a few seconds, and I start to feel a little steamy under my poorly planned polyester shirt.

But the showdown finally ends with a heavy sigh and a jerk of the chin from my opponent.

I scurry to a seat in the corner where I alternate between pretending to read a magazine and staring uncomfortably at my black Converse until a nurse calls me toward the back. I do *not* look in Harriet's direction.

"Mabel Willis, we're ready for you."

I nod and set down the *Cosmopolitan* magazine in my hands on the communal coffee table and follow the blonde's lead.

She looks to be close to my age, her name tag reads Sara, and her teeth are so white I start to have flashbacks of that *Friends* episode where Ross gets his teeth bleached.

"Once we get you settled in, the surgery itself shouldn't take more than an hour." The nurse smiles, and the room brightens.

Literally brightens. The whiteness of her teeth defies logic, and they appear to emit their own light source.

"Well, that's good news, I guess."

"Go ahead and take a seat right there," she says as she points to the dentist chair in the center of the room before heading to the counter and washing her hands at the sink.

The plastic leather of the chair squeaks and groans as I slide my yoga-pants-covered ass into place. Another blond, female nurse steps into the room to assist Sara.

The two women rummage around in the cabinets and drawers surrounding the sink until they're content with their medical loot, and then move toward me.

For the second time since my arrival to this office, instructions fly at me like dicks in a dildo factory.

"First, we're going to take your vitals."

"Then, we're going to start an IV."

"We need the IV so we can sedate you for the surgery."

"Do you have any allergies?" Sara asks, but it takes me too long to answer for her liking. So, she asks again. "Mabel, do you have any allergies?"

Holy hell. "Um…no."

Her responding smile nearly blinds me. "Fabulous."

Fabulous? That's an odd word to come out of a medical professional's mouth…

Molly, the other nurse, scrubs at my right arm with something that smells like alcohol, and Sara takes my left arm and wraps a blood pressure cuff around it.

Holy crap, they're coming at me from all angles.

"It's just going to be a little stick, okay?" she asks, but she gives me zero time to respond.

No countdown. No warning. No time is apparently being wasted today at this medical practice. *Taking teeth is our name, and fast is our game.*

Without preamble, Molly shoves a sharp needle into my arm, and the pain is so instant, so intense, I damn near levitate off the dentist chair.

"Holy flapjacks!" The words shoot from my mouth, and I have to bite my lip so I don't start screaming out in pain.

Is she starting my IV with a shiv?

"Sorry about that. I'll be done in…" I'm expecting her sentence to actually finish with something like *in a jiff*, but instead, it trails off into nothingness. Panic sets in immediately.

"You'll be done in…?" *Soon? For the love of everything, tell me you'll be done soon.*

"Hmm…" Molly mutters to herself while she fiddles around with the needle that's *still* in my arm.

To the left, to the left. To the right, to the right.

If I didn't know better, I'd think she was trying to reenact the Electric Slide with a needle dancing around inside my arm. It's not even that fun of a dance at weddings, but at least then there's alcohol!

Jiminy Cricket! I yell in my head as Molly rotates the needle again.

"Sara," Molly whispers, making weird eyes down at me and then back up again. Feeling like a third wheel at my own goddamn surgery date, I decide to just shut my eyes while these bitches do whatever it is they're doing.

"Yeah?" Sara responds.

"Does this look right?"

"Uh…" Sara pauses. "Yeah, I think so?"

I think so? Holy shit.

"I guess I'll just hook it up to the fluids to see," Molly responds, and I feel a small tug and pull on my arm.

"Oh my God," Sara says a little too loud, and my eyes pop open. "I think you put it in her artery instead of her vein."

Wait…*what?*

I glance down at my arm and follow the blood-red path of IV tubing until it reaches the bag of fluids hanging above me. I know zip about medical shit, but I've watched every single episode of *Grey's Anatomy*, and I'm pretty sure, unless you're getting a fucking blood transfusion, IV tubing shouldn't have blood inside it. Nor should it be filling the IV fluid bag.

The room turns to chaos in a matter of seconds.

"Shit," Sara mumbles and quickly yanks the IV out of my arm and holds pressure. The blood-stained IV fluid shoots out of the tubing and onto the floor, and Molly scrambles around for gauze pads and God only knows what else.

Circus music plays inside my head, and blood loss aids in the hallucination of an elephant or two on my chest.

"Sorry about that, Mabel," Sara says and grabs more IV supplies, which I can only assume will be used on my opposite arm.

Surely, the first arm is momentarily out of blood.

"Sometimes these things happen with IVs, but we'll get you all set here in a few minutes."

Freaking Bruce and freaking Groupon. After this, I am *done* with questionable discounts on retail.

I mean, what's next? Is a monkey with cymbals going to bounce into the room to remove my tooth?

Fuck, I hope not.

Dear God, it's me. Maybe. Please get me out of this surgery alive.

"Not going to lie," I whisper past the nausea that is now creeping its way up my throat. "I'm not feeling so hot right now."

"Oh dear." Sara's eyes go wide when she makes eye contact with me. "You look a little pale."

I'd say that's par for the course at this point.

"Just take some deep breaths," Molly encourages like she knows what she's doing. She talks a good game compared to her actual skills. "Once we get a fresh IV in you, we'll give you some medicine to make you feel better."

My eyes turn to saucers. "You're going to do another IV?"

"This one will work," Molly responds with confidence that is truly mind-blowing after the serious fuckup she's still trying to clean up. "Just close your eyes and try to relax. This will all be over soon."

"I just have one request."

"And what's that, sweetie?"

"Please don't kill me."

Both nurses chortle like I'm joking, but I'm not.

Seriously, God, please don't let them kill me.

"Time to wake up, Maybe," someone whispers into my ear, but they sound like they are talking underwater.

I open my eyes, and everything is blurry and fogged.

I take several blinks, but nothing clears up.

Am I alive?

"Hello?" I ask into the blurred void of my surroundings. "Is anyone there?"

"I'm here. You're going to be okay."

I try to figure out where the voice is coming from, but all I can see is a dark blob with blond hair. And Good Lord, it's terrifying.

"It's time to go home," the voice says again, but this time, the blob is gone and a bright white light fills my view.

Oh shit. Is that *the* light?

The "you just kicked the bucket, and now it's time to cross over to the other side" light?

Ah, fuck. I knew it! I knew this shit was going to go sideways!

Those damn nurses killed me, and I'll never even get the chance to yell at them for it! It's not like they'll get punished. Bruce is way too cheap to hire a lawyer to initiate a medical malpractice lawsuit. Plus, there's probably some fine print in that Groupon that prevents it.

"Here's your phone and your belongings," the voice says and sets a bag in my lap.

As if I need my phone now.

I mean, AT&T has always given me pretty great service, but I doubt their cellular networks are good enough that I'm able to browse Instagram in the afterlife.

"He's going to be here any minute. You can just relax your eyes for a bit, okay?"

He? As in God? God is coming to get me now?

Who would've thought He even has the time to meet and greet every new arrival?

Consider me impressed.

Also, though, slightly panicked too. I know He created me, but I would prefer to meet Him when I've had time to put on some damn makeup or fix my hair.

But the fatigue that apparently comes with death keeps my ass firmly planted in whatever place it currently resides. So, I just let my eyes fall closed and wait for God to come pick me up.

Surely, he'll understand that death by Groupon surgery isn't the easiest to bounce back from.

Something vibrates in my hands, and I pry my eyes open to find a plastic bag in my lap and a cell phone flashing with something on the screen.

Whose phone is this?

Is this my phone?

Or, like, my heaven-allocated phone?

I inspect it with clumsy fingers, but eventually, I figure out it's mine.

Is this like prison? I get one phone call or text message before God gets here?

I shrug and figure it's worth a shot.

It takes a serious effort to see past the light—*which, by the way, is even brighter than I imagined*—and takes forever for me to unlock the damn thing. But once I do, I start scrolling through my missed text messages while a Neil Diamond revival concert starts to filter into my ears.

If I didn't know better, I'd think I was alive and my dear old dad was playing DJ, but like the voice said, God is coming and momma is about to head to her final home.

When I tap to open the text message inbox, I find a few missed text messages from my mom and another one from Evan.

Man, they're going to be so sad when they find out the news.

Evan: I hope you don't lose too much blood today. LOL. But seriously, let me know how everything goes.

Looks like that rat bastard will be eating his words when he finds out I lost a death-worthy amount of blood...

I somehow manage to pull up my contacts and try to figure out who my last and final text message should go to.

I scroll through the list, but when I reach one name in particular, I stop.

Holy hot fudge, Milo Ives.

I want to fuck him. Well, wanted to fuck him.

This dead-ass virgin can't fuck no more.

I wish I could've touched his penis, though.

I bet it's a beautiful penis. Like a beautiful painting of a penis, but without the paint. Just the penis. The whole penis. Not just the tip of it.

If I'd known I was going to take my last breath in a dentist chair during a minor surgery, I wouldn't have been such a chickenshit the other day at the shop.

I would've told him who I was, and then said something smooth like, "I got the feels for you, baby."

Well, smooth but classy and sophisticated too.

Like, Shakespeare kind of words...

"Good day, dear sir gentleman. It is I, Maybe. Doth thou enjoying the day?"

Yes, something exactly like that for sure, but even gooder.

More gooder?

Betterer?

More better?

Meh. Tomato, tomahto.

These are my final words *ever*, and I majored in books. No doubt, I'll come up with something grand.

FIVE

Milo

My Tuesday started at the crack of dawn. After a lengthy interview with Rosemary, and an even lengthier phone call with my mother, I didn't have the brain power left last night to prepare for the list of meetings I have today. But I couldn't go into them unprepared, and thus, the necessity to be an early riser was born.

I've never seen a more hideous baby.

But despite the exhaustion and the insanity that is my busy-as-fuck day, I carve out time around ten a.m. to head to St. Luke's Hospital to meet my cousin Emory's brand-new baby girl—who I'm absolutely positive will be a whole lot prettier than her metaphorical relative.

My mom texted a few pictures of Hudson Blair Black as soon as she was born a few hours ago, but it's so hard to see any real distinguishing features in the shaky pictures of joy that come immediately following the miracle of new life. I'm hoping to take a few of my own that don't look like they've been shot mid-parajump from a 747.

The elevator dings its arrival on the fourth-floor maternity ward, and a herd of excited family members with balloons and stuffed animals and flowers steps out in front of me. I wonder briefly if I should have stopped in the gift shop to get something for Emory and the baby, but then I remember who I'm dealing with.

Emory is a good person, but she's also snooty as all hell. If I was going to get her a gift she'd appreciate, I should have done it well outside the walls of this hospital.

Crying babies and busy medical staff create a chaotic background melody as I get buzzed through the secure doors that provide a layer of protection against babynapping, and a swirling mix of bleach and sterile medical equipment rounds out the olfactory element of the ambiance.

"Excuse me," I say, stepping up to the nurses station right inside the doors.

The obviously busy brunette nurse at the computer keeps typing but looks up at me at the same time. "Yes?"

"I'm looking for Emory Black's room. Room 407?"

She nods and gestures to the right with just her head. "It's right down the hall there. It'll be on your left."

I smile as I say "Thanks," but I'm already nothing but a memory. She's got shit to do, and it's all a whole lot more important than dealing with me.

I head the direction she instructed, and after a short walk down a long hallway lined with black-and-white photos of newborn babies, the room is there, on the left, just as she said it'd be.

The door is cracked a tiny bit, so I push it open slowly, knocking lightly at the same time. I feel like I have to announce my arrival somehow, but being the asshole who wakes up a sleeping newborn doesn't seem like the kind of thing I want to add to my resume.

Emory's best friend, Greer, is the first to notice me from her spot next to Emory's bed on the other side of the large room, and she waves me in with a friendly hand.

She's been in Emory's life almost as long as I have and has spent more than her fair share of holidays with our family. Up until two or three years ago, she was always a part of Christmas Day.

I smile, jerking up my chin in greeting, and walk slowly through the crowd of people toward the bed.

"Well, well, well...look what the fucking cat dragged in," Caplin

Hawkins says loudly from the corner I couldn't see when I came in. He is way less concerned with the consequences of waking a sleeping baby than I am, apparently. "If it isn't Mr. *Forbes* Billionaire."

As a reflex, I give him the finger. As my company's lawyer, Cap's been a part of my life since I was twenty-three. He has a brilliant mind and a real knack for corporate law, but he's also a pain in the ass. Which is probably why he's morphed so easily from the role of lawyer only to my friend.

"It's hard, isn't it?" I tease back. "Always having to compare yourself to me? Do I need to arrange a strategy with your assistant for hiding articles when they come out about me?"

Cap laughs in a way only Caplin Hawkins can—*maniacal and calculating and a sure sign I should expect some form of ridiculous payback*—but I refocus on the reason I'm here.

My cousin and the beautiful baby she created.

"Congratulations, guys," I say, stepping toward the hospital bed. One peek at a now-sleeping Hudson in her father Quincy's arms, and I grin. "Goddamn, what a beauty."

Perfect, angelic skin, full pink lips, jet-black hair, and long dark lashes, this little lady makes the Gerber baby look average.

"Obviously, she gets her looks from me," Emory says, but her best friend Greer is more than ready to offer a sarcastic retort.

"Honestly, it's hard to tell with all that makeup you've got caked on your face."

Emory's responding look is a glare that could penetrate walls. "At least I met my daughter without looking like I just rolled out of bed."

"You and I both know that is exactly how I will meet my future daughter." Greer laughs. "And you know I'm just kidding, Em. You look gorgeous. Kim Kardashian's glam squad fucking wishes they could make her look that good post-birth."

I roll my eyes. This is a typical Emory and Greer snark-war. I've been witness to it more times than I can count.

Greer's main squeeze, a guy I've met only a time or two, Trent

Turner, grins at her adoringly. I snort under my breath. Obviously, he's painfully in love.

Cap laughs, this time innocently, as far as I can tell, but Emory snaps. "Don't even start, Cap." One more wrong move by my buddy and I might have to find a new lawyer.

"I didn't say a word," he says defensively, raising both hands in a show of submission. I bite my lip to stop a laugh from escaping, but the pleasure I get out of the exchange must be evident on my face because both Emory and Cap glare.

It's safe to say my favorite cousin is a little quick on the draw this afternoon, but all things considered, it's understandable. The woman just had a baby. In my book, that's the ultimate free pass.

It isn't long before the conversation switches back to the baby, and I take the opportunity to get back in Emory's good graces. Hudson is still in a doting Quince's arms, but I address Emory directly. "Can I hold her?"

Emory nods at Quincy, and I jog over into the corner to put some sanitizer on my hands. Quincy is waiting when I get back and doesn't hesitate to make the transfer as I hold out my arms.

Hudson sighs the sweetest little baby sigh as I arrange her in my arms and pull the tiny warmth of her body into my chest.

God. *How can something so tiny make my heart feel so big?*

Like it's programmed to do it, my body develops a small bounce and sway as I stare down at her gorgeous face.

There's a whole story—a whole goddamn world of events—that led up to the creation of this perfect human being, and the cosmic power of it all makes my chest squeeze.

I glance up at Emory and Quince and then back down at the baby. This moment feels so acutely destined.

I've never focused on fate. Hell, I've never even focused on love.

But ten minutes of holding the result of human connection has me wondering what the world could have in store for me.

Hudson gets a little fussy, waking from her slumber and turning her lips down in disquiet. Quincy jumps to take her back, and Greer informs us it's time for everyone to exit the room. "Okay, it's time for you bastards to get out of here. Emory needs to get her tits out."

"Jesus Christ," Emory mutters. "Stop saying that, G."

"Fine. Emory has to get her *boobs* out."

Emory rolls her eyes. "I have to breastfeed."

I grin and step forward to give Em a kiss on the forehead. "Congratulations, cuz. I'm so happy for you."

She smiles. "Thanks, Milo."

With my congratulations officially given, Cap and I are the first ones to leave the room and head down the hall, back out the special doors, and over toward the elevators.

"Where are you headed now?" he asks.

"Back to work."

He groans and taps the down button for the elevator. "That's fucking boring."

I laugh as the elevator arrives, and we step on.

"Is Evan really getting married?" he asks, and something about the tone he uses makes me tilt my head and meet his eyes as the doors close shut.

"Yeah."

"And how do you feel about that?"

I search his eyes. "I mean, he's been engaged for nearly a year. Seems like the natural next step."

"First, Quince. Now, Evan *and* Trent." Cap sighs and runs a hand through his hair. "Goddamn everyone's dropping like flies."

I laugh at that. "Well, if that isn't the worst way I've ever heard anyone describe marriage…"

"You know it's true, dude. Marriage. Babies. Shit is going down within our friend circle."

"Aw," I tease. "You feeling left out, sweetheart?"

"Shut the fuck up," Cap retorts on a chuckle. The hall from the elevator to the lobby is surprisingly empty, and in a weird way, it makes his words seem even more dramatic, like I've found myself a party to an after-school special. "I'm terrified...*for them.*"

"*Oh...*" I pause, and a smirk makes itself known on my lips. "So, you're just scared for them. Not scared in general? Or projecting your commitment fears on to them? Of course, that makes total sense."

"You bet your ass, it does," he says without a second thought. "I don't have any fears of commitment. I just prefer not to commit."

"So, this is more of an altruistic kind of concern you're harboring, then."

He nods. "Exactly."

"If that isn't a good friend, I don't know what is," I tease, and he rolls his eyes.

"You know, I almost forgot how much of a fucking smartass you are."

Truthfully, I'm just getting warmed up. His remarks have given me so much ammunition. But luckily for him, my phone pings three times in quick succession from inside my jacket pocket before I can give him any more shit. I pull it out to check the screen.

Maybe: Great day, dear gentleman.

Maybe: Are you there, good sir?

Maybe: I appropriate your time and constipation in this matter.

What in the ever-loving hell is happening right now?
Why is Maybe texting me? Did Evan give her my number too?
And what the hell is she talking about?
Before I can even *try* to decode the messages, another one comes through.

Maybe: I may be but a mere innocent maiden, but I have desires that flow deeper than deep. I want to jump in your pool water and float on your big noodle raft.

And another.

Maybe: I have a delicate, desiring request to ask of you, good gentle sir.

And then, she drops a fucking bomb.

Maybe: Deflower me, please?

"What the hell?" I question out loud before I can stop myself. Cap's overly curious gaze moves to my phone.

"Everything okay?"

"Yeah," I say, but I shake my head at the same time. I stare at the screen, trying to make sense of it, but impressive article in *Forbes* and billion-dollar company or not, I'm coming up blank.

Cap's curiosity only grows the longer I stare, though, and he moves strategically to try to get a glance. I bend it like fucking Beckham to ensure that doesn't happen.

"What the fuck, dude?" he questions in near outrage. "What is it?"

"It's nothing."

He grins. "That doesn't look like nothing."

"Trust me. It's nothing."

Nothing I can make sense of and absolutely nothing I'm going to share with Caplin Hawkins.

He holds out his hand. "Let me see."

"Fuck no." I lock the screen of my phone and slip it back into my pocket. I may not know what's going on, but now, while I'm so closely located near the billionaire equivalent of a peeping tom, is not the time to try to figure it out.

"Someone sending you titty pics?" he asks with a grin, and the sheer thought of Evan's little sister sending me pictures of her breasts has me choking on my own saliva.

"Don't be a fucking dick."

"What?" he asks and raises both of his hands in the air like he's the most innocent, well-mannered man who's ever lived. "It's a valid question."

In Caplin Hawkins's world, it is.

And, hell, maybe a few years ago, it would've been a valid question for me too.

But not now. And not *Evan's little sister*.

Good God.

When I get out of the hospital, away from Cap's prying eyes, and inside the privacy of Sam's Escalade, I pull out my phone and reread her messages. Instantly, an absurd laugh escapes my lungs when I read the last one.

Deflower me, please?

Maybe Willis is a virgin?

No. I shake my head. *Surely, this is just some sort of fun prank... right?*

But the simple idea of Maybe, Evan's little sister, sending out these kinds of text messages, no matter the reason, to random bastards in this city makes my gut churn with discomfort.

I guess it's a good thing Evan asked me to reach out to her...

I'll be contacting her sooner rather than later, that's for damn sure.

Chapter SIX

Maybe

The sounds of a garbage truck slamming trash cans around startles me awake, and I pop up like a freaking jack-in-the-box to look at the clock.

A bright, glowing, red eleven shines back at me.

Holy moly. It's already 11:00 a.m.?

Thirty-six hours since my surgery and I'm finally starting to feel like I'm no longer a cast member of *The Walking Dead*. I'm still a little groggy, but I'm more aware of the real world.

And apparently—*and this really is news to me*—I'm not dead. What I thought was the lobby for heaven was actually the recovery room, and as it turns out, God does not, in fact, look like Bruce and drive a Hyundai Elantra.

Who would've thought a single tooth removal could turn into such a shitshow?

Yesterday, I slept for sixteen hours straight and only woke up to pee, take some meds, and sleep-eat a bowl of vanilla ice cream. Being comatose came in pretty handy though, I can see now, as my mom evidently texted forty times asking me to "rate my pain" on a "scale from one to ten."

Thankfully, the pain *is* subsiding, so I make a mental note to switch out this morning's dose of Vicodin for Tylenol.

I toss my phone down on the pillow of my bed and slide over to the side to put my feet on the floor. My body protests as I drag it off the mattress, but by the time I make it over to my dresser to reread the doctor's post-op instructions, everything seems to be limbering up. Now that I'm lucid, I can feel a layer of filth from the trauma covering my skin, so I make my way into the bathroom to gargle with some salt water and wash my face.

One glance at my reflection and I startle like that possessed chick from *Paranormal Activity* is living inside my mirror.

Holy mother of dragons. I touch my image cautiously. *I look like shit warmed over.*

My lips and cheeks are puffy, I have what must be two days' worth of drool dried to my chin, and don't even get me started on my hair. My brown locks are tangled on top of my head and down my shoulders in a fashion reminiscent of Edward Scissorhands.

Seriously. If Ratatouille were into styling hair, he'd sure as shit nest his way inside this catastrophe.

Without a second thought, I turn on the shower water and hop under the warm spray.

Fifteen minutes later, I'm scrubbed and rejuvenated and, thanks to the expensive leave-in conditioner I *procured* from my mom's bathroom on one of my visits, the bristles of my hairbrush glide through my wet locks with ease.

I grab my phone from my room and head into the kitchen to make some oatmeal, but before I can get a verse and a half into "Wild Oats" by the Rainmakers—*the song I always sing while making oatmeal, obviously*—the stupid smartphone pings from its spot on the counter.

I grab it cautiously, a niggling feeling that it contains evil forming in my belly and swelling.

A text message. From my mom.

I roll my eyes, smile, and breathe a sigh of relief at the same time. I mean, she's being a pain in my ass, but a *caring* pain in my ass.

I don't know why, but I thought it was going to be something *much* worse. I'm not sure what, but—

I lift my finger to tap on her name in my text inbox, but I stop in midair when I see a new message thread two rows down. With *Milo Ives.*

What in the ever-loving crapola is this? Did he text me?

Oh hell. I glance out the window quickly to see the sky looking eerily red. *Red sky in the morning, sailor take warning.* My heart pounds wildly inside my chest, and I start to wonder if he somehow put two and two together and figured out I was the "new employee" at the shop the other day.

Jesus, that would be embarrassing.

Still, I can't *not* click open the conversation.

This is Milo Ives. My longest, deepest, most wildly inappropriate crush, and he's *texting me something.*

Unfortunately, when I get a look at the messages within the thread, my heart pretty much stops beating.

I am horribly, terribly, catastrophically wrong.

He didn't text me. *I* texted *him.*

For the love of everything, what did you do?!

I scroll furiously, reading the evidence of my self-sabotage with a painfully earnest self-awareness. Harry Potter in a handbasket, I asked to…to ride his pool noodle?

I drop the phone onto the counter and my head straight into my hands and let out one of the most painfully pitiful groans known to man.

I am an idiot. The idiot to end all idiots, and for the love of Pete, I think there might be *more* messages.

I grab the phone again, swift and purposeful like the removal of a Band-Aid, and scroll down to the end of my text ramble.

I lose the ability to breathe, and all blood officially leaves my head.

Deflower me, please? I said.

Oh. My. God.

How many times is it possible to die in a seventy-two-hour period? I have to know. Because if I wasn't dead before, I surely am dead now.

I scroll up and down again, hoping it's a figment of my imagination.

But ohhh boy, it's real. So real that right below the final message sits a read receipt from two days ago.

He. Read. Them. And for fuck's sake, he just *had* to be the type of person to leave read receipts on text messages.

The panic is intense for a minute and a half. I pace my kitchen, yank at my wet locks, and bump into every piece of furniture I've never owned—*thank you, Evan.*

But when I finally reach the end of my initial breakdown, I remember one, tiny, glorious detail.

Milo Ives *doesn't* have my number. Bruce and Betty were all about keeping shit real with their kids, and I had to hold out for a phone until I was fifteen. Two long years after the disappearance of Milo.

Thank God *he doesn't have my number.*

If he did, I'd have to ask Bruce for the inside track on a two-for-one coupon for resuscitations on Groupon.

Chapter
SEVEN

Maybe

Two days later and I'm well on my way to a full recovery. I'm no longer injured, bleeding, swollen—or contemplating creating a scenario where I could achieve that status again, thanks to the text-pocolypse.

All in all, I'm back to normal, can eat solid foods without my gums bleeding, and am actually feeling better now that I don't have constant oral pain. Unfortunately, that means I'm back to working with my parents.

"Betty!" my dad shouts from the back room of the shop, thirty seconds away from starting World War III, Floral Edition. "Have you had a chance to check these shipments?"

"Could you stop yelling!" my mom *yells*. "What if we had customers out here?"

"Do we?"

"No, but if we did, they would've hightailed it out of here because you're an idiot!"

"You're giving me shiitake mushrooms because my yelling would have driven off the customers *we don't actually have*, and *I'm* an idiot?" Bruce shouts back. At the reminder of his funny little practice of using other, somewhat ridiculous, versions of curse words when he's at work, I close my eyes and let my head fall back. "If you would've looked at these shipments, I wouldn't have to be back here yelling!"

Man, I'm so glad I decided to move back to New York and work at my parents' floral shop while I try to find a job.

Probably the best idea I've ever had.

No, no, my mind taunts. *Not the* worst *idea you've ever had.*

The pure thought of the godawful anesthesia-blissed-out deci-sion to text Milo with a sexual proposition makes nausea clench my gut. I immediately will my mind to other things.

Ariana Grande's new album.

How many days there are until my brother's wedding.

How many tacos can I actually eat at Taco Bell? Like, if I really apply myself? Four? Five?

Fun-size candy bars are too damn small to be fun.

You name it, and I'm thinking about it.

Problem is, every time I finish thinking about something else, I start thinking about the embarrassment again.

I mean, what in God's name could he be thinking? He didn't say any-thing. Is that some sort of *don't have anything nice to say, don't say any-thing at all* type of thing? Or did he assume I was just some desperate harpy, looking for my stake of his billion dollars?

My mom shoves the cash register shut with her hip and pulls me from my painful inner monologue. For once in my life, I'm grateful that my entire family consists of unusually loud people.

"I'll kill him," she mutters under her breath. With a roll of her eyes and a heavy sigh from her lips, she turns on her heels and pushes open the door to the back room with both hands.

"You are driving me crazy!" Her voice bounces off the walls of the shop, just before the door swings closed behind her.

"Ditto, Betty!"

Filled with the disquiet of my embarrassment and a euphemistic bucket full of uncertainty, for the first time, maybe ever, I find com-fort in my parents' bickering. It's annoying, sure, but it's also consis-tent. I'm fortunate enough to have parents who've been willing to fight with each other for over thirty years. That doesn't happen much anymore.

I smile to myself and carry a bushel of fresh cut sunflowers toward the front of the shop and proceed to stock a few of the water-filled glass bowls that sit in our DIY-bouquet section.

My parents' bickering penetrates the walls of the back room, and from what I gather, this week's shipment of lilies and roses looks like total shiitake mushrooms. Bruce's words, obviously, not mine. And, evidently, this has been a far-too-frequent issue with one of our shippers.

I'd say in about ten minutes, an irate Bruce will be telling the shipper in question where to shove their shiitake mushroom flowers—right up the grasshole. Again, his words, not mine.

One-by-one, I pull the sunflowers out and place them in the display. And just before I add the final ten stems to the water, my phone pings in my back pocket, and I pull it out to find a text message notification.

My lock screen reads, *Text Message from Milo Ives,* and my heart migrates out of Chestville and into Throatstown. And, hey, it might as well do some apartment shopping while it's there because it seems like it's seriously considering relocating.

I wonder if the universe has something against me. Have I invited bad karma into my life somehow? Done some dirty deeds I'm unaware of? Strong-armed an old lady unknowingly?

A million questions roll through my mind, and I realize they're most easily answered if I'd just find the strength to tap the fucking screen and look at what he sent.

Sunflowers completely forgotten, I brace myself for impact. Locked knees, vomit bucket at the ready.

Milo: Hello, Maybe.

Sweet Jesus, Mary, and Joseph, he knows it's my number! How in the h-e-double-hockey-sticks does he know it's my number?!

He knows I'm the one who sent those crazy fucking text messages.

I almost put the bucket to use immediately, but I don't have time for it because another text message comes through.

Milo: Evan reached out on your behalf the other day. He thinks I might be some help in your job search.

Oh. God.

Milo: What do you say we grab lunch this week?

When I don't respond within a few minutes, he sends another.

Milo: I'm free Wednesday around noon. You?

Shit. I *need* to answer him. The last thing I need is to actually face him right now.

Just play it cool... Who knows, maybe the read receipt was just some kind of weird error and he never actually got the text messages?

Smartphones are good, but they're not *infallible* good.

And wouldn't he have mentioned it? I mean, insane text messages like those aren't exactly easily ignored or forgotten, no matter who the recipient is...

With a deep, anxious breath, I tap my fingers across the keypad.

Lunch would be great, but I'm super busy these days, you know, with my stupid boring life...

Delete.

What IS lunch, exactly?

Delete.

I've actually given up eating all food. Very new age diet. All the rage.

Delete.

Hey, Milo. Ha-ha-ha. Lunch? With moi?

Shit. I sound like a vagrant foreigner, and technically, *I* shouldn't know who is texting me. I stole his number from the flapjacking computer and proceeded to solicit sex! Bruce & Sons ethical code has been all but destroyed.

Delete.

Me: Hi...um...mind telling me who this is?

Finally, I settle on unadulterated ignorance and send off a response. His reply chimes in a minute later.

Milo: It's Milo. Ives. And no, I didn't mean to say that in a Bond, James Bond kind of way.

Oh my God, he's so funny, my heart yells. *I love him!*

I flash a flyer for a two-bedroom with rent control in Throatstown at my heart and tell it to shut the hell up. This isn't a time for its opinion. This is a time to use my brain.

I contemplate the structure, cadence, and simplicity of his reply in forty different ways, and again, even after all of my analysis, I can't help but notice that he *doesn't* mention the anesthesia-fueled brain misfire.

Is he just being polite, or did he really, somehow, not get those messages?

Holy hell, the uncertainty is ball-shriveling. I mean, you know, if I had balls to shrivel.

Oh, for fuck's sake. Get it together, you psycho! You can't go through with this. You sent the man a ramble of text messages that included asking him to devirginize you!

I'm right. I *can't* go to lunch with him.

Actually, I can never come into contact with him for the rest of my life.

Not tomorrow. Not next week. Not next month. Not one-hundred-fucking years from now.

No flipping way. I'd rather cut off my left tit than have to face him.

And I love my left tit. It's the perkiest of the set.

I know it's not exactly an easy feat since he's my brother's best friend and friends with my family and living in the same flipping city as me, but I'll walk around in camouflage and start living like a damn vampire if I have to.

Two a.m. grocery shopping at the Quickie Mart up the block.

Wearing a bag over my head on the subway.

You name it, and I'll do it.

Before I can overthink this situation to death, I type out a response.

Me: That's really nice, Milo, but I'll have to get back to you on it. I'm not free this week, and I'm not sure of my first available date after.

Yeah. I'll get back to him in exactly one million years.

Milo: All right, well, I have to head into a meeting, but let me know if your schedule clears up.

Me: Will do.

More like, will *don't*.

I might have to forgo my job search and enter myself into the witness protection program, but I will never see Milo Ives again. *Never ever ever.*

Chapter EIGHT

Milo

At a little after noon on Saturday, the bell above the entrance door chimes as I step into Bruce Willis & Sons Floral.

Now that Emory and Quincy are settled at their New York apartment—*yes, they have one in more than one city, thus requiring a distinction…rich people problems*—a gift of ostentatious, over-the-top, snooty cousin-approved flowers is in order.

And maybe, since I'm here, I'll send another surprise bouquet to my mother just to push my brownie points over the top.

I could use a little goodwill in the son department, and Betty and Bruce will no doubt have some information about how to track down Maybe.

With her dodgy text messages yesterday about being too busy to meet me for lunch, I'm not sure how else to go about helping her make connections for work.

Gut instinct tells me she's in the avoidance stage after sending me those insane—*and honestly, when I think about it, pretty damn hilarious*—text messages, but I have a feeling when we have a laugh about them and put it behind us, she'll really appreciate the leg up I can give her in the publishing industry.

Bruce strides through the door from the back room, and a big ole grin crests his lips when he meets my eyes.

"Milo!" he bellows, just like the old days. "Well, I'll be darned, son, you sure are a sight for sore eyes! How ya been?" he asks and steps around the counter to pull me into a hug and clap a steady hand against my back.

The familiarity of his hugs is still a welcome feeling, even at thirty years old.

"Pretty good."

He steps back to assess me further, and a sly grin spreads across his lips. "You in here to buy some flowers for a lady friend?"

Lady friend. I chuckle. "My cousin, actually. And maybe my mom too. Is it true that you can never send your mother too many flowers?"

"You bet your grass!" Bruce says enthusiastically, and I smile.

"Great. Maybe you can recommend a couple of arrangements, then."

"Of course, son. What are ya lookin' to spend?"

"It doesn't matter." Bruce's eyes start to gleam, and I love the look on him. With how infrequently I see my own parents, this exchange with him feels like it's filling a little bit of the void. "Something *really* obnoxious for my cousin Emory."

He rubs his hands together and moves to step behind the counter, remarking, "Oh, you just wait."

I put a quick but gentle hand to his arm to stop him before he gets too involved. "I'm also hoping you might know where I can find Maybe. I've been trying to get our schedules to line up, but it just hasn't seemed to work out."

He quirks a brow and, instantly, I feel the need to add some details. It's not like Maybe and I have hung out over the years. I can imagine me asking for her now feels a little out of nowhere. "Evan asked me to help her get in contact with some publishing houses in the city."

"Ah, okay," he clucks with a pat to my back. "She's in the back. Let me grab her for ya."

She's in the back? As in, she's here?

Instead of physically going to the back, Bruce shouts, "Maybe! Come out front!"

I laugh a little to myself. *I guess she's in the back.*

"Dammit, Bruce! Stop shouting like a banshee!" Evan's mother, Betty Willis, shouts from somewhere in the shop. Her voice seems disembodied and omnipotent—which is a little creepy—but I'm guessing it's just the acoustics of the building.

He is completely unfazed by her request. "Would ya tell Maybe to come out here? She's got a customer." He elbows me in the arm and winks.

"Oh my God! You're killing me today!" Betty moans dramatically.

"Women, you know." He shrugs. "Can't live with 'em, can't live *with* 'em."

My eyebrows draw together. "Don't you mean can't live *without* them?"

He chuckles boisterously, even grabbing his chest at one point, he's laughing so hard. "Oh, son. No. No, I don't."

All I can do is grin, and thankfully, before Bruce can dive headfirst back into yelling, the back door pushes open and the gorgeous brunette from the other day comes through with a bucket of fresh flowers.

Her head is down, her eyes fixated on juggling the container in her hands, but I have to admit, I'd recognize her body anywhere. The subtly luscious curves made that big of an impression. "Jesus, Dad!" she snaps. "Could you be any more Effie Trinket right now?"

"Who the fun factory is Effie Trinket?" Bruce thunders back. He's obviously confused by the reference, and honestly, I might be too if I were paying more attention.

But I'm not. I'm fucking fixated on *her.*

Maybe was the one who took my order the other day. The goddess with the big brown eyes and perfect skin, the woman with the figure I've been thinking about ever since the first time I saw it, the awkwardly adorable store employee—*this* woman—is Evan's little sister. And it's fucking jarring.

Between one breath and the next, my whole world slows down.

This is really Maybe Willis?

This *can't* be the lanky, unsure thirteen-year-old girl who was obsessed with books and Janis Joplin and ate an entire box of Sour Patch Kids a day.

"It's a *Hunger Games* reference," she says to Bruce through a snort without looking up. "And it is *not* flattering."

Either she's been through one of the biggest transformations known to man, or my foggy memory of her *really* didn't do her justice.

Long golden-brown locks flow past her petite shoulders and halfway down her back, and fuck, those chocolate eyes of hers could swallow galaxies.

Her skin is cream and ivory and silky smooth save a few tiny freckles that outlasted her adolescence and still dot her nose and cheeks. Her lashes are long and dark, and her lips are so full and pink, I'd think they were photoshopped if I weren't witnessing them in person.

A small waist is hidden beneath a red ribbed top, and her darkwash blue jeans fit perfectly over her curvy hips.

Maybe Willis isn't a girl anymore.

No. She's *all* woman.

"Where in the heck have ya been?" Bruce asks—*loudly*—and grabs my attention before my thoughts head toward places they shouldn't be.

"In the back." She rolls her eyes. "Working like a normal person."

"Well, Milo is here to see ya," he says. She stops mid-step and snaps her shocked gaze to mine.

"W-*what?*"

Her big brown eyes grow wide, her lips part into a perfect little O, and her cheeks turn a bright shade of red. Recognition has set in, but unlike me, it's painfully obvious she's known who I was all along.

Man, she must think I'm a real prick. Talking to her the other day like she was a goddamn stranger.

I'll apologize for it at some point, but right now, with Bruce playing witness, I don't see much of an option other than diving headfirst into the fray.

"Hi," I greet, and I don't miss the way her throat bobs when she swallows. "I'm here to take you to lunch."

"Y-you're what?"

"I'm here to take you to lunch," I repeat, taking a step toward her.

She takes a noticeable step back. "But I-I'm working…"

"Don't be ridiculous," Bruce chimes in. "Go to lunch with him, Maybe. You and I both know we're always slow on Saturdays."

Her mouth opens and closes a few times, but words don't come out. I don't know if she's mad about how cavalierly I treated her as a stranger or if she's still embarrassed about the messages, or hell, maybe the two are directly related. But I'll never know if I don't get her out of this building.

"Come on." I step toward her to take the bucket of flowers she's visibly forgotten about from her hands. "It'll be nice to catch up."

She doesn't say anything as I set the container on the counter, but her stunned silence is in no way a deterrent.

"We can catch up and talk about some publishing contacts I think you'd be interested in."

"Look, I really appreciate your effort to help me out and everything, but—"

Bruce takes it upon himself to chime in again.

"Stop being so stubborn, Maybe," he says. "Let the man help you get wet."

My eyes go wide automatically, and Maybe freaks.

"Oh my God! *Dad!*"

"What?" Bruce questions with a shrug—like he didn't just say something insanely inappropriate. "Everyone needs a little help getting their feet wet in a new career. These days, it pays to know people, if you know what I'm sayin'."

Apparently, Evan's dad is still in the business of putting his comically wrong spin on popular sayings, and since he's not *my* dad, I don't think it'll ever get old.

When we were sixteen and headed to prom, right in front of Evan's date, he said, "Now, don't go too hard on her, son. Treat her like the virgin she is, okay?"

Mind you, he was talking about his *car*, not Evan's sixteen-year-old date—who, ironically, was actually a virgin. I still laugh to this day when I think about it.

But I know it's not ever as funny when it's your parent. "You sure have a way with words, Bruce."

"Betty and Maybe call them Bruce-isms."

"Trust me," Maybe interjects. "That's *not* a compliment."

I smile. Evan would say the exact same thing.

Bruce, however, is completely unfazed. "Meh." He is quite literally the definition of zero fucks given.

"So, to lunch?" I slide my hands into the pockets of my jeans and meet Maybe's now-narrowed eyes.

"Apparently, I don't have a choice…"

"Nope. Not really." I smirk, shake my head, and shrug good-naturedly. "But I'll let you choose where we eat."

"Wow," she mutters and grabs her purse from behind the counter. "So generous."

She doesn't slow as she heads for the door, so I quickly tell Bruce to send whatever he thinks is best to my mom and Emory, ask that he give my hello to Betty, and follow after Maybe dutifully.

It takes almost a block to catch up with her—the speedwalk she's employed completely unrelated to getting away from me, I'm sure—and we walk the final three silently, shoulder-to-shoulder.

I smile to myself when we stop in front of Ruth's, her choice that just so happens to be one of my favorite lunch spots in the city. I wrap my knuckles around the handle of the shiny chrome-embellished door and hold it open for Maybe to step inside first. A young hostess with a blond ponytail and pink-painted lips greets her, asking how many people will be dining today, and that's when the silent treatment she's giving me becomes acutely noticeable. Sure, we've been keeping to ourselves, but not even answering the hostess? A line has been drawn.

Before, I figured it was smart not to push or pry and just give her some space. No need to poke the already annoyed bear cub before at least feeding her lunch first. But that's changed now. Now, I intend to push. Hard. For as long as it takes to get a reaction.

"A table for two," I step up to say with an almost obnoxious level of assertion.

Maybe may think she can avoid this encounter, but she's wrong. I've got years of experience in the snake pit that is the business world on my side.

Without delay, the young girl makes quick work of grabbing menus from her stand and taking us to a table.

Maybe sits down in the seat across from mine, fidgets with the napkin-wrapped cutlery, and then opens her menu on a sigh.

She stares at the lists of dishes and kitschy pictures like they hold the key to promptly removing herself from this situation.

I can't stop myself from being amused by her. And I thought the awkward bumbling of the other day was cute; her irritation is a whole other level.

My menu still prone on the table where the hostess placed it, I cross my arms over my chest and lay it all out there. "I'm sorry I didn't recognize you the other day. I can't imagine that made you feel great."

She purses her lips and scoffs under her breath, but for the most part, stays silent.

I push onward. "Is that why you sent those text messages? A prank to get back at me?"

Her eyes skitter upward so quickly, they almost seem out of control. But for the first time since leaving Bruce & Sons, she's making direct eye contact.

A rosy smear of color deepens on both cheeks, and she tucks a piece of hair behind her ear nervously. "Oh. Those. I guess you got them."

I smirk. "I did, indeed."

Her head quirks to the side just slightly, and then her shoulders square. "You know what? Yeah. I sent them as a prank to get back at you."

"Why didn't you just tell me it was you?"

"I don't know." She shrugs and has to avert her eyes from mine for the briefest of moments. "I guess I was too surprised to see you there looking grown and successful and *not* remembering me."

I cringe. "Shit, I feel like a real asshole."

"Because you were," she teases with a little grin. "You were all," she says and drops her voice to mimic mine, "'*I know the Willis family. They're good people.*'"

I can't help but laugh at her ridiculous impression. "And all the while, you were just standing there like, hey, you idiot, I am a Willis?"

She shrugs and offers up a cheeky grin. "Pretty much."

My chest blooms. Finally, she's starting to let her guard down.

"Well, for what it's worth, I'm sorry. You look..." I pause, steeling my voice against making my next word sound as depraved as it is in my head. "*Different.*"

If her blush is any indication, though, I'm pretty sure I fail.

"So...uh...do you know what you're getting to eat?" she asks, changing the subject to something innocuous—thank God—while looking up at me from beneath the long curves of her full, feminine lashes.

"You can never go wrong with their Reuben on rye."

A small smile quirks up the corner of her soft pink mouth. "So, I take it you've eaten here before?"

"Only once a month for the past two or so years."

She giggles, and I kind of hate how much I enjoy that sound coming from her lips.

I feel like a bit of a bastard for being so...observant when it comes to her.

Observant? More like enamored.

Fuck. This is *my best friend's little sister.*

The one who had permanently red lips in the summer from eating her favorite cherry popsicles and had posters of Joan Jett in her bedroom.

Needless to say, I shouldn't be thinking about her in any way besides friendly. Neutral. *Unaffected.*

Yeah, but what you should be doing and what you're actually doing are two different things, you bastard.

I'm so curious about her that I find myself lifting up my glass of water and taking a drink just to distract myself from my thoughts.

I can't remember the last time I was this intrigued by a woman.

It's probably just nostalgia, I tell myself. *That's all this is.*

Yeah. This is just nostalgia. It has to be.

A waitress named Karen stops by our table and takes our order—Reuben on rye with fries for both of us—and when she leaves, I lean forward and turn faux serious. "I have a question for you."

She licks her full lips nervously but doesn't let our eye contact flounder. It seems, now that we're getting the initial awkwardness out of the way, she's finding a little more confidence. "And what's that?"

"Do you still listen to Kate Bush?"

She nearly chokes on the drink of water in her mouth. *"What?"*

"When we were kids, you always used to sing 'Wuthering Heights' in the morning..."

At the top of her lungs, every single morning when she was getting ready for school, and it was miserable for everyone inside the house. Maybe never quite grasped that she couldn't hit those falsettos like Kate.

Her brown eyes pop wide open. "You heard that?"

I grin. "I'm pretty sure everyone in the whole neighborhood heard it."

"Jesus Christ." The apples of her cheeks flush red, and amusement fills up my chest like a balloon. "I was what, like, twelve? And, apparently, believed I had a budding music career ahead of me."

My grin grows wider. "So, I take it that's a no?"

"Uh…definitely a no, *and* I'd like to make a rule for this lunch."

I quirk a brow. "A rule?"

"Yeah." Her nod is firm, and her eyes turn serious. "No talk of memories that include me being an awkward and embarrassing teenager."

"You weren't awkward and embarrassing."

Honestly, she kind of was, but wasn't everyone? If you don't have an awkward phase of adolescence, you must have some kind of contract with the devil. And considering I already have some strikes against me, agreeing with her on this one is *not* the way to go.

"Uh…yeah, I was."

"I thought you were pretty cute."

She rolls her eyes. "Because I was Evan's little sister."

A smile crests my lips. "Speaking of Evan, he's really confident in your ability to do big things in publishing. That's why he reached out to me to work some of my connections."

"Right. Publishing," she says, her voice seeming the barest hint disappointed. I search her eyes to try to figure out why, but she shakes her head quickly and picks up the corners of her lips into a genuine smile. "Thank you, Milo. I could definitely use the help. I've sent out more than a hundred resumes, but not a single one has called me for an interview."

I wave my hand. "That's because there are a lot of stodgy snobs working in the publishing industry." I laugh, and she barks a startled bout of the same. "Luckily, I'm friendly with a few of them."

She smiles.

"I'll work on getting a few options together and reach out to them."

She nods. "Thanks. I know this is probably inconvenient for you. I mean, you're a really busy guy. I'm sure you don't just have tons of spare hours lying around to help your friend's sister."

I frown a little at her insinuation that I'm only here because of

Evan. Sure, it was the catalyst, but I genuinely want to be here. With her.

I shake my head and reach out to touch her hand. Unfortunately, at the searing burn of awareness the simple contact sends up my arm, I realize touching her may not have been the best idea. I move slowly to undo my mistake, so she doesn't take it the wrong way. "I'm glad to be having lunch with you, Maybe. Happy to help and happy to see you."

Before anything else can be said, Karen brings our food, and Maybe and I spend a few silent minutes devouring our sandwiches. There really isn't anything better in Chelsea than a Reuben on rye from Ruth's.

But I can't in good conscience let the entire meal go on without bringing up the thing that's been plaguing me about those messages of hers ever since I got them.

"So, about those text messages..."

She glances up from her plate, the width of her eyes eating away at the other features of her face. A blush once again stains the apples of her cheeks, and I hate to admit, it looks *really* good on her.

Dangerously, *treacherously* good. Which, of course, is all the more reason I have to have this discussion.

"Which ones?"

Which ones? Funny, kid.

"You know which ones."

Maybe doesn't respond. Instead, she takes what has to be the biggest bite of Reuben she can fit inside her mouth and holds it there.

I have to bite my lip to fight my laughter.

"I take it you don't want to talk about them?"

She shakes her head. Her mouth is *conveniently* still too full to form words.

"Can I just say one thing?" I ask and, hesitantly, she nods.

"I know they were in good fun, but I think it's important for you to understand the New York dating scene is a little different from what you're probably used to," I state. "Text messages like that could get a pretty woman like you into a hell of a lot of trouble."

Her eyes narrow, and mouth still precariously full of food or not, she finds her voice. "What is that supposed to mean?"

It's one thing for her to send me a "deflower me, please?" text message.

But it's a whole other fucking thing for her to send that same message to some random douche she met in a bar. There's no telling what might happen to her.

"Look, I'm not trying to offend you," I say softly. "A lot of the men in this city are bastards, Maybe. I don't want to see anything bad happen to you."

She searches my eyes for a long moment, and then she spits the remainder of her gargantuan bite into a napkin and glares. "You do realize I'm not a child, right?"

Uh oh. Where exactly did I go wrong here?

NINE

Maybe

Is he really sitting here lecturing me on the New York dating scene? Like I'm an actual child?

Like he's my *father* or something?

God. Not even Bruce would be so condescending, and he's an emotionally underdeveloped gorilla!

Before I know it, I'm glaring, spitting my food into a napkin like an honest-to-God heathen and giving Milo a piece of my mind.

"You think I'm just out there sending offers for my virginity to every Tom, Dick, and Harry?"

He sits back in his chair, obviously surprised at my ire, but I don't let up. Now that I've channeled all of my embarrassment into anger, I couldn't stop if I tried. "What? You think I'm trying to sell it on the corner like some X-rated lemonade stand?"

His hands go up in a defensive posture, but I keep on rolling.

"Like a black-market auction to give my most delicate flower to the highest bidder?"

My voice is a little too loud now, I can tell by the way he's shaking his head and looking at the people around us at the same time, though I have no choice but to see it through.

"Well, I'm not! I'd never be so cavalier. I sent those text messages while I was all hopped up on anesthesia and thought I was heading to the other side. I thought I was dead, for Pete's sake!"

"Maybe, calm down," he says softly, doing his best to wrangle the beast I've become. "I...I shouldn't have said anything. It's not my place."

"You're damn right, it's not your place!"

"Maybe," he says calmly, reaching out to grab both of my hands with his own. At the contact, every raging brain cell in my mind shuts down. I am immediately, *frighteningly*, at peace. "I'm sorry."

"Yeah...well...good."

I look down at our hands—hands that are still gloriously touching— and take a deep breath to steady myself. I'd need a hell of a lot more than ten fingers to count how many times I've imagined what it would feel like to have Milo Ives's hands on me. Now, I find myself wondering what he would taste like, what he would sound like when he comes. What those hands would feel like when they're touching *other* places.

All of my teenage fantasies come rushing back in a tsunami-like wave, and I almost laugh. Just like Milo himself, my delusional daydreams about him have grown up.

I snap my eyes away from our hands, and they land right on his mouth.

His stupid, sexy mouth.

I move my gaze *again*, but this time end up lost in his insanely beautiful blue eyes.

I'm starting to wonder why God decided to give Milo Ives all the good stuff. It feels like some sort of sick joke.

"So...what exactly did my brother ask you to do?" I use the brief pause to redirect the conversation to something other than those damn text messages. "Just use your rich people contacts to connect me with publishing houses in the city?"

He smirks. "Rich people contacts?"

"Oh, come on, Billionaireman," I retort. "I'm surprised you can even walk in the city without men and women falling at your feet and financial advisors picketing for your investment money."

He rolls his eyes but chuckles. "Does the role of Billionaireman come with a cape? I've always wanted a cape."

I snort. "If you want a cape, clearly, you can afford to buy a cape."

"You don't think that'll get me funny looks?"

"In this city? With your money? It'll be the next big fashion trend. You'll see capes on every blessed corner."

He shakes his head. "Better stick to suits, then."

I smile—a big, dreamy smile that could easily cross over into creepy if I don't monitor it closely. Unfortunately, we've gotten off topic enough that I have to go out on a limb *again*. "So, besides the rich people contacts, what else did he ask of you?"

His beautiful blue eyes narrow slightly. "What else do you *think* he asked me?"

"I don't know…" I pause, and a thousand different scenarios play out in my head. "Ev is fucking nosy sometimes. I wouldn't be surprised if he asked you to help me make friends or date or something insane like that."

"Help you date?" His eyes go wide. "I can assure you that was not requested of me."

"Well, I'm shit at dating." The words just kind of fall out of my mouth before I can stop them. "So, it wouldn't exactly be unwarranted."

"What makes you say that?"

"Because I am," I answer honestly, and before I know it, I'm pouring my heart out like this is a goddamn Jackie Collins novel.

It's annoying as hell. But not anything new.

Even as a kid, Milo could pretty much get me to tell him anything.

I fondly recall being eleven years old and telling him about a fight I'd had with Emma—my best friend at the time. It was the usual catty girl stuff, but it was putting a serious rain on my adolescent parade, and Milo ended up being the only person in my house who was willing to listen.

After that, I trusted him.

And evidently, over a decade later, I still do.

"You didn't date when you were at Stanford?" he asks and pops a fry into his mouth.

"A few times, I guess." I shrug. "But nothing of substance. Most guys my age weren't into a quiet night of Netflix. They wanted frat parties and bar-hopping."

"Sounds like you've been dating the wrong guys, Mayb."

I snort. "So, what you're telling me is that basically every guy I came into contact with at Stanford was the wrong guy?"

"No." He laughs. "Well, maybe. I don't know who you were around. But a college frat party isn't a great place to meet a guy, base case."

I nod, though I suppose it's happened for some people.

"And what about you?" I ask before finishing off my last bite of Reuben.

"What about me?"

"Are you dating anyone?"

"No." He tilts his head toward his shoulder, and he smirks. "Nothing steady anyway."

Another snort escapes my nose. "I'm not surprised."

"What's that supposed to mean?"

I laugh. "I mean I'm not surprised that you're doing a lot of *not-steady* dating."

"I didn't say I was doing *a lot* of it," he defends pitifully.

"Oh, c'mon, Milo," I retort. "Back in the day, you always had a revolving door of pretty girls. When you were living with us, you once came home from one date, only to go on *three* more in the same night. With three *different* girls."

He chokes on his water. "I did not."

"You definitely did." I nod, eyes serious.

"How the hell did I even fit that much activity in?"

"You and Evan were in your senior year of high school, and you said it was, and I quote, *conditioning.*"

"No!"

"Getting in shape," I say, using finger quotes, "for prom." The vivid nature of my memories of him would probably be more disturbing if he weren't so horrified by his own actions.

"Well, fuck. What an asshole, seventeen-year-old-kid kind of thing to say." He runs a hand through the dark locks on top of his head. "I have to admit," he says with a tiny smile. "I'm a little disappointed in myself."

I shrug.

"How in the hell do you remember this kind of shit?"

Because, when it comes to you, I remember everything. Sigh.

"I don't know… So, yeah, it's safe to say I'm not surprised you have fuck buddies now."

"Fuck buddies?" he coughs, choking on his water.

"Yeah. A fuck buddy. Friends with benefits. That sort of thing."

"Jesus," he says through a chuckle. "I know what a fuck buddy is. Just hearing the words leave your mouth is…well, disconcerting."

I roll my eyes. "Surely, I'm not the only person in New York saying fuck buddy."

"Yeah, but you're Evan's little sister."

A deep sigh leaves my lungs. "I'm not thirteen anymore, Milo."

"That's becoming more apparent by the minute."

God, is he always going to see me as Evan's baby sister?

What is it going to take for him to really realize I'm not a little girl anymore?

Suddenly, a lightbulb goes off over my head, and I spout the words without a second thought. "Why don't you help me with more than just a job?"

"Help you with more than a job?"

"Yes. Help me navigate the New York dating scene. You said yourself I'm not really in touch with it anymore. I need someone with the inside track."

It's a shot in the damn dark, but one I have to take.

For the love of God, what if he says yes?

"Jesus," he says on a sigh. "Help you date?"

I nod, and he scowls slightly.

I don't know what to make of his expression, but after a few seconds of silence, he finally makes up his mind. "How about we start with connecting you with publishing houses and go from there?"

It isn't a yes.

But it isn't a no either...

Maybe he'll be more open to it the more time we spend together.

"Fine," I agree and point a teasing index finger toward his face. "But you better have some damn good connections, buddy."

He winks. "Trust me, kid. I've got the right connections you need to land your dream job."

Kid. He called me kid.

Every single piece of me knows I should be irritated, but for some strange reason, the way it flows off his tongue with affection and amusement, I don't hate it all.

Chapter TEN

Milo

"**M**r. Ives, your nine-thirty just called to say he's running twenty minutes behind schedule," my assistant Clara's voice echoes from the intercom on my desk. "And just so you know, Caplin Hawkins has called twice."

Of course he has.

"Thanks, Clara," I respond. I haven't spoken to Cap since I saw him at the hospital, but when it comes to him, there's always a calm before the storm. He may be silent for weeks at a time, but when he decides to make contact, he *always* comes on strong.

Women, I fear, see it as part of his appeal.

I toss the file for GlossBit, the firmware company I was scheduled to meet with at nine thirty, onto my desk and pick up my phone to scroll through some of my publishing contacts.

I never have much time during a busy workday, so the twenty minutes I've just been granted is the perfect time for trying to figure out who would be the best fit for a connection for Maybe.

Or it would have been, if my phone didn't start ringing in my hand.

Incoming FaceTime Call Caplin Hawkins.

Jesus Christ, this guy is like a bad rash.

Despite my better judgment, I tap accept and then transfer the call to my computer.

"Goddamn, Milo. You're so hard to get ahold of, I was almost fooled into thinking you're someone important," Cap greets. "But, well..." He gestures at me and the computer and the fact that he has me on the line mockingly. "Apparently not." I give him the finger, but he pays it no mind as he conferences Evan in.

On a sigh, I brace myself for the kind of call I can only imagine this will be.

Evan's image shoots dramatically onto the screen, filling half of it next to Cap.

He smirks immediately at the sight of me. "I told him you had meetings all day, but you know he's hard of hearing."

"Only when it's something I don't want to hear," Cap clarifies before laughing raucously. "Anyway, I think the point Evan is trying to make here is that you should always answer Old Cap-i-tain's calls."

"Isn't it supposed to be the other way around?" I question in amusement. "Shouldn't I be the one always trying to get my lawyer on the phone?"

Cap chuckles. "You would think that, right? I mean, I *am* the bigger deal out of the two of us." I shake my head and Evan snorts. "But you know I'm a hands-on kind of guy in *and* out of the courtroom."

"Ninety-nine percent of the women in New York can agree with that sentiment," I announce.

"One hundred," Evan corrects.

Cap's grin grows wider.

"Like you bastards should talk. Up until the last few years, we were nose-to-nose with conquests. Evan's got a thick chain around his ankle that links to only one pussy—"

"Hey!" Evan snaps.

"But what about you, Milo? You come down with a sudden bout of impotence or something?"

I smirk. "We can't all continue to stick our dicks in everything that walks. Some of us have to grow up to be men, you know."

"Grow up to *be* men or grow up to *like* men?" Cap muses. "You know I'm a supporter of all walks of sexuality, bro. Say the word, and I'll get suited up to walk in the parade with you."

"Is it just me, or is everyone wondering how in the world Cap has yet to be disbarred?" Evan remarks.

"I haven't been disbarred because I am a magical specimen of a man with skills heretofore unmatched in the field of corporate law. Hence the reason why I've been trying to reach you bozos all fucking day."

"All fucking day?" I chuckle. "It's not even ten a.m., Cap."

"Do you want to hear it or not?"

"Hit me with it," I respond.

"The contract with Birkin Industries is a go. It's just a matter of signatures at this point."

"Seriously?" I question, forgetting all about Cap's inappropriate tendencies. Birkin Industries is an app development company we've been trying to buy out, but fuck, they've been resistant. So much so that I nearly gave up on the prospect.

"Consider Birkin your bitch."

"Damn, Cap," I say. "That's incredible." *He* really is incredible. It's no wonder he's so sought after.

"Well, shit," Evan mutters. "And for a minute there, I almost forgot why you're our lawyer."

"You both know I'm the best lawyer money can buy, and I *always* have important shit to talk about."

"A month ago, you interrupted one of my meetings with an urgent call."

"It *was* an urgent call."

"You called to ask me if you could fuck Kelly Booker."

"Because she was your ex-girlfriend. I was sticking to Bro Code, bud. You should be thankful I'm such a thoughtful guy," he explains. "Trust me, I made the mistake of accidentally getting up close and personal with one of Quince's ex-girlfriends, and I felt like a real bastard."

"Accidentally? How does something like that happen accidentally?"

"I didn't know she was his ex-girlfriend until after the fact." He shrugs it off. "I knew her name was familiar, but her face drew zero recognition. Honestly, for all I know, she had some plastic surgery done or some shit."

"For the love of God, stay away from my sister," Evan chimes in, and Cap tilts his head to the side.

"You have a sister?"

Jesus, Evan. Big mistake bringing her up. Huge.

"Yeah, and she's off-fucking-limits."

Cap grins. No offense taken at all. "But like, she's free rein on nights and weekends, right? Like an old phone plan?"

"I swear to everything that's holy, you better keep your hands—"

I'm not sure how Maybe ended up a part of this ridiculous conversation, but I cut him off in an attempt to change the direction of the conversation to something a little less volatile. "By the way, Ev, I had lunch with her on Saturday."

"You did?" he asks, and a genuinely warm smile crests his lips. "How did it go?"

"Wait a fucking minute," Cap interjects. "You're telling me your sis is off-limits, but you're thrilled when this bozo takes her out to lunch?"

"Because he knows she's off-limits and is helping her out."

Cap grins like a dirty bastard. "Oh, I'm sure he's *helping* her out, all right..."

Internally, I cringe when I think about how Maybe basically asked me to help her get laid.

She said date, my mind interjects. *Getting her laid is just what you were thinking about.*

"Don't be a sick fuck," Evan retorts. "Maybe is trying to get a job with a publishing house, and Milo has contacts that could help her get a foot in the door."

"And I don't have contacts in publishing?" Cap asks, offended. "You do realize I'm a corporate lawyer, right? I have my hands in all-the-fucking pots."

Evan chuckles. "Yeah, well, I don't want your dirty-fucking-hands anywhere near my baby sister."

"I still don't see why I can't help little Miss Maybe out..." Cap grins a devilish smile. "I'm very accommodating."

The mere idea of Cap and Maybe within 100 feet of each other makes my gut churn.

"Mr. Ives," Clara's voice chimes through the intercom. "Your nine-thirty is here."

"All right, well, I'd like to say it was great talking to you bastards, but I prefer not to start off my Monday with lies."

Evan smirks. "Thanks again for helping Maybe out."

"Of course. No problem."

"And what about me?" Cap asks, and I laugh.

"What about you?"

"Don't I get a thank you? A lunch date? Some-fucking-thing for all of the hard work I've put in for you dicks?"

"Aw, you feeling left out, bud?" I ask in a sugary voice. "How about I take you out to lunch next week? Will that make you feel better?"

His pout turns serious. "Somewhere nice?"

"Don't worry, sweetheart. I know you're a five-star restaurant kind of lady."

"As long as we're on the same page," he retorts, and I click end on the call before he can rope me into another ten minutes of ridiculousness.

But in typical Cap fashion, before I even have the chance to let my nine-thirty appointment into my office, he insists on having *additional* last words via text.

Cap: Why don't you go ahead and bring Maybe along? I'd love to meet this off-limits sister of Evan's...

I roll my eyes. Always the shit stirrer.

Me: Lunch is canceled on account of you being a dirty bastard.

Sadly, my message doesn't give me the satisfaction it should. If anything, it's a stark reminder of the way I've been thinking about a very grown-up Maybe since the first time I saw her.

If anyone's a dirty bastard, it's me.

Chapter ELEVEN

Maybe

After a short ride on the E train to SoHo and a five-block walk through a quiet side street of unique storefronts, I spot the sign for Charlie Bird—a cool, new-American eatery that Lena chose.

I locate her quickly, seated at an outdoor table with a half-drunk glass of white wine sitting in front of her. I nod my direction at the hostess and head straight for my delightfully weird new friend.

"Looks like you already got started without me," I say by way of greeting and sit down in the seat across from hers. "I hope you weren't waiting too long. There was a delay on the E."

"Not at all." She shakes her head. "You're just on time."

Just on time? Pretty sure I'm fifteen minutes late, but who am I to argue?

I order a coffee from a fauxhawk-sporting, emerald-eyed server named Grady, and Lena frowns in disappointment.

"Really?" she questions. "Coffee? You're not going to have something fun with me?"

"Trust me, I'm three cups behind my usual four-cup quota for the day. It will benefit both of us if I drink coffee."

She laughs, shakes her head, and sips her wine while we both peruse the menu. It feels weird to have silence with a virtual stranger feel comfortable, but she's so at ease with it, I can't help but be the same.

By the time Grady comes back with my coffee, we're both ready to order.

"Burger and fries, please," I say and hand him my menu. "But I do have one very special request."

Grady grins. "Hit me with it."

I loathe coming across as difficult, especially when I'm at a restaurant, but this is one thing I can't help but be difficult on.

"Please keep any and all onions away from my plate," I say in the nicest way possible. "I'm truly not trying to be a pain in the ass here, but I'll literally puke if they accidentally end up in my food."

"Got it," he says with a soft smile. "No onions."

"I am forever grateful."

Once Lena orders and the waiter heads toward the kitchen, she flashes a secret grin my way.

"You are flipping adorable."

I furrow my brow. "What are you talking about?"

"Trust me, even our server would agree with me on this. You're adorable."

I groan and scrunch up my nose. Adorable is the last thing I want to be. Gorgeous, sexy—even hot. Now those are adjectives I can get behind.

"What's wrong with adorable?"

"Adorable is for puppies and kittens. I want to be seen as a grown woman."

"There's nothing wrong with adorable." She grins and takes a sip of wine. "Trust me, honey. Adorable for a *grown woman* is good. Guys blow their loads over adorable."

I snort. "They do not."

"Oh yes, they do." She nods. Eyes serious. "Being able to combine innocence and secret sexpot is dick kryptonite."

"Secret sexpot?" I question on a laugh.

"I have a good eye for these things." Her smirk is both knowing and devilish. "I can tell, beneath those cute little jean shorts and Converse and beautiful girl-next-door face, there's a total freak just waiting to come out."

I don't know how to respond to that. At all. But I don't need to because Lena is apparently well-versed in the art of keeping conversations going all by herself.

"Trust me, our server Grady is probably in the back adjusting his boner for your adorableness as we speak."

A shocked laugh escapes my throat. "He is not!"

"He totally is." She laughs again. "Just stick with me, and I will enlighten you on all things men."

With her long blond hair and bohemian dress and hippie-chic vibe, Lena is the epitome of confident goddess. She is the sun, and cool girl vibes are her rays of light, radiating from her every action and word.

No doubt, I could certainly use her wisdom when it comes to men.

"So, you just moved back to the city and you're on the job hunt?"

I nod.

"Did you grow up here?"

"Yep. My family owns a floral shop in Chelsea." I nod, pouring two sugar packets and a bit of cream into my coffee and stirring it with a spoon. I finish stirring and take a sip of coffee to test it out. "What about you? Have you always lived in New York?"

She nods. "Born here. I'll suffer through life here. And no doubt, I'll die here."

"You make it sounds so wonderful."

"I'm kidding." She snickers. "But I'm a New Yorker through and through. It's my home."

"And how long have you worked at Jovial Grinds?"

"Actually, I own it."

"Wait..." I tilt my head to the side. "You own the coffee shop?"

She nods. "My dad bought it for me as a high school graduation present."

I nearly choke on my enthusiasm. "That's some present."

She snorts. "Yeah. My dad is all about grand gestures of

affection." She rolls her eyes. "Since my brother is a big hotshot lawyer with a whole lot of his own money, my dad has to expend most of his efforts on me."

Ha. Sounds like a serious hardship. I bite my lip to keep from saying my opinion aloud. "Does your brother live in the city too?"

"Yep," she says and softly pops the P. "And he's a total pain in my ass."

"He sounds a lot like my brother, Evan. But he lives in Austin, so the distance keeps his nosy ass in check."

"If only my brother would relocate..."

I grin. "So, let me get this straight...you own Jovial Grinds, yet you also work as a barista there?"

She nods.

I pause to consider if I should really ask my next question, but she smiles as if to encourage it.

"Why?"

"I might be a trust-fund baby who grew up on Park Avenue, but I refuse to turn into some debutante who organizes fancy dinners and hangs out with snooty bitches. I did college, I did the travel, I did a bunch of other odd jobs, and then last year, I decided to work there."

"But you're not the manager?"

She shrugs. "I have no fucking clue how to manage a coffee shop."

Her explanation only makes me like her more.

"Where do you live now?"

"I have a loft in Harlem."

A loft in Harlem? I mean, I know it's up-and-coming, but still... I'm not sure I understand that one. She might be one of the most intriguing, mysterious people I've ever met.

"So, tell me something about yourself, Maybe," Lena says, leaning forward with a sparkle in her eye. "One thing about you I need to know."

"Jesus." I snort. "No pressure or anything."

She smiles and leans one shoulder into an exaggerated shrug. "It's not as hard as it sounds. I feel like we all usually have something specific in our hearts at any given time that we should consider our priority. If we stop ignoring it and acknowledge it—let the universe acknowledge it—we'd get a lot further in the quest to do something about it."

It's insane—totally, unequivocally nuts—but when I think about what she's said and apply it to myself, the one glaring thing that feels unresolved to me comes barreling to mind. "You're going to think it's crazy."

She shakes her head. "My *one* thing I need to get control over is my flightiness. It makes me unsure of what I want. Where I want to be. I need direction."

I swallow at her candid answer, and she jerks her chin. "Now, you go."

My lips stick together and my mouth fills with cotton, but somehow, I force the words through anyway. "I'm a virgin. And I don't want to be anymore."

My chest inflates as a weight lifts off it. It feels good to admit it.

She doesn't react at first, and my stomach starts to tense up. But when she finally speaks, she does it with a smile, and it's worth the wait. "I dig it."

"Shut up," I retort. "You're just saying that."

"I can promise you I never just say anything," she says. "And it makes complete sense to me."

Before I can offer up some sort of response, my cell phone starts vibrating across the table.

A text message from Milo. Immediately, butterflies flutter around inside my belly, and curiosity has me unlocking my screen and reading it.

Milo: Do you have time to stop by my office today? I have some publishing contacts to give you.

When I read the second half of his message, all my little winged friends fly away.

What did you expect, crazy? For him to ask you if you wanted to fuck on his desk?

I sigh, but before I can type out a response, Lena's voice grabs my attention.

"Who is that text from?"

I shrug. "No one important."

"You're such a liar." She narrows her eyes. "Seriously. Who is it?"

"Just a guy I know."

"What's his name?"

"Milo."

She stares at me long enough that I start to get self-conscious. "What? Why are you looking at me like that?"

"Because there is *so obviously* a story with this Milo. It's written all over your face."

"No, it's not."

She nods enthusiastically. "Uh-huh. I could tell the instant you read his text. I swear to God, your eyes flashed with a thousand different emotions in a matter of seconds."

"They did not."

She looks at me pointedly, and I find myself caving to her demands.

"Fine." I sigh. For some strange reason, Lena's confidence and open-mindedness hold the key to unlocking all of my secrets. It's like I *have* to trust her. It's disconcerting but unavoidable. She's obviously cast some sort of spell on me. "Milo is...my brother's best friend."

Her entire face lights up. "And why exactly is he texting you now?"

I sigh again. "Do you really want to know all the gory details?'

"Are you kidding me?" she damn near shouts. "Tell me *everything.*"

So, I do. I lay it *all* out.

The age difference, the pining, the text messages, the encounters we've had since I've been back—everything.

She is smiling and laughing and one-hundred-percent riveted through the whole tale.

But when I tell her about our lunch a few days ago and how he's supposed to be helping me get a job with a New York publishing house, she stops me.

"Wait a minute," she says with one hand raised in the air. "So, he asked you to come to his office this afternoon?"

I nod.

"That sounds a little overboard, doesn't it?" she questions and waggles her brows.

I roll my eyes. "Trust me, he's not into me."

"Girl, he's asking you to come to his office to give you information he could have just fucking texted to you. He's into you, whether he wants to admit it or not."

"Don't be ridiculous."

"Let me ask you a question," she continues. "When you asked him about helping you out with the dating scene at lunch the other day, why did you do it?"

I shrug. "I don't know."

"Yes, you do." Lena searches my eyes. "Was it because you wanted to date men in New York or because you want to date *him*?"

I don't respond. I don't know how to respond.

But the truth is most definitely evident to both of us in my silence.

"It doesn't matter why I did it," I eventually respond. "Even if I wanted to date him, I wouldn't know the first place to start, nor am I stupid enough to think he'd actually go for it. He still sees me as his best friend's little sister."

"Pssh," she says with a wave of her hand. "You're friends with me now. And I *do* know dating. I know it like the back of my fucking hand." She looks at the time on her phone. "Okay, text him back and tell him you'll be at his office around four."

"Okay…" I pause. "Why four?"

"Because we're going shopping first."

I raise a brow.

"Consider this day one of Maybe's seduction of Milo." She winks.

A shocked laugh spills from my throat. "You can't be serious."

"Oh, but I am," she singsongs. "And we're going to make damn sure that you're showing off those killer curves of yours when you step into his office this afternoon."

Seducing Milo Ives? This is crazy. I mean, it would never work… right?

But what if it *could* work…?

"Don't overthink this." Lena's voice pulls me from my thoughts. "Just text him back and prepare yourself for magic to happen."

So, I do the only thing I can do. I text him back.

Me: I'm currently at lunch with a friend, and we're going to go shopping for a bit afterward. Mind if I stop by around four?

Milo: That works. See you then.

He follows that text up with another one that includes nothing but the address of his office, and at the sight of it, my hands get clammy with the sweat of reality.

See you then, he said.

Holy hell.

What was it that Lena said the day we met? *There's no time to change like the present?*

I guess she's right. If I don't go after what I want now, I never will.

Ready or not, here the new Maybe comes.

Chapter
TWELVE

Milo

Like normal, it's been a day full of meetings and phone calls, one after another, but at some point later in the day, Clara grabs my attention from the glass door at the front of my office with a wave and a whistle.

I'm on the phone with Frank Wright—the CEO of a successful baby products company by the name of Simply Baby—but I wave her in anyway. If she waits until I get off the phone to tell me what she needs, it'll most definitely be too late. Ole Frank *loves* to chat.

Clara stops on the other side of my desk and lowers her voice to a whisper. "Mr. Ives, I have a Maybe Willis here to see you."

Is it four o'clock already?

I glance at my watch, smile—*I can't help it*—put my phone on mute, and answer her in terms that can't be misconstrued. God knows I don't have the patience to play a mind-blitzing game of charades trying to convey my message silently.

"Thanks, Clara. Send her on back, please."

Clara nods and scoots out the door, and Frank keeps right on going, blissfully unaware of my multitasking. "I'd really love to have our new software up and running by the end of next month. We've had too damn many security issues, and with over fifty new products in development, we need the team collaboration tools as soon as possible."

We haven't had a relationship with Simply Baby for long, but it's more than enough time to figure out one thing—Frank Wright is the kind of man who can never get enough reassurance and updates. If he's told me this information once, he's told me one hundred times, but he's paying Fuse a lot of money for our expertise, so all I can do is channel my inner Gandhi and coddle him via phone conversation five days a week.

Still, I'm definitely regretting giving him my number as his point of contact instead of Evan's. If Simply Baby's headquarters were in New York rather than Chicago, I imagine I'd be getting daily pop-ins a la the style of a nosy neighbor.

Knowing exactly the pep talk I need to give to get Frank off the phone expediently, I start into my spiel.

"I understand your concerns, Frank, and I know your company's especially vulnerable during this growth. I can assure you—"

The glass door to my office swings open again, but this time, the woman walking in steals the air right out of my chest and puts a stop to any and all words before they leave my mouth.

Good *God.*

Unconsciously, a hand goes to my chest.

She is...*stunning.*

Long, sleek, shiny brown hair gathers in the center of her shoulders and flows down her back, and her lips are painted a lush, almost merlot red. Her legs must be a mile and half long to show that much skin in her tastefully short white dress, and the nude stilettos on her feet make me imagine what they'd look like wrapped around my back.

Fuck. This isn't good.

But there's also something about her that has nothing to do with the clothes or the hair or the makeup—it's in the way she carries herself across the marble flooring of my office.

It makes my heart beat so hard it's hard to breathe.

She flashes a grin and mouths a "hi" my way before she sits down and crosses her legs in the seat across from mine.

She's self-assured to the point of *bold,* and the change of pace sets my blood on fire.

Confidence looks *good* on Maybe Willis.

"Milo? You still there?" the voice in my ear questions, and I have to blink a few times to understand where in the hell it's coming from.

"Milo?" he asks again, and I finally snap back to reality.

The call with Frank Wright.

I find my voice as quickly as possible and work tirelessly to steady it. "I'm still here, Frank," I say, holding up one finger in Maybe's direction.

She nods her understanding and glances around my office curiously. It takes all of my willpower not to watch her with avid interest.

"I can assure you, Frank, you have nothing to be worried about. We'll have you up and running three weeks before your deadline."

"That's great news."

I smile with satisfaction and toss Maybe an unplanned wink. Her endless, warm eyes hold mine so intently, I find it hard to swallow.

"I'm going to get you in contact with my CFO, whose Austin team is actually the one working on your software. That way, he can keep you abreast of all progress to make sure you're at ease until everything is done," I tell Frank, making a command decision to fork the problem off on to my best friend—something I should have done two months ago.

I patch Frank through to Clara to give him Evan's number and email, and then thankfully, end the call.

"Passing off your difficult clients to my brother?" Maybe teases, her lips curling up into a sexy grin.

I shrug and hold her eyes. "Sometimes, it pays to be the boss."

She laughs at that.

"So, I take it lunch and shopping went well?" I ask, and she glances down at her dress and heels.

Twisting a foot inward so that her knees touch in the center and her hip sticks out, then lifting her arms meaningfully at her sides, she tilts her head to her shoulder and challenges, "You tell me."

"You look..." I start to pay her a compliment, but when words like *sexy* and *gorgeous* and *fucking beautiful* pop into my mind, I pause to search for something a little less...*intense.*

This is Evan's baby sister, and I haven't been able to stop ogling her since she walked through the door. The last thing I need to do is give my mind permission by saying something I shouldn't out loud.

"I look?" she asks when I don't finish, searching my eyes. "I look what?"

"Uh..." I clear my throat and scrub a hand through my hair. "You look very nice."

My dick calls me a chickenshit liar in four different languages. Which is really impressive since I only speak the one.

Her face falls ever so slightly, but she recovers quickly. "Thanks." Unfortunately, it's still too slow to hide her disappointment completely, and I feel like a prick.

Nice? I may as well have been giving a compliment to my mother.

I clear my throat and try again. "What I meant to say is that the clothes look very nice. *You* look *beautiful.*"

Her cheeks flush my new favorite color—a perfect mix of peachy pink and red—and she stares up at me from beneath her lashes. "You really think so?"

"Yes," I answer without hesitation. I can't pussyfoot around the truth too much, and quite frankly, I won't. Maybe should know— she should always know—she's more than a stylish dress and good makeup. "You always look beautiful, kid."

Her eyes widen and her mouth parts, and I suddenly have a vivid picture of what she'd look like staring up at me from her knees.

Jesus, Milo. Stop. Stop right now.

Before Maybe can respond—and before I can mentally undress my best friend's little *and* off-limits sister, I direct the conversation to the whole reason I had her stop by my office today.

"Tell me...if you could work for any publishing house in New York, which one would you choose?"

She doesn't even have to think about it. "Beacon House."

"That was a quick answer."

She shrugs. "I put a little bit of thought into this over the past six years while I slaved away at Stanford."

"Well, good. I have an excellent connection at Beacon, but that's not who you'll be interviewing with first," I say immediately, scribbling down notes on the edge of my desk calendar. Now that I know what her ultimate end game is, I know exactly the direction to go.

She quirks a brow, and I continue.

"I'm going to line up an interview for you at Rainbow Press next week."

I don't miss the slightest hint of a frown that mars the smooth surface of her forehead. "Rainbow Press?"

"Yep."

Rainbow Press is a moderately successful publishing house whose editor in chief, Cassandra Cale, went to Yale with Evan and me. And the truth is, I already lined up an interview for Maybe there this morning. When I spoke with Cassandra and told her about Maybe, she told me they were already on the hunt to add three more junior editors to their staff. I knew they'd be the kind of stepping stone we'd need to get us any other place Maybe could dream up.

"Oh. Okay. Well...that's great."

I grin at her stapled-together, blandly polite response, and she rallies a little harder, thinking I want more from her. "I would be happy to have a job at a publishing house like Rainbow Press."

"Yeah, but it's not good enough to achieve your dream," I tease slightly, and she shakes her head.

"No, it's fine."

I laugh. "I appreciate your attempt at being diplomatic, kid, but Rainbow Press is not where you're going to end up."

She tilts her head to the side, and I watch the way a few long locks of her hair slide across her shoulders. She worries her bottom lip with her teeth, and then finally, shrugs her defeat. "I'm confused."

"Think of this interview as a practice interview," I explain. "I'm certain you'll get the job, but I don't want you to actually accept the job."

"Wait…" She pauses and searches my eyes. "You want me to go to this interview already knowing I'm not going to accept the job?"

I smile and wink. "Bingo. That's exactly what I want you to do."

"You realize that makes no sense, right?"

"Just trust me on this. You're going to hold out for something that's bigger and better. Something like Beacon House." I smirk. "But you're going to need an offer on the table in order to do that."

"You sound insanely certain."

"Because I know how a thriving company like Beacon House works," I answer with conviction. "I already know they're not currently looking to add any editors to their roster, but I also know they don't want to miss a new, up-and-coming, *sought after* editor who graduated from a prestigious school like Stanford."

She stays quiet for a long moment, and I watch her closely. I might not know much about women, but I know Maybe looks damned beautiful when she's deep in thought.

"You really think this is a surefire plan?"

I lean back in my leather chair. "I didn't turn ten thousand dollars in credit card debt into a thriving billion-dollar business without having this kind of foresight. Stick with me, kid."

"Okay," she finally agrees, raising both fists above her head in a pathetic excuse for a cheer. "Beacon House, here I come."

I laugh. "First stop, Rainbow Press. Next stop, the job of your dreams."

Her responding smile lights up the damn room. "God, I hope you're right."

"I am," I say with the kind of confidence you can't fake. "You're going to do big things in the publishing industry."

An adorable snort escapes her nose. "You're just saying that."

"I'm saying it because it's true," I correct her and proceed to grab a piece of paper from my desk and jot down the information for her interview.

Next Tuesday 2:00 pm with Cassandra Cale, editor in chief at Rainbow Press

"When you get to the lobby, ask for her," I explain and slide the paper across the surface of my desk until it meets her fingertips.

She takes it into her hands, scanning it quickly. "I thought you hadn't set this up yet?"

I shrug. "I guess I fibbed."

She grins and waves her hands around the office at my photographs with celebrities, Business Bureau Awards, and original Pollock paintings. The one solid wall of my office is covered from corner to corner, and the other three are made of glass. "You better watch that nose, Pinocchio. There's a whole lot of valuable, *breakable* shit in this room."

I smile, stand from my chair, and circle the end of my modern black desk to lean into the other side—*closer to her.*

"What are you up to for the rest of the day?" I ask as a means to distract myself from reaching out to grab her trim waist.

"Uh...I don't know... Go home. Take these heels off. Figure out TapNext."

"TapNext?" My eyebrows draw together.

"It's a dating app," she explains, but it's not the app I don't know. A good friend of mine by the name of Kline Brooks created that hugely successful dating app many moons ago. It's based on the standard dating model, but it's undeniably better in every area possible. More secure. More clients. And the highest match success rate in the country. "My friend Lena, the one I went shopping with, wants me to try it out with her."

Discomfort comes out of nowhere and fills my throat, but I swallow it down. She doesn't need some asshole raining on her parade.

"Anyway, Lena is convinced my dating card is about to be so full I won't even know where to begin." She rolls her eyes, and then a tiny, nervous smile kisses her lips. "I'm not sure if I should be excited or terrified."

I nod, but I don't need a mirror to know it's *stiffer* than normal.

"What's that look for?" she asks, noting my sudden silence.

"Nothing."

She quirks a brow. "It doesn't seem like nothing."

It *is* nothing. It's a simple attraction to a beautiful woman I've known most of my life. It's not anything to get worked up over, for God's sake. Right?

Still, it's not like I can say that to her. "I'm just happy I'm not the one who's about to set up a profile on TapNext," I improvise instead.

"You don't like dating apps?"

I shake my head. "Not for me anyway."

"Because you loathe dating," she says with a little smile.

"I don't loathe dating. I just don't have time for it."

But apparently, I loathe the idea of you dating, which is fucking insane.

"You totally do," she retorts, and I just brush it off with a laugh.

"Just do me a favor, yeah?" She raises her perfectly shaped eyebrows pointedly and waits for me to continue. "Be careful who you agree to go on a date with."

She laughs. "You afraid I'm going to end up in someone's trunk?"

"Jesus, kid. That's a terrifying thought."

"Don't worry, Milo," she says with a wink. "I'll make sure the FBI does background checks on all of my prospects."

A tiny grin curls the corner of my mouth as I shake my head. "Smartass."

"Yeah, well, someone had to lighten the mood here."

"Says the person who just mentioned ending up in someone's trunk."

"It was a joke!" she excuses on a laugh.

"A *horrible* joke."

"I guess maybe Bruce is rubbing off on me."

"*Also* a terrifying thought."

"Fine," she says with a cheeky grin. "I take back the trunk joke."

"It's a little late for that."

She rolls her big brown eyes. "If I didn't know any better, I'd think I was sitting across from Evan right now."

"Yeah, well, since he's in Austin, I guess someone has to keep an eye on you."

Clara's voice fills my office suddenly and interrupts our banter. "Mr. Ives, I have Mr. Frost with Berkin Industries on the line for you."

Maybe smiles slightly and jerks a thumb toward the door. "I guess I'll leave you to run your empire, Billionaireman."

"Very funny."

She grins. "Thank you for the sage career advice."

"You're welcome," I say, and the genuineness in my tone can't be missed. "Let me know how it goes with Rainbow Press next week. And if you have any issues figuring out where you need to be, give me a call."

"Will do."

I watch with dismay as she disappears, out of my office door and down the hallway and most likely home to start a goddamn dating profile on TapNext.

Son of a bitch. The idea of it makes me cringe.

But Maybe Willis is off-limits. So, I have no choice. All I can do is sit back and watch the real-live nightmare happen.

Chapter THIRTEEN

Maybe

I have an interview today.

An *I'm going to interview but not take the job* interview, but an interview all the same.

Thanks to Milo, I am meeting with Cassandra Cale, the editor in chief for Rainbow Press—a publishing house located in Manhattan.

It's supposed to be a laid-back meet-and-greet where I'll introduce myself, she'll ask me some questions, and then tell me about the job opportunities that are available within the company.

Funny how that still translates to what must surely be a heart attack.

My chest is tight and my hands are fidgety, and if my knee would stop bouncing for just one fucking second, it'd be nice. And jaw pain. Women having heart attacks usually have jaw pain, right?

Anxiety, party of one!

I take a deep inhale and force myself to walk down the steps of the nearest subway station. My new pair of pale pink heels click-clacks against the concrete what sounds like assuredly, but my legs are so shaky, I have to do something I never do—grip the dirty, grimy, bacteria-infested banister to the left of the steps—to prevent myself from falling face first.

I make a mental note not to touch my face with my germy hands before I can wash them at the very first opportunity.

The noon subway crowd is chaos, and people are everywhere.

Rushing. Waiting. Running. Walking fast. Walking too slow. It's a swirling sea of hipsters, homeless, and upper middle-class worthy of that movie *Sharknado*.

Despite the variety of backgrounds, when it's crowded like this, people have no distinction. They are just things in your way. Moving, smelling—good and bad—sometimes accommodating but a lot of times rude *things*.

An older gentleman in khaki shorts with his belt basically fastened to his neckline bumps me as I step onto the platform, and I teeter on my heels.

He doesn't notice, though. I am, like him, just a thing.

With a whine and a displacement of air, the train arrives, and I hurry on with the rest of the New York crowd. Belt man bumps me again to find the only open seat left and plops his khaki ass down like he owns the joint.

I, on the other hand, am left standing beside one of the metal poles.

Promptly, the train shuts its doors, leaving anyone outside of its threshold stuck in the muggy station air, and starts its path toward the next station with a jolt. Unsteadily, I grip the coolness of the pole to keep my balance.

One hand free, I pull my phone out of my purse and do what everyone else on the train is doing, I scroll through social media.

Facebook first.

Then Twitter.

And for the briefest of moments, I search the TapNext app that Lena has been badgering me about for the past week. But when I locate it in the app store, I can't get myself to download it.

What in the hell would I do on a dating app?

The only thing I can imagine is disaster.

Yeah. Definitely not doing this today.

I move right along, and by the time I pull up Instagram, I'm what those new age parents refer to as *overstimulated*. I scan the train

110

surreptitiously, keeping one eye to my Instagram feed as a means of pretense until my attention catches on the phone screen of a young woman seated right beside the metal pole I'm holding on to. Wearing a cutoff pair of jean shorts and sporting curly blond hair, she looks to be about my age.

I watch as her fingers tap excitedly across the keypad and wait for something of interest to show up in response to her succinct prompt of *Tell me.*

I shouldn't be looking. Or reading, for that matter, but I can't help it.

After all the peptalking I've had to do to avoid throwing myself directly onto Milo's penis, I have zero willpower left.

I want to spread your legs wide, slowly, and kiss down the inside of your thighs.

My cheeks heat at the simple sentence, but I have to blink three times just to steady myself when the next message populates.

I fucking love how wet you get.

Holy mother of subway sexy times.
My mind takes off at the pace of a Derby horse.
Who the hell is the dirty talker on the other end of her phone?
Is he even a fraction as attractive as Milo?
Does she know how flip-flapping lucky she is?!
Her fingers tap across the keypad, and a few seconds later, her response pops onto the screen of her phone.

I'm on the subway, and my back is arched just thinking about this. I'm craving you so bad right now...

God. I want that.

I want the low-ache, can't-breathe, skin-scratching feeling of someone talking to me like that. I want to be wanted so badly, a man can't stand the thought of waiting another second to tell me what he's going to do with me.

I want to sext and be sexted and live out every single word in real life.

I've never even come close to experiencing a sliver of what the NSFW blonde has.

Am I missing out?

I suppose there's still time to change it, but is it even possible for a twenty-four-year-old virgin to sext?

I'm not completely naïve, but I can't deny I'm still *pretty damn naïve* at the same time.

Without a second thought, I swipe the lock screen on my phone, click into my messages, and pull up the straightest shooter I know.

If there's anyone who'll know what to do—know how to take control of this part of my life and change it—it's her.

Me: Do you like sexting people?

Lena responds a minute later.

Lena: Definitely. Though, I've had some seriously weird sext conversations that I'd prefer to never experience again.

Me: Like what?

Lena: Oh, honey. You don't want to know.

Me: Yes. I do.

I nod to myself as I send it just to punctuate my words with completely useless emphasis.

Lena: Well, I've had guys send me pictures of things I didn't want to see and go into explicit detail on things I would never even type into Google, and I've been looped into a group conversation with some swingers with questionable choices in camera angle.

Me: But you do sext. I mean, you've for sure sexted before and you've liked it.

Lena: Lol. Yes, I've sexted and, yes, I've liked it.

God, I want to sext message someone.

You want to sext Milo.

No. Not Milo. Well, not specifically him. Obviously, it'd be great if it were him, but I just want to experience it in general.

Hello, denial! Nice to meet you! I'm a big fat liar otherwise known as Maybe!

God, my inner subconscious is such a snarky biotch sometimes.

Lena: So...mind telling me where all this is coming from?

Me: I'm sitting here on the subway watching this cute girl sext message with someone. I kind of saw them...on accident.

Sort of. I mean, the first message was definitely an accident, but the next four or so were more of an intentional eavesdrop. Those are minor details, obviously.

Lena: Adorable and a little voyeur? I swear to God, you are too much. I fucking love it.

Before I can respond, another text message pops onto the screen.

Lena: Stop eavesdropping on other people's sext convos, and do it for yourself. You need to sext message Milo. Tonight.

The mention of his name makes me gasp and choke at the same time, and the sound comes out kind of like a bark. The man to the left looks at me, and his mouth turns down at the corners. Obviously, he was hoping to find a cute Yorkshire Terrier or the like, and instead found a virginal, odd girl.

I turn my back on him and go back to typing on my phone.

Me: WHAT? No.

Lena: You gotta be crazy if you want to get what you want in the end. And you want Milo. Scoot out onto that sexting limb and reach for him.

Me: OMG. You're serious. YOU'RE SERIOUS???

Lena: Consider this Phase 2 in Maybe's Seduction Plan.

Me: Phase 2? HAHA. I'm still trying to uncover my eyes in Phase 1.

Lena: Just trust me, okay?

Me: I wouldn't know the first fucking thing to say.

Lena: Let me guess, he's already told you he wants you to let him know how your interview goes today, right?

Me: How in the hell do you know that?

What the hell? Did she bug me before I left Bergdorf's with her last week?

Lena: I'm telling you…I have a real sixth sense about these things. The man is into you, Maybe. He's currently trying to fight it, but the proof is in the pudding. He wants to see you. Talk to you. And, after your sext conversation tonight, he's going to want to bang you.

Me: *Your confidence is terrifying.*

Yeah, but you're one-hundred-percent smiling like a loon right now, so what does that say about you?

I groan inwardly at my own ridiculousness.

Lena: *Have I steered you wrong yet?*

Me: *Technically, no. But I'm chalking that up to luck more than anything.*

Lena: *You have no reason to doubt me.*

Me: *You do realize it's not as simple as me just sexting him, right? To do that, I would have to know something ABOUT sexting. The closest I've ever come to dirty talk is the end of the year exam in sex ed.*

Lena: *LOL. Relax. You're not going to start a sexting convo with him. You're going to text him about your interview. And THEN, you're going to segue it into the sexting.*

I furrow my brow.
And she really thinks I'm capable of something like this?
Apparently, she's lost her mind.

Me: *How in the hell am I supposed to do that? Everything I'm coming up with revolves around, "Oh, so, by the way, would you care to engage in a little sexting with me?"*

Lena: *HA! Yeah, definitely don't do that.*

Me: See? I cannot be trusted to handle Phase 2. I'm completely incompetent.

Lena: Take a breath, girl. You can do this. You're attracted to Milo, right?

I frown at my phone.

Me: Obviously, yes.

Lena: Then you've got the tools. When something you want to do to him comes to mind, just type it instead of keeping it to yourself. And, trust me on this, it does NOT take much.

The subway whines as it slows down at the next stop—my stop—and just before I can shoot Lena another message about how awful of an idea this is, a new text message comes through.

But it's not from her.

Milo: I glanced at the clock and saw the time. I hope you're not nervous about today, but if you are, just know you have no reason to be. You're going to do great, kid.

God, it's like his ears were burning or something.

My fingers hover over the keypad, tempted to tap out a reply, but I decide to wait.

I'll text him after the interview.

And then maybe, just maybe, if I can find the damn nerve, I'll put Phase 2 into action.

But right now, I need to focus.

Off the subway and up the stairs, I head toward my fate.

My first official interview with a publishing house.

Here's to hoping Cassandra Cale actually likes me.

Chapter
FOURTEEN

Milo

Time flows like hardened cement as I sit inside a meeting about our upcoming mergers and acquisitions.

It's all very important shit we've been working on for a long time—shit I do, in fact, care about—but the guy leading the meeting, Earl from Finance, has the vocational charisma of a sloth.

His voice moves like molasses—so much so that I'm pretty sure Ambien is in the process of studying its chemical makeup—and he uses no gestures to accompany his words whatsoever. I can't help but picture him as the male version of Elaine's coworker on *Seinfeld*, played by Molly Shannon, who didn't move her arms when she walked.

Across the large pine conference table, Laura, Fuse's Head of Marketing, blinks her green eyes slowly, the top of her head starting to sag in a sleepy tilt forward before jolting upright again.

I bite my lip to fight my grin as potential drug names for an Earl-based sleep aid come to mind.

Monotonetelix.

Boresnorevidel.

Noinflectionplex.

Another glance around the table shows a large number of people at the end of their ropes. There might as well be invisible jail cells inside this conference room for all the enjoyment these people are getting. They're doing ten-to-twenty-five, and the only option left is to bide their time.

I squint across the room.

Is that…is Jeanine from HR making a license plate?

I make a mental note to put Earl on projects that only require his numbers-genius brain and nothing else in the future. No running meetings, giving presentations to clients, or public speaking engagements of any kind.

Sadly, I'm responsible—I called this meeting. I'm the jailer *and* the fucking prisoner in this situation, and yet, I have no recourse.

I make eye contact with Lyle, my right-hand man in New York, and the agony on his face is almost comical.

"For the love of God, finish him!" his furrowed brow—a bushy, uni type that could have its own zip code—yells like we're inside the game *Mortal Kombat.*

I shake my head on a smile. This is important. We both know it's important.

Earl is giving the eighteen most important people working at Fuse's New York offices the rundown on how we're about to move further into the international market.

Taiwan. Tokyo. Rome. Melbourne.

They're all on the cusp of the next big tech bubble, and Fuse is going to be at the helm of software safety for all of them.

We *have* to have this meeting. Still, Lyle's mime-like depiction of shoving a pencil through his eye isn't unwarranted.

Earl has started in on his *detailed* financial plan for the next six months, and if I'm not mistaken, I hear a flock of buzzards start circling above us.

My phone vibrates inside the pocket of my jeans, and I take it out without hesitation. Normally, looking at my phone during a meeting is a big fat no, but today…today, I'm thankful for *any* distraction.

A text message notification shows on my lock screen, and a smile curves my lips when I see who it's from.

Maybe: Thank you for the pep talk earlier. It made all the difference in my efforts not to come across as one of the characters from Girl, Interrupted.

I bite my lip to keep myself from laughing out loud while Earl reads from his list of figures. My phone is under the table, but a laugh during this meeting would undoubtedly give me away.

Me: So, it went well?

Maybe: I *think* it went well. God, I'm not sure. But you'll have to help me overanalyze it later tonight when Bruce isn't on a rampage about roses. "If I see one more wilted petal on these thorned beaches, I'm gonna shiitake mushroom all over that godspam pitiful excuse for a supplier!"

Me: LOL. Sounds like a plan. And sorry about Bruce...I'm praying for you.

Maybe: HA! Great. Hopefully God takes Billionaireman seriously as a character reference. This is supposed to be a freaking flower shop, but I'm in the weeds here.

She's so funny, a smile slips past my defenses, and Lyle notices. His superbrow draws together again, but I shake my head subtly.

Not only is the catalyst for my happiness none of his business, I'm afraid I couldn't explain it to him even if I wanted to.

I mean...*what am I doing here?*

Am I still just doing Evan a favor?

Am I looking out for a person I'm fond of?

Are Maybe and I friends?

I'm dangerously aware that there might be even *more* to it than friends, but I refuse to open that can of worms now by allowing the thought to fully form.

The guilt alone would take days to sort through.

All I know is that the promise of talking to her tonight makes me feel like a kid again—like the tree is decorated, the presents are wrapped, and later tonight, Santa's going to give me the gift I've been waiting for all year.

Fucking hell. Life sure is starting to feel complicated.

Chapter
FIFTEEN

Milo

"**I**t that all you got?" I taunt my trainer, Claude, like some kind of workout masochist.

He swings at my head once, twice, three times, and I duck like I was born to fucking quack.

My feet move quickly to the right, and I bend my upper body to the left before swinging an unexpected right hook right into the fleshy part of Claude's ear.

He smiles—*because while I'm a masochist, he is an outright sadist*—and lures me in for more.

I stutter-step forward, my eyes on his hands as he moves them expertly to block every punch I throw, and breathe through the aching stitch in my side.

No matter how many training sessions he puts me through, no matter how in shape I *think* I am, I still leave the gym feeling like someone just ran me over with a truck. Tonight will be no different.

I round out the dance between us with a spin and a double hit to his stomach, and he swings up and around to land one last strike to my shoulder just as the timer he set on his phone rings out with mercy on me.

I head for the side of the ring to grab my towel, and Claude follows.

"Nice workout, bro," he says, his accent a heavy mix of old-school German and millennial-influenced American. "I'll see you Wednesday."

I mentally flip him the bird but outwardly nod toward him after I take a swig of water. "See ya, man. Thanks."

I'm not thankful at all—at least not right now. I feel like a real prick for paying someone to torture me.

But two days from now, I'll be craving more. It's an endless cycle that keeps the three-time heavyweight boxing champion on my payroll.

Yep. Definitely a workout masochist.

Claude slides out of the boxing ring, out of the room, and toward the entrance to the gym, and I finally feel free to drop my tough guy act a little.

"Ow," I whisper, rolling my shoulder around on itself.

With only the final remnants of adrenaline flowing through my veins and a real ache starting to set in, I grab the rest of my shit from one of the chairs in the far corner of the ring and make my way toward the locker room.

I push through the heavy wood door easily enough, but when its swing is almost complete, the weight of it disappears and my body jumps forward.

Right into an actual giant.

"Milo!" he shouts, his voice jovial and *loud*. While I startle at first, it doesn't take me long to smile.

Thatcher Kelly is a larger-than-life kind of guy. *Literally.* He makes me look tiny in comparison, and I'm not even pulling an ego card when I say I'm not exactly a small guy—I'm six foot two inches of *mostly* muscle.

He looks like he ate me for breakfast. A Milo Protein Bar, if you will.

"What in the fuck have you been up to?" he asks, slapping me on the back with almost frightening strength. "It's been a while, dude."

While I've known Thatch for a few years—since the day he barreled his way into my meeting with Kline Brooks and turned it into a meeting about him—I don't have much occasion to see him outside of work. I think it's been at least six months since I've even run into him here at the gym.

"Working. Traveling. You know, all the same shit," I respond with a grin. "How are you? How are Cass and the kids?"

"Everyone is good. Crazy, but good."

I laugh. Thatch's wife is, in fact, crazy. Outspoken, impulsive, and sometimes unpredictable, she should come with a "may cause serious injury or death" warning like a firework.

The last time I spent time with the two of them, we met up for drinks at a cigar bar in SoHo and somehow ended the night in Midtown with Cassie doing a white-girl-wasted version of "Girls Just Wanna Have Fun" in a bar that didn't even have karaoke.

"How's Kline?"

"Boring as-fucking-ever," he says with a smirk.

I laugh. Anything tamer than doing ninety on a dirt bike, and Thatcher Kelly thinks it's boring.

"When are you settling down and tying the knot like the rest of us pathetic bastards?"

I smile at the gossipy question, and he pounces.

"Ah, a smile! So, when can Cass and I meet her?"

"Meet whom?"

"Your wife-to-be."

"Slow your roll, dude," I say with a laugh. "Pretty sure I have to find her first."

"You're not dating anyone?"

I shake my head, and he narrows his eyes.

"No man ever smiles at that question unless they've got the lady in mind."

An image of Maybe pops unbidden in my head, and I jump on that shit like a member of the goddamn WWE.

Holy shit, why would I think of her right now?

I try to steady my racing heart and answer the inquisitive giant as normally as possible. "No lady yet. But I'm thirty, Thatch. Pretty sure I've got time."

He snorts. "Yeah, well, I'm well *past* thirty. I'd like to attend the wedding before I get arthritis."

"I'll do my best," I say with a laugh, and he smiles.

"See that you do. And listen, I'm thinking about starting up a poker night. Boys-only kind of thing once a week. You interested?"

I shrug. "Yeah. Sounds good. Let me know when you get it set up."

"Will fluffing do, Lo-Dog."

I shake my head at his ridiculousness and give him a chin jerk goodbye. I'm sure I'll be seeing him for poker soon, though. When it comes to Thatcher Kelly, you learn pretty quick that once he sets his mind to something, it's a guarantee it will happen.

By the time I make it out of the gym and toward the subway station, it's nearing eight and I'm so hungry, I'm contemplating asking the guy sitting across from me for a bite of his Chipotle burrito.

Thankfully, my place is only one station away.

Sure, I could have used my driver, Sam, but his daughter had a dance recital tonight, and I'm not too keen on being responsible for scarring children emotionally. Her dad should be there, and I have two feet and can handle the short subway ride and walk on the rare occasion when he can't drive me.

Fifteen minutes later, I step inside my apartment, grab the menu from the cabinet and call in an order from the restaurant across the street, and jump in the shower.

They're usually quick with delivery, and I don't like to mix food and sweat.

Luckily, I finish up and am pulling a white T-shirt over my boxer briefs when the bell rings, indicating someone's arrival. I head down the hall, and the elevator door slides open to my doorman, Gill.

"Hello, Mr. Ives. Your food order."

I reach out to take it from him with a smile. "Thanks, Gill. Still have money, or do I owe you some more?"

To keep things more secure—you wouldn't believe how many weirdos there are out there trying to get my address off the internet—Gill acts as a middleman for me on deliveries. I keep a rolling supply of money with him to pay for everything.

He smiles and shakes his head. "I'm all set, Mr. Ives."

"Thanks. Don't forget to tip yourself," I remind him.

He nods once and steps back onto the elevator.

I spread out the contents of my bag on the counter—broiled salmon, broccoli, and lemon-butter rice—and grab a plate from the cabinet. But before I can serve it up, a message alert makes my phone buzz on the marble countertop.

I move to it quickly and scoop it up. I can't even pretend I haven't been waiting for this message all night. And thankfully, since I'm home alone right now, I don't have to.

Maybe: *flashes Billionaire signal on buildings all over New York City* Are you there, Billionaireman? I'm ready for your help fighting my neuroses.

My smile is so big, I feel it all the way at the corners of my eyes.

Me: Here and at the ready, my distressed friend. Lay it on me.

Maybe: Okay, so, I *think* I made a good impression with Cassandra. I mean, she didn't kick me out in the first five minutes, and I didn't make ANY references to My Little Pony. She even happened to know some of my work from the Stanford Gazette.

I shake my head as I type out a reply, wondering how one human being can amuse me so much.

Me: Was referencing My Little Pony an actual possibility?

Maybe: I don't put anything past myself when I'm nervous.

Me: Well, you can relax now. It sounds like she loved you.

Maybe: Let's not get too ahead of ourselves here, buddy.

Me: Tell me this—did she tell you when she'd call you?

Maybe: She said I'd hear from her in the next day or so.

Me: She loved you.

Maybe: How in the hell do you know that? You weren't even there! Can Billionaireman see through walls now?

I picture her getting all amped up, and it makes me laugh into the silence of my apartment. It comes out sounding a little evil, but there's no one here to hear it, so I don't waste time focusing on it.

Instead, I type out another message and hit send.

Me: I've known Cassandra for a long time, and she isn't one to say something she doesn't mean. She's a straight shooter. Like the John Wayne of publishing.

Maybe: Hmm… exactly how well do you know her? Like, are you guys friends, or are you guys "friendly"?

My eyebrows draw together.

Me: Is there a difference?

Maybe: Yes. Friends is friends. But friendly? That could mean all sorts of things. Like when Jimmy Thompson's mom was "friendly" with the mailman when I was in second grade, and he ended up with a dog-phobic half-brother.

I laugh.

Me: You're making that up.

Maybe: Maybe I am, maybe I'm not. The story doesn't matter, Milo. What matters is that "friendly" means something different than friends.

I shake my head and type out a response. I glance over at my food. It's got to be cold by now, but that's what microwaves are for.

Me: We are just FRIENDS, kid. She went to Yale with me and Ev.

Maybe: Ah, okay. Not that it matters or anything. You're free to be friendly with whomever you want. And she's a pretty lady, so being friendly with her probably wouldn't be bad.

Me: Maybe.

Maybe: Wait...are you saying my name or saying maybe it wouldn't be bad being friendly with her?

Me: MABEL WILLIS, I have no intention of being friendly with Cassandra Cale now or ever.

Maybe: Oh. Well, all right. None of my business.

I shake my head and laugh out loud. I can't help it. She's a lunatic. A fucking adorable lunatic, but a lunatic nonetheless.

Maybe: Well, I just want to say again, thank you for getting me that interview and helping me with this. I am forever grateful.

Me: No thanks needed. I'm glad to help.

Five minutes pass by without her saying anything else, so I dish out my food onto a plate and put it into the microwave. Just as the microwave announces it's done, my phone buzzes again. I leave the food and pick up my phone again.

Maybe: Can I ask you something?

With the way this evening's conversation has gone, there's absolutely no telling what's on her mind. And honestly, that's kind of the fun part.

Me: Shoot.

I grab a bottle of water from the fridge and take a swig while the bubbles of her message that indicate she's typing whirl.

Maybe: How often do you sext? A rough calculation is fine. Round up, round down, that sort of thing.

I spew water all over myself and the counter, and then quickly wipe it away from my face with the sleeve of my T-shirt.
She's asking me about sexting? Where in the hell did this come from? Was it a typo?

Me: I'm sorry...did you say sext? As in text messaging about sex?

Maybe: Yes.

Part of me is thrilled about the prospect of talking about sex with this gorgeous woman. It's so thrilled, it's giving the idea a big ole standing ovation.
I groan and adjust my pants before rubbing at my eyes to try to make myself think with other, more rational parts of my body.
Maybe Willis is Evan's little sister. I should *not* engage in talk about sexting with her.

Me: I don't know if I'm really comfortable talking about this, kid. Sexting can get...intense.

Maybe: So, you have done it. You do it.

I groan and type out what I think is a fairly innocuous message. If she's not going to drop it, I'll just have to keep things in check.

Me: I mean, it's not on my appointment calendar, but it's happened before.

Maybe: What do you say when you sext?

Fucking hell. I bite my lip as my mind automatically plays through a list of things I want to say to her.

I dare you to rub your fingers over the top of your panties. But do it exactly how you love to touch yourself when the panties aren't in the way.

Slide a finger inside yourself. But imagine it's me. Imagine it's my hard cock filling you up.

If I were there, I'd taste you. I'd slide my tongue inside you and feel how wet you are. And I'd rub my cock on your clit, make you beg me to slide inside you.

Shiiiit. I'm in so much trouble here.

I take a deep breath to recenter myself and succumb to the fact that I'm going to have a rock-hard cock until I do something about it later tonight.

I can't tell her the things I want to say, so I go with something a little more textbook than romance novel and hit send.

Me: I don't have pre-planned sext messages that I send out to women, Maybe. It's more of an in-the-moment kind of thing.

Maybe: I think I want to do it. Sext message, that is. It's time.

I rub at my face roughly. *Good God, she's trying to kill me.*

Me: It doesn't exactly work like that. You don't just start randomly sexting people.

Maybe: I KNOW THAT. I'm just saying I want to experience it.

Before I can respond, another text message pops onto the screen.

Maybe: Why don't we just do some sexting now?

Me: WHAT?

Maybe: C'mon, Milo. It's not a big ask. Just help me practice a bit.

She wants me to practice sexting with her? I open and close my eyes just to make sure what I'm seeing is real.

But it is. And she doesn't hesitate to continue her crazy campaign to make it happen.

Maybe: Evan asked you to help me!

I laugh. Outright.

Me: He asked me to help you find a job in publishing. I'm absolutely positive he did not ask me to sext with you. I don't even think Evan's ever used the word sext in conversation.

Maybe: It's not like I'm going to send you pictures of my boobs and demand dick pics. I just want to rehearse. Like a sound check.

Sound check. *Christ.* The fact that she's never done something like this before and wants to experience it for the first time with me is almost too much to handle.

Why does she have to be so goddamn irresistible?

Maybe: It's either you or some random dude on TapNext.

TapNext? Fuck. I abhor the thought of her sexting some asshole on a dating app.

Maybe: What are you wearing right now?

She's relentless. I sigh. But I also smile.

She's so damn disarming, I don't even know what I'm thinking anymore. It's like I've lost all control of myself.

Maybe: Please, Milo.

Me: You're not giving up on this, are you?

Maybe: Nope.

Son of a bitch. This is a bad idea.

I *know* this is a bad idea.

But despite my better judgment, my fingers tap across the screen slowly while my heart speeds up in my chest.

Chapter
SIXTEEN

Maybe

Okay, so I don't think I started Phase 2 exactly like Lena explained.

In fact, I'm pretty sure I did the exact opposite of what she advised.

But when absolutely no natural segue came to mind, I found myself reciting a lesson from my childhood with Betty Willis over and over again in my head—*honesty is always the best policy.*

The fact that I used Betty's advice on something as unorthodox as sexting Milo is completely disturbing, but there's no going back now.

All I can do is wait.

Nervously.

When two minutes pass, I start to freak out and throw myself face first into the comforter on my bed. The down material compresses at my face, allowing my continued breathing with ease. When a third minute comes to a close, I start to wish the material were a little more unyielding.

Jesus. What have I done? I completely fucked Phase 2, and now he is probably never going to speak to me again! Abort! Abort the mission!

I'm seconds away from typing out a rambling apology when my phone vibrates in my hands.

Milo: Boxer briefs and a T-shirt.

Oh. My. God. He's doing it.

We're doing it.

Well, we're not actually doing *it*, but we're doing sexting, the virtual form of doing it, and holy hell, I cannot breathe.

Calm the hell down! Take a breath, you lunatic.

I force myself to breathe and read his text message with slightly less crazy eyes.

Boxer briefs and a T-shirt.

Milo in just boxer briefs and a T-shirt?

Yeah, that's hot.

Shit. Okay. Sexting. Sexting.

What in the hell do I say next?

Are they big boxer briefs?

What the hell? That doesn't even make sense, Maybe.

Delete.

Do you have a big ole ball bulge?

Seriously?

Delete.

After another four awful attempts, I come up with something I *think* seems appropriate and hit send.

Me: Can I see?

Milo: Only if you show me too.

I swallow hard and look down at my stupid pizza pajama pants and white camisole.

Oh. My. God. I'm an idiot. Who wears pizza pajamas to a sexting party?!

That's another Betty lesson I should have paid attention to—*always be prepared!*

Me: *Uh... I feel stupid now. I should've dressed better for this conversation.*

Milo: *I can assure you, kid. I'll be happy with whatever your wearing.*

Me: *I don't know about that...*

Do I take them off?
I lift the elastic of my pants up and peer down at my underwear.
Pink boy shorts.
Okay, they're not bad.
I jump up off the bed and wiggle my pants haphazardly down my legs. Breathing hard, I bounce back on the bed and settle in again. But before I can contemplate my next move, my phone vibrates with another message. A picture message.

Taken from the chest down, it's a picture of him, sitting on his couch, with exactly what he said on—a white T-shirt and black boxer briefs.

And yes, there is a bulge.

A *big* bulge.

Holy. Flapjacking. Shit.

It's at this exact, inopportune moment that I realize Bruce's creative cursing has rubbed off on me.

Jesus, Maybe. Do you really want to think about your father right now?

I shake my head, trying to physically force the ridiculous thoughts to fall out, and throw myself backward. I bring the arm with the hand holding my phone up to cover my eyes when it vibrates again.

Milo: *Now, it's your turn.*

Fuck. My turn.

Just go with it. You may never get another opportunity at this.

I lift my phone up, snap an angled picture from my chest down and send it before I can back out.

The longest minute of my life passes by before my phone vibrates with a response.

Milo: Monday panties on a Tuesday?

I glance down to see he's right, I am wearing my days of the week underwear, and they are, in fact, sporting the wrong day. For some reason, the fact that he focused his message on that makes me relax a little. I even laugh as I type out a response.

Me: I like to live dangerously.

Milo: If you really want to live dangerously, touch yourself and tell me how it feels.

Holy. F-bombs.

Time slows down and my brain starts to bleed, and I think I'm really going to pass out this time.

Did Milo Ives just say that to me?

Did *Milo Ives* Just. Say. That. To. *Me*?

I swallow hard against the nerves moving up my throat, but at the same time, I do as I'm told. At least, the touching myself part. The ache between my legs all but challenges me not to. Giving him the details, though, that's probably going to take me a minute.

I work on typing out the words as shakily as I can. How I'm rubbing my clit in tight, round circles and putting pressure on the top each time.

My thumb hovers over the send button for the briefest of seconds, just long enough to take a deep breath, but that's all it takes for Milo's message to come in and stop me cold in my tracks.

Milo: *And that's how you sext, kid.*

My hand arrests and my adrenaline crashes. I wanted Milo to teach me how to sext, and he taught me, all right.

He taught me so well, I almost believed it was really happening.

Chapter
SEVENTEEN

Milo

Maybe stands in front of me, completely bare, and my eyes turn hungry. Greedy. Fucking ravenous to take in every inch of her soft, perfectly tanned skin.

God, she's something. My brain can't even put together words to describe the sight of her naked, wanton, and waiting for me to make a move.

"Milo," she whispers, and I don't miss the way her teeth bite into her bottom lip or the way her thighs tremble as she fidgets underneath my gaze.

"What do you want?" I ask her, but she doesn't respond.

She just looks at me with those big brown eyes of hers and traps me in the never-ending depths.

"Maybe, what do you want?" I prompt again.

"You." One word. Three letters. And powerful enough to make my cock harden and twitch beneath my boxer briefs.

I act on instinct, on desire, on fucking need, and I'm on my feet, striding toward her.

We're in my bedroom.

And before I know it, we're on my bed, Maybe beneath me and my boxer briefs a distant memory on the floor.

My cock is at her entrance, the tip sliding through her wetness, and I groan at the painfully delicious feel of it.

Fuck, I want her. I've *been wanting* her.

Since the moment I saw her in Bruce & Sons and didn't even know it was her.

A day hasn't gone by where I haven't wondered how this would feel.

How she would look, how she would taste, what she would feel like wrapped around my cock.

"Please," she begs, and her hips gyrate from side to side. Her movement pushes the tip of my cock inside her, and I come unglued.

I can't resist her anymore.

Not for even a second longer.

I'm *going* to slide inside her and make her mine.

Slowly, so slowly I had no idea I had it in me, I slide my cock inside the perfect heat of her tight pussy. I'm halfway inside and so close to bliss I can taste it when a persistent, annoying-as-fuck sound picks up a steady beat and volume.

I don't know where it's coming from, but goddamn, it needs to stop.

I blink my eyes with the intent to look down at Maybe, but she's no longer beneath me.

What the hell?

I blink my eyes again, and her smell disappears.

Piece by piece, my world falls away, the sound getting louder and louder and louder until…*I wake up.*

Fucking motherfucking hell.

I reach out toward my nightstand and slam my palm against my alarm, permanently ending the obnoxious sound.

My cock screams inside my boxer briefs, and my stomach aches with the need to come and do it hard.

I check the time to see it's already ten past seven.

I was dreaming. About Maybe.

Which is no surprise, given how far I let it go last night like a *fucking idiot.*

With my heart pounding inside my chest and my breaths

coming out in erratic pants, I look down at my primed cock and groan.

I rub at my eyes and take deep, steady breaths until my heart slows down to a normal pace.

What in the hell was I thinking?

About Maybe's perfect, untouched, tight pussy, you bastard.

Completely unsure what to do with this insane realization, I scrub a hand over my face and stand up from my bed. I adjust my now half-hard cock beneath my boxer briefs and head into the hall and toward the kitchen to make some coffee.

As the pot brews, I grab my phone from the kitchen counter and scroll through work emails. But before I've even managed to pour myself a cup of coffee, I've found my way back to my text conversation with Maybe.

And that's how you sext, kid.

Such a douche thing to say, I almost choked on it.

I just didn't know how else to stop my one-way train to hell.

I set down my phone on the counter and pour myself a coffee before I do something stupid like text her to explain.

But my distraction technique only works for about two minutes. I pick up my phone again, ready to lay it all out there when it pings with a text.

Only this time, it's not her. It's *her fucking brother.*

Evan: Mind if I conference into the morning meeting today? I have some things I want to update the marketing and finance teams about related to Simply Baby. And you're a real dick for passing the torch on crazy Frank Wright. LOL. His daily calls are a true joy. Right up there with a root canal.

Evan: Oh, and I talked to Maybe yesterday after her interview with Rainbow Press. Just wanted to say thanks for helping her out. I owe you big time, bro.

Oh yeah, you helped her out, all right, you dirty bastard, my mind taunts.

Jesus Christ, I am in *serious* trouble.

Chapter EIGHTEEN

Maybe

At exactly noon, I let Bruce know I'm taking a long lunch and head to Jovial Grinds.

I've been a powder keg of nausea and excitement and uncertainty since last night, and a morning full of Bruce, his -isms, and his favorite Doo Wop CD have *not* done anything to help the situation.

I know the whole sexting thing with Milo ended unconventionally, but no matter how much I dissect our every exchange for technical merit and artistic value, I can't forget that he did, in fact, request an actual picture of me in my underwear and sent me one of his own.

That *has* to mean something.

Practice-run, instructional-value-only sexting shouldn't include show-and-tell...*right?*

RIGHT?

It's the second, intense-inflection *RIGHT?* that has me here, in search of another opinion.

And oh baby, I'm getting it. From the instant—and I do mean *instant*—I stepped through the door, Lena has been in full investigation mode regarding what she calls "Phase 2" of the plan.

Thankfully, there's only one customer inside the coffee shop, a sixty-year-old regular by the name of Winston who loves naps as much as he loves coffee.

While he snoozes behind the *New York Post*, I sit across from Lena and ramble through the events of last night as calmly as humanly possible.

Which is to say…not in the least bit calmly at all.

"I don't think I did the whole segue from interview talk into dirty talk like you probably pictured… I mean, I *know* I didn't. We were joking and stuff like usual, and then I pretty much just asked him how often he sexts with people. He didn't really give me an answer, but I asked him to sext with me. He seemed hesitant in the beginning, but eventually, he did it. I mean, we did it. We sexted," I spit out in a rush. "I actually sexted with him, Lena. He even sent me a picture of his bulge, and dear *God*—"

"Wait a minute." Lena stops me mid-sentence, and a giant, amused smile spreads across her lips. "You mean to tell me you actually sexted with him last night? Full-on junk pictures exchanged, dirty-talking sexting?"

Eyes as wide as saucers, I nod. "The pictures were in our underwear, but yeah." I pause briefly before jumping to add, "And he ended it abruptly."

She waves a hand wildly and then smacks it down on the table so hard, Winston jumps, snorts, and then falls back to sleep.

"Don't worry about the ending. If you were in the throes of pictures and pornographic material, he was invested. He probably just panicked."

"Panicked? Why in the heck would *he* panic? I'm the one with no experience here!"

She laughs. "You're his best friend's little sister. They probably swore on a blood pact that he'd never touch your lady bits when they were kids, and now, he's exchanging soft-core pictures with you."

Her overzealous joy spurs a laugh from my lips. "You're insane."

She shakes her head. "Nah, girl, *you* are insane—in the best damn way. I am so *proud* of you!"

I giggle shakily and take a sip of coffee. "Man," I jabber. "I still can hardly believe I did it. I mean, I had to read through our conversation again this morning just to make sure that it was real."

"Fast learner, you are, Obi-Wan."

Her response makes me snort. "First of all, I don't think that reference is right." She shrugs. "And let's not get *too* ahead of ourselves here. I mean, I don't even know if he…you know…enjoyed it."

"Did *you* enjoy it?"

"What?"

"Come on. Don't be a prude," she says with a grin. "Were his messages focused on making you come?"

Uh. *Ha.* Yeah. I mean, I *was* touching myself at his command when he ended it. When my cheeks start to heat, she points an index finger in my direction.

"You adorable little hussy!"

I fall face first into my palms, and she puts her hands on my shoulders and shakes them consolingly.

"If you enjoyed it that much, I can guarantee he enjoyed it too."

"How in the hell do you know?"

"Because phone sex, text sex, any kind of virtual sex, is the ultimate two-way street. None of it is tangible, it's all imagination. In order to say things to you that get you excited, he has to be able to see them in his mind. And if he sees them in his mind, I *promise* you, as a male member of the human species, he was feeling them in his dick. He probably wanked himself to all manner of thoughts of you right after you guys were done."

Milo masturbated to thoughts of me?

Holy. Shit. My cheeks flush again, and Lena doesn't miss a beat.

"Yes, friend," she says, and her full lips turn up in a knowing smile. "And guess what? Because of last night, you just successfully put yourself into your crush's fantasies."

It's nearly too much to process.

She grins. "Have you spoken to him today?"

I shake my head.

I mean, I've almost texted him at least fifty times, but no, I haven't *actually* texted him.

Nothing seemed quite right.

Thank you for the orgasm last night!

You're a great sexter!

How 'bout that sexting last night? Pretty awesome, right? Want to do it again tonight?

Delete. Delete. Delete.

But, seriously, what do you say to someone after that?

Fuck if I know.

But apparently, Lena does.

"Phew." She lets out a giant breath from deep down in her lungs. "Okay, that's good news."

My eyebrows draw together, rife with skepticism. "Why is that good news?"

"Because your next text to him cannot, *and I mean cannot*, be about sexting or anything remotely involving what happened last night."

Jesus Christ. Why does everything I learn about dating seem like it adds a side to an already impossible-to-solve Rubik's Cube?

"Then what in the heck do I say?"

"Something really boring and mundane. You need to make him feel like last night was no big deal in your mind."

The first thing that comes to mind is the email Cassandra Cale sent me this morning. Evidently, I wowed her yesterday—so much so, she didn't waste any time offering me a job.

"Well…Rainbow Press sent me a job offer… Will that work?"

Lena's face lights up. "That. Is. Perfect."

"Okay, so I'll text him and let him know about the job offer."

Easy peasy.

"Ah, ah, not so fast, honey," she responds with a devious smile. "First, the job offer. Then, you're going to make him sweat a little."

Make him sweat?

"What?" I tilt my head to the side. "You want me to work out with him?"

"*No.*" She damn near cackles. "Not actually sweat, but metaphorically sweat."

I furrow my brow. "I'll be honest, you lost me back on sweat. I truly have zero clue what you're talking about at this point."

"It's all very simple," she says and briefly glances over her shoulder to watch Winston rise from the sleeping dead, toss his empty cup into the trash, and walk out the door without uttering a single word.

"You need to make him feel like whatever happened last night is no big deal. Now isn't the time to be a stage-five clinger. Now is the time to put yourself out there with other men and make it clear to him that you're not just sitting around and waiting for him to make the next move."

"And how exactly do I do that?"

"Did you download TapNext on your phone?"

I cringe. "Not yet…"

"Jesus," she mutters and holds out her hand. "Give me your phone."

"What?"

"Give me your phone, Maybe."

On a sigh, I unlock the screen and hand it to her.

It takes ten minutes, but by the time I leave the coffee shop to head back to Bruce & Sons, TapNext is downloaded on to my phone and Lena has set up an entire dating profile for me. Bio, photo, the whole-fucking-shebang.

When I go into the back room to put my apron back on, my nerves get the best of me, and I send a text to Lena.

Me: *I don't think I really want to date random guys I meet on TapNext.*

She texts back immediately.

Lena: Don't panic. You're only using it for one date.

Me: One date? You went to all that trouble making the profile for one date?

Lena: Yep. It's all you're going to need. You're going to go through your matches and find a nice guy who looks like you'd be able to suffer through a dinner with him.

Me: You're a complex woman, Lena. And I don't understand you one bit.

Lena: Just trust me, okay? You're not really going to date the guy. You're just going to make Milo think a bit. Because before you officially go on your date, you're going to send Milo a few text messages asking him for "advice" about your date.

Me: This sounds suspiciously crazy.

Lena: Because it fucking is. But it's also going to work.

I can't decide if she's giving me the best advice I've ever been given or if she's sending me on a seriously scary journey that's going to end in disaster.

Another text of additional reassurance comes in from her just as I need it. The timing is so perfect—*I was a literal second away from completely losing my shit*—I'm hoping maybe, just maybe, it's a little bit of a text from God too.

Lena: I promise you, it's all going to work out better than you can even imagine.

Better than I can even imagine?
I'll settle for good as long as it's not too good to be true.

Chapter NINETEEN

Milo

After a long-as-hell workday, I leave the office and head to the gym.

It's Friday. The weekend is here. And I'm going to do everything in my power to avoid the office and my emails until Monday morning.

Sadly, I tell myself this every Friday evening, but here's to hoping I actually follow through this time.

I step into the lobby of the gym, and the sounds of chatter, music, and the clinking and clacking of weights fill my ears.

The young girl behind the reception desk nods her recognition and buzzes open the doors that lead to the main area of the gym.

It's busy for a Friday evening, but after a quick change in the locker room, I manage to snag a treadmill on the second floor and start my workout off right with some cardio.

With Rage Against the Machine playing through my earbuds, I turn up the speed and dive straight into the session.

But twenty minutes into my run, the screen of my phone lights up inside the cupholder, and my attention is officially pulled to the exact place it shouldn't be. The exact place I've been trying like hell to avoid for the past week.

Maybe: I need your help.

I look up from her message and meet my reflection in the floor-to-ceiling mirrors of the gym to find myself smiling like an idiot.

Shit. I cringe at my absurd reaction to seeing her name in my inbox.

It's been five days since Maybe innocently tricked me into a sexting conversation that went way too far, and every-fucking-night since then, I've woken up smack-dab in the middle of all sorts of *explicit* dreams about her.

It's all completely fucked.

She's my best friend's little sister. And one-hundred-percent off-limits.

Yet I can't stop trying to picture what she looks like when she comes.

And Evan was worried about Cap helping Maybe out...

Son of a bitch.

Maybe: Earth to Milo. Come in Milo.

On a sigh, I type out a response and offer up a silent prayer that she's still just overthinking the whole Rainbow Press situation.

Me: Kid, I already told you. There is no need to feel guilty about not accepting the Rainbow Press job. Cassandra Cale isn't mad. She knows it's not personal. It's business. And, honestly, she's probably still holding out hope you'll end up reconsidering after you interview with other publishing houses. She doesn't know what I know about Beacon's track record for jumping on her prospects, but they don't know you've already declined her offer either. This is a case of "what they don't know benefits us."

In between all of my insane fantasies about Maybe, I've still been the guy on the publishing industry sidelines, helping *and* reassuring her that she's making the right moves.

At least you're still managing to do the one and only thing Evan asked you to do...

Yeah. Fuck. At least I'm still doing that.

Maybe: *I appreciate that, but it's not the help I need. This has nothing to do with business, Billionaireman.*

Me: *I'm not sexting with you again.*

Good God, you idiot. I groan two seconds after I hit send and see my far-too-inappropriate words populate in our conversation.

Apparently, it seems I just can't help my-fucking-self when it comes to her.

Maybe: *HAHA very funny. Not that kind of help. I need advice for a date.*

Me: *A date?*

She's going on a date?

I nearly trip over my own fucking feet, and instantly, I tap the console on the treadmill several times until the speed slows down to a leisurely jog.

Maybe: *I have a date tonight with someone I met on TapNext.*

Me: *Seriously?*

Maybe: *Why would I lie about something like that?*

Me: *When did you meet him?*

Maybe: *Yesterday.*

Me: You're going on a date with a guy you met online yesterday?

Maybe: Yes, Billionaireman. Keep up. Aren't superheroes supposed to have unparalleled cunning, strength, and wit?

I scowl.
What in the ever-loving hell? Has she lost her mind?
Maybe going on a date with some random stranger sounds like the worst idea I've ever heard.

Me: Do you even know anything about this guy?

Maybe: I know his name is Jess. And, not gonna lie, I love the name Jess because of the Gilmore Girls. I've been 100% Team Jess since the instant he stepped foot in Stars Hollow.

I furrow my brow. *Should I know these women?*

Me: Who are the Gilmore Girls?

Maybe: YOU DON'T KNOW WHO THE GILMORE GIRLS ARE??

Me: Do they live in New York?

Maybe: Oh my God! I don't have time to get into all things Gilmore Girls with you, but one day, I will enlighten you. Right now, this date is my priority, and I have no idea what I should wear. Help. Me.

Me: You mean your date with a potential serial killer is your priority.

Maybe: He's not a serial killer!

Me: How do you know? You've only known him for 24 hours via a dating app. He could be a serial killer...or at the very least, a catfish.

Maybe: Pretty sure the length of time you know someone doesn't help deduce whether or not they're a serial killer. I mean, Jeffrey Dahmer's family knew him his whole life, and they had no clue. Ted Bundy's wife didn't know either.

I sigh. Always the sassy smartass...

Me: And that reasoning is supposed to be reassuring how?

Maybe: Don't rain on my date parade, Milo. Just help me. Tell me what is appropriate first-date attire.

Me: Pretty sure you're supposed to consult girlfriends for this kind of advice.

Maybe: But I don't want a woman's advice. I need a man's advice. I'm sending you three options. Be honest. And flipping stop thinking about serial killers and tell me which outfit is the best choice.

Thirty seconds later, three photos upload inside our conversation.

Hesitantly, I open the first one.

It's Maybe standing in front of her bedroom mirror with a pile of clothes sitting on her bed and several shoes strewn across the floor behind her. Her long brown locks are tossed up into a messy bun, and an uncertain smile shapes her full pink lips. Her body is clad in a little black dress, and nude stilettos cover her petite feet.

She looks good. *Too* good.

Option one is not the right choice.

Option two is more of the same. A short, floral summer dress that rests a little too high on her thighs, and the pale pink heels on her feet only add to the elongation of her toned legs.

Nope. Not that one either.

The last and final photo is more laid-back and the clear best option of the three. Jeans, a little white blouse that shows just a slight hint of her lower stomach, and a pair of flats.

I waste no time at all in giving her my choice.

Me: The jeans but with a different shirt.

Maybe: What? Why? I thought the white blouse was cute. It's fun and flirty.

Me: It shows too much.

Maybe: You're nuts! It doesn't show anything. Maybe I should just wear one of the dresses.

No. Way.

With the things I'm thinking about doing to her in those dresses, I can only *imagine* what some low-life catfish will be thinking about doing.

Me: No. Definitely the jeans.

Maybe: Fine. Jeans it is. But I'm sticking with the blouse. Thanks for the advice!

I should end the conversation, but I literally *can't.* The phone is attached to my hand permanently now and will forever be a part of my body. At least until she's home from the date, that is.

Me: When is he picking you up?

Maybe: I'm meeting him at a restaurant in Greenwich Village.

I almost chastise the bastard for not picking her up for the date, but then I realize it's a good fucking thing he isn't going to see where she lives.

Unless she decides to take him home...

Me: Are you planning on bringing him back to your place for a nightcap?

A nightcap? For fuck's sake, I sound like my dad.

Maybe: A nightcap? LOL. If you're asking me if I'm planning on some kind of first-date hookup, I don't know. I guess I'll just see how the night goes.

Oh God. I *do not* like that response.

Me: Just be safe, okay?

Maybe: You got it, dude.

Two seconds later, a Michelle Tanner GIF with a thumbs-up populates under her message.

Maybe: And you be safe too.

I furrow my brow. What is she talking about?

Me: Safe doing what?

Maybe: I don't know. I figured you probably have a big night out planned with one of your "friendly" lady friends.

I'm equal parts amused and terrified at where this conversation could lead.

Me: *Here we go again.*

Maybe: *HA. I could have said fuck buddies, but I was trying to be cognizant of your delicate sensibilities.*

Me: *Smartass.*

Maybe: *So, you DO have a "this is not a date" date tonight?*

Four minutes ago, I had nothing going on. Paperwork, Netflix, and a bottle of scotch to smother the inappropriate fantasies about my best friend's sister. But now that she's going out, I can't stay home. I'll lose my fucking mind.

Me: *I have dinner with a friend, yes.*

Maybe: *A friendly lady friend.*

Me: *I can confirm it is a woman.*

Maybe: *A fuck buddy.*

A laugh bubbles up from my lungs. I knew she could only hold that in for so long.

Me: *Jesus.*

Maybe: *LOL. All right, I'm going to go get ready for my date. I hope you have fun on your non-date date tonight.*

Me: Thanks. I really hope your TapNext date isn't a serial killer, but I'll make sure Bruce creates a nice arrangement for the funeral if he is.

Maybe: LOL. Very funny. Goodbye, Milo!

When our conversation comes to an end, I feel...uncomfortable. She's twenty-four years old. She should be going on dates. She should be putting herself out there.

This is a *good* thing for her.

It just doesn't feel good for me.

Truthfully, it doesn't feel so good at all.

Now I have to figure out something to do.

After scrolling quickly through my contacts, I text Senna Flick, a friend who's been a casual monthly fling for the last two years. Where I'm busy running Fuse, she's busy traveling around the world doing marketing for a wealthy media conglomerate that owns two major television networks and produces movies on the side for a popular online streaming website. Getting together has always been uncomplicated and mutually beneficial.

No-strings-attached sex and sufficiently intelligent company.

Tonight, as a whole, feels different, but the text exchange is simple, just as it always is.

Me: Dinner tonight?

Senna: I'll be ready at 8.

I sigh when I read the text but do the nice, gentlemanly thing and type out a response.

Me: See you then.

Senna: Can't wait. ;)

I sigh again.
The woman is the same, the game is the same—it's all the same.
So why does it feel so different?

TWENTY

Maybe

Is that him?

Oh, never mind, that guy is wearing a uniform. Pretty sure no one would schedule a date during their flipping shift.

Or wait…is that him?

Unless he didn't offer up the information that he has a wife and a baby who he's bringing to dinner with him, that's probably not the right guy.

While sitting at the bar of the restaurant, I've been playing the "which guy is my date?" game for the past fifteen minutes, and I honestly can't remember what he's supposed to look like anymore.

This is exactly what you get for arriving twenty minutes before the date is supposed to start.

Definitely one of those times where fashionably late is the way to go, Maybe.

I pull my phone out of my purse and discreetly bring up the TapNext app and proceed to study Jess's profile picture.

Okay. Just remember…Blond hair. Brown eyes. Fairly broad shoulders.

I memorize the basics of his attributes like I'll be tested on them later.

You can do this. You can and will remember what your date looks like.

I slip my phone back into my purse just as the bartender steps up and asks me if I would like another glass of wine.

I glance down at my now-empty glass and immediately shake my head.

Considering I guzzled that thing down in a matter of five minutes and I hardly ever drink alcohol, another serving will pretty much guarantee I'm a slurring, rambling hot mess during my date.

"No thank you," I say, conscious of self-preservation and safety. The bartender nods his head in understanding and moves to the other end of the bar to wait on a new customer.

Another few minutes go by like one of those time continuum movies, where a second feels like a year, so when I glance at the door and see a blond-haired man striding in, I immediately stand to my feet.

That's him. I'm sure of it.

He stands at the hostess counter, most likely letting her know he's looking for someone—*me*—so I decide to make it easy on everyone and walk straight up to him.

"Hi," I say, and he looks up to meet my eyes.

"Hello."

Shit…now what?

Do we shake hands? Or do we hug? Or do I curtsy?

Jesus…don't curtsy.

Impulsively, I go with the hug, stepping forward and wrapping my arms around his shoulders. "It's so great to finally meet you in person," I say, and I note that he just barely hugs me back.

"Uh…"

Shit. Did I just infringe on his personal boundaries?

Is hugging during the first-date introduction a big hell no?

God, why am I so awkward at these things?

Desperate to smooth it over, I search for something else to say.

"You're even more handsome than on your dating profile."

"Your *what?*" a female voice behind him shouts, and I tilt my head to the side in confusion.

"Uh…" The guy looks back and forth between us. "Wait…no…"

"You have a fucking dating profile?" the woman asks, her voice practically shaking with the need to kick his ass.

"Wait…no… I don't know…" His blue eyes go wide.

Ah, *shit.*

His *blue* eyes.

Not, as my study guide failed to help me remember, *brown.* Sure, I remember now, but that doesn't do this guy's balls a whole lot of good. Seriously. If the vein in this woman's forehead is any indication, she's about to go Jackie Chan on them any second.

"What in the hell is going on?" his wife, I'm now figuring out by the giant rock on her finger, asks.

"Honey, just calm down for a second," the man—a man who is most definitely not Jess—says. "I don't know this woman. I have never seen her before in my life!"

"She sure seems to know you!"

"Oh God," I mutter, a quivering hand coming up to cover my mouth. "I am so, so, so sorry. I thought you were my date. But you're not."

"No," he says in a firm, extremely pissed-off voice. "I am *not* your date."

"He's not my date," I repeat myself, but this time, I meet his wife's eyes. "He's not my date."

She glares.

"I'm so sorry. He looks like my date, but he's not my date." I look at Not-Jess again. "You're not my date."

The man shakes his head. "I'm definitely not your date."

"My date's name is Jess, and your name isn't Jess."

"My name is Tom," he says with conviction to female Jackie Chan—like his wife doesn't know what his fucking name is.

"How about we go on down to the courthouse?" she yells. "Get Peeping added in front of it."

Oh. God. This shit's gone severely sideways.

"Again, I'm so sorry," I apologize and jet. I really don't have any interest in waiting around to tell them how to spell my name for the irreconcilable reason on their divorce papers.

I hightail it away from the hostess stand and push through the doors of the women's restroom. Once I've safely locked myself inside one of the stalls, I pull my phone out of my purse and call Lena.

She answers on the second ring.

"Hey, girl."

Already worked up from nearly breaking up a marriage, I skip the pleasantries altogether.

"Holy shit, I'm on a date and I just went up to the wrong guy and hugged him and he is here with his wife and fucking hell why am I so awkward, Lena? Seriously, I think I might have just inadvertently caused trust issues in someone's marriage. I can't believe I just—"

"Take a breath, girl." She cuts me off on a laugh. "You're literally talking a million miles a minute."

I inhale a deep breath. "Sorry. It's just that shit went down out there by the hostess stand."

"Okay, so what happened, exactly?"

I explain it to her again, but this time much slower, and by the end of my story, she is laughing her ass off.

"Lena! It's not that funny!"

"Oh, but it is," she retorts. "It's hilarious, Maybe."

"God help me." A groan jumps from my lungs. "I should never be allowed out of my apartment."

"It's going to be fine," she reassures. "And anyway, you need to remember that it doesn't matter how this date actually goes. What matters is if Milo knows you're on a date. You can be a total hot mess on this date, and it doesn't matter."

The realization is liberating. "Okay, you're right."

"I know," she says with her signature confidence. "So, does Milo know you're on a date?"

"He knows. I asked him for help picking out my outfit."

Lena doesn't respond right away, and it makes me freak out a little.

"Wait…oh God…is that bad? Did I screw up Phase 3 of the plan?"

"Honey." She laughs. "You're a damn genius. Making him pick

out your outfit for a date with another man? Jesus Christ, I hope you sent him pictures in lingerie."

A laugh of relief leaves my lips. "Not quite, but I did sample a couple of cleavage-boosting dresses."

"Brilliant."

I smile. "So now what do I do?"

"Go back into the restaurant and try to find your date. This time, don't start hugging and schmoozing and shit until you're sure it's him."

"And then?"

"And then just enjoy the free dinner."

"That's it?"

"That's it," she says, and I can hear the smile in her voice. "Just go back inside the restaurant, eat a giant bowl of fettuccini alfredo, and try to enjoy yourself. No use sitting through a dinner in misery, you know what I mean?"

My stomach growls in the name of fettuccine, and suddenly, I'm at ease. If there's one thing I know how to do, it's eat a bowl of pasta.

"Yeah, for once, I think I *do* know what you mean."

Chapter TWENTY-ONE

Milo

At exactly eight o'clock, I pick Senna up from her apartment in Midtown, and we head toward SoHo where I reserved a table for two at one of my favorite steakhouses.

Senna is all long legs and red lips and long blond hair flowing down her back in a mane of curls and waves. And her tight white dress is probably illegal, even after Labor Day.

When we were escorted from the hostess stand to our table, she turned heads the entire way, and her familiar display of flirtatious eyes and long lashes has been in full effect since I picked her up.

Not to mention, her apparently bare foot is already rubbing against my jeans-covered leg.

She's happy to see me.

And like with all of our previous "dates," she's expecting for things to lead toward sex at my apartment by the end of the night.

"How is your steak?" she asks, her voice slightly purring with her words.

"It's good."

"Can I have a bite?"

"Uh...sure," I respond and go to put a piece on her plate, but in a dramatic display of her cleavage pushed out between her arms, she rests her elbows on the table and opens her red-painted lips, urging me to feed it to her.

So, I do.

And she moans her approval.

"You're right," she purrs and licks at her bottom lip. "It's *really* good."

I should be one hundred percent enjoying this display.

Should be being the operative words.

But instead of enjoying the ease of our no-strings-attached relationship and the sexual satisfaction we've been known to give each other in the past, my mind is about twenty blocks away. In Greenwich Village. Wondering how Maybe is doing.

Is her date going okay?

Is he actually a stand-up guy?

What are his fucking intentions?

That dickhead better not be expecting sex from her tonight...

Every single question and thought bouncing around inside my head only make me more uncomfortable.

When Senna excuses herself for the ladies' room, a sigh of relief escapes my chest, and I pull my cell out to send a quick message.

Me: How's it going?

Thankfully, she responds not even a minute later.

Maybe: He's not a serial killer. At least, I don't think he is.

Me: That's reassuring.

Maybe: LOL. It's fine. No red flags so far.

Me: If any red flags arise, you know you can call me if you need an excuse to escape the situation.

Maybe: Are you offering me a date out?

Me: A date out?

Am I really so old that I don't know the terms the kids are using anymore?

Maybe: Yeah. You know, where you already make an arrangement with your friend to call in a fake emergency or something if the date goes to shit.

Me: Do you need a fake emergency?

Maybe: LOL. I'm good. And I thought you were on a non-date date tonight?

Me: I am. But I just wanted to make sure you're okay.

Maybe: It's all good in the hood. Go enjoy your dinner with your lady friend who may or may not be a fuck buddy.

All good in the hood. A part of me wants to laugh, but the part of me that's worried about her is far too great.

Me: Are you sure? It'll be a real bummer if you end up as a Missing Girl on Dateline.

Maybe: LOL. I'm fine, Milo. Promise. No need to play the big brother role.

Big brother role?
Is that what I'm doing?
It sure as fuck doesn't feel like that to me.

Me: How about this? Text me when you get home tonight so I don't have to worry about you being locked inside some weirdo's apartment.

Maybe: What if the weirdo finds my phone and pretends to be me and texts you false assurances?

Me: Jesus, kid.

Maybe: I've seen **Law & Order**, *Milo. That's how it works.*

Me: Well, then I guess you'd better send me photographic evidence.

Maybe: I can handle that.

I read her text message and wait for the relief and satisfaction of our agreement to take over, but it never comes.

It's only when another text comes in thirty seconds later that I know exactly what I have to do to make tonight right.

Maybe: This time, I'll be wearing the right day of the week. ;)

As soon as I can get away from this dinner, I'm going home... alone.

Chapter
TWENTY-TWO

Maybe

Another Saturday at the floral shop and I'm so bored, I might start beating my head against the wall just to spice things up. Unless it's Mother's Day weekend, Bruce has yet to fully grasp the sad and incredibly slow pace that is kept on the weekends.

Well, either that or he simply doesn't care.

He is obstinate in keeping a full staff scheduled, even though he knows we'll mostly be twiddling our thumbs. Hell, one of our regular delivery drivers, Stan, is here with nothing to do. He finished all of his deliveries before eleven this morning, and now he's just sitting outside on our back patio—*where all the staff takes breaks in the spring and summer months*—and talking to his girlfriend while chain-smoking cigarettes.

Martha and Rosaline, two of our back room staff members, have cut more bouquets than we need, and I went ahead and told them to take a long lunch. What Bruce doesn't know won't kill him.

For most of the morning, I focused on cleaning up the shop. Dusting, sweeping, wiping down everything with a surface. But once I smelled like bleach and even the walls were fucking shining, I gave up the good fight on trying to stay busy and plopped myself down behind the counter to suffer through the monotony by browsing social media and looking at YouTube videos of jumping goats and mischievous puppies.

The things we do for boredom.

YouTube no longer a suitable distraction, I pull up my Kindle app and dive back into my current read—*The Other Side* by Kim Holden. I've been a fan of hers since I read *Bright Side*, and only a few chapters in, I'm certain this book is going to be the beautiful, emotional, addictive ride I've come to expect with any of her books. She is just one of those authors who holds the power to tear you to shreds, and yet, by the time you reach "The End," she's put you back together again in the most awe-inspiring, life-changing way.

Seriously. It took me three years to not think about Kate from *Bright Side* on a daily basis.

Ten more pages in and I'm hooked. *Riveted.*

Until my phone dings with a sound that I've come to learn is TapNext.

I pick it up to find a message from Jess—my date from last night.

Showcasing blondish-colored hair, dark brown eyes, and a one-dimple smile, his profile picture stares back at me as I read his message.

@NotYourUncleJess-E: Just wanted to say I had fun last night and hope we can meet up again soon.

Have. Mercy.

Fun last night? Were we even on the same date?

By the time I located my correct date, the night didn't exactly go swimmingly.

When it comes down to it, Uncle Jesse and I didn't jive.

When I zigged, he zagged.

When I laughed at our server's silly joke about meatballs, he stared at me like I'd lost my mind.

And when he cracked himself up over a vulgar story about his friend losing his credit card while trying to swipe a stripper's breasts, it was my turn to question his mental stability.

And it wasn't that hearing about him and his buddies being at a strip club bothered me, it was more the way he commented about the woman's appearance. And I'm not talking nice compliments here. By the end of his stupid story, I knew the exact locations of Lacey Lou's cellulite and stretch marks.

You'd think Jess was some kind of perfect specimen without any flaws, but obviously, that's not the case. *No one* is perfect. Jess is a bit of an egotistical prick. And I guarantee Lacey Lou is damn beautiful in all of her stripper glory, cellulite and stretch marks and all.

The rest of the evening stayed smack-dab in the middle of awkward. I spilled marinara sauce on my white blouse. And when he asked me if I wanted to head to a bar to continue the night, I made up some lame excuse about having to be at work in the morning.

Technically, I wasn't lying. I mean, I *am* at work today, but it wasn't even nine o'clock by that point in the evening. Unless I was a seventy-year-old woman who calls it a night before the evening news, I was one hundred percent exaggerating my usual bedtime.

Needless to say, it was a sad, sad dating experience, and I'd rather strip with Lacey Lou than repeat a date with Uncle Jesse.

Instead of messaging him back, I click out of the app and call the one person who needs to hear what went down.

Lena answers on the second ring.

"I was literally just about to call you."

I grin. "Is that so?"

"Of course, girl," she responds. "I need to hear about your date last night."

"There is nothing to hear."

"What do you mean?"

"Jess is literally not worth talking about," I comment.

"That bad?"

"I was home by nine."

A laugh fills my ear. "That's never good."

"Tell me about it," I mutter and pick at a few pieces of lint on my jean shorts. "I don't care what you say, I refuse to go on another date with that man."

She laughs again. "Well, good news is that who you went out on the date with doesn't matter. The point was that Milo knew you were on a date. Which he did, so it's safe to say our goal was achieved."

"He actually texted me last night."

"Who texted you last night?"

"Milo. During my date. He was texting me to make sure I was okay."

"Well, hot damn, momma!" she exclaims. "I did not expect that to happen."

"It doesn't matter, though," I add. "He was out last night too. With a woman."

"Yeah, but he was texting you."

"So?"

"*Girl*," she says, and her voice rises three octaves. "He was texting you while he was out with a woman. If that isn't a fan-fucking-tastic sign, I don't know what is."

I grin. I can't help it. The excitement in Lena's voice is like crack. "Have you talked to him since?"

"He made me text him when I got home last night, but other than that, no. I haven't talked to him today."

A picture message, mind you, in which I couldn't stop myself from throwing on my *right-day-of-the-week* panties, my cutest tank top, and snapping a picture of me lying on my bed before hitting send.

Surprisingly, his response back was almost immediate and didn't disappoint.

No living dangerously, kid? I'm almost a little sad about that. But definitely happy to know you made it home safe and sound, in the right apartment, and without the risk of ending up in some psycho's trunk.

And my far-too-hopeful, swoony-eyed little psycho took that as a good sign that his non-date date wasn't anything to write home about.

Wishful thinking? Probably.

But it seems I can't help myself when it comes to him.

It seems? HA. More like it's been that way since you were eleven.

"Let me get this straight." Lena pulls my attention back to the present. "He texted you during your date, and then he told you to text him when you got home from your date?"

"He wanted to make sure I got home safely."

She snorts. "Oh yeah, I'm sure that's all he wanted."

"What are you getting at here?"

"He may have been saying it under the pretense of your safety, but the fact that you were on a date with some guy, a guy who was not him, was seriously screwing with his subconscious."

"I think you might be exaggerating this a bit here..."

"I know how men think. And Milo is trying like hell not to think about you in the way he really wants to think about you."

Her comment leaves me speechless, and I stare at the bucket of pink roses near the front door of the shop. It's equal parts too much to process and hard to believe.

But my inner swoony-eyed little psycho is apparently having no issues comprehending it all. She's grabbed a pair of pom-poms and is cheering, "I. Told. You. So!" inside my head.

Ugh. It's all so confusing.

"Stop overthinking this, Maybe. The man is into you, whether he is wanting to admit it or not." The certainty in her voice is mind-boggling. "And now, we must move on to the next step in our plan."

I quirk a brow. "And what's that?"

"You're going to come to a party with me in SoHo on Friday," she starts. "And you're going to talk Milo into meeting us there."

"You can't be serious."

"Just trust the process, honey. Everything is coming up roses."

After we make plans to grab lunch together tomorrow, we end the call, and I'm left with the task of trying to talk Milo into going to some house party that is apparently a friend of a friend of a friend of Lena's.

Sheesh. Sometimes I think she overestimates my abilities with shit like this.

I stare down at my phone and contemplate the best way to start this conversation.

But instead of letting my overthinking tendencies get the best of me, I dive right in.

Me: Just so you're aware, you have a party to go to Friday night. It's a big deal and really important for you, and just because you'll be lonely if I don't, I plan to come with you.

To my surprise, he responds a few minutes later.

Milo: So, really, YOU have a party to go to, and you want MY company.

Me: I guess you COULD put it that way.

Milo: Do I get a say in any of this?

Me: Think of it like that lunch you forced me to go to with you, but instead of choosing the restaurant, I'll let you choose what time you want to meet me there.

Milo: That's mighty generous of you.

I'm smiling like a loon as I type out my response.

Me: I know, right? Add some rosary beads around my neck, and I'm basically Mother Teresa.

Milo: Mind telling me what kind of party this is or even where it is? That might come in handy if I'm meeting you there.

Me: *I don't know…it's a party in SoHo. One that will most likely have booze and too loud music and, by midnight, a lot of drunk people.*

Milo: *That sounds horrible.*

Me: *Yeah, but do you really want to leave me on my own to navigate a party like that by myself? If you think the ratio of me to serial killer is high on a date, think of what it must be at a party.*

Milo: *Jesus. You drive a hard bargain.*

Me: *I'll text you the address when my friend Lena sends it to me.*

Milo: *I thought you said you were going to be on your own?*

Me: *Lena doesn't count. She's a girl. I need some muscle to back me up if shit goes down.*

Milo: *Who is throwing this party? The mob?*

Me: *HA. Very funny. But I really don't know the host, and this IS New York. So, it could be. I'll see you Friday night.*

Milo: *You're a real pain in my ass, kid.*

Hmm…and I thought this Saturday was going to be total shit…
It seems like Lena is right. Everything *is* coming up roses.
Milo-colored roses.
Milo-roses.
Milo-oses.
Yeah. Okay. That's enough play on words, you weirdo.

Chapter
TWENTY-THREE

Milo

A little after ten, I step off the elevator and directly into the spacious penthouse of a young New York socialite by the name of Daphne Ares. Apparently, Maybe's new friend Lena has friends in the highest of places in this city.

Not that I give two shits about schmoozing it up with the famous names of New York—I'm only here at Maybe's persistent request.

Yeah, right, you bastard. You would have swindled your way into coming to this party the minute you heard she was coming—even if she didn't invite you.

It's only been a week since she demanded my attendance tonight, and for the last five or so days, between our constant text messages and occasional phone calls, she hasn't let me forget that I agreed to be here.

So, despite my better judgment, here I am.

And I wish I could say I'm dreading it, but when my heart kicks up in speed at the thought of seeing her here, it's apparent dread isn't even in my vocabulary tonight.

I walk down a long, marble-floored corridor, and the instant I reach the main space, I'm hit with the thumping bass coming from the speakers of the DJ at the center of the room.

The room is filled with mostly twentysomethings dancing and laughing and just living it up on someone else's dime.

Fucking socialite parties.

It only took one of these shindigs thrown by a trust-fund baby for me to realize this was not and would never be my scene. I was twenty-six, Fuse had just started to gain success in the tech market, and Caplin Hawkins had dragged me to Tribeca to party it up with a young heiress to a hotel chain.

Her name was Christina Hellman, and if my memory serves me right, Cap fucked her in the bathroom while I fended off three twenty-year-old girls who wanted me to go snort coke with them on the balcony.

Personally, I've always been more of a fan of my brain cells and sobriety than the temporary high that drugs and alcohol can provide.

I'd make a perfect D.A.R.E. spokesperson. Just say no to drugs and all that.

Once I make my way through the throng of drunken dancers, I spot Maybe in the corner of the room, a smile on her lips while she chats with a blond-haired woman and a man wearing a fucking Fedora and a douchebag smile.

God, I might be only in my thirties, but I feel entirely too old for this crowd.

The instant I reach their little group, Maybe's big brown eyes meet mine, and my chest tightens at how damn beautiful she looks.

Long brown locks brush against a flowy pale-pink top, tight jeans hug her little ass and long legs, and a pair of nude stilettos have her standing a few inches taller than her normally petite height.

She looks like a fucking treat, and I mentally chastise myself for enjoying the view so much.

"You're here," she says, and she steps past her friends to wrap her small arms around me in a big hug. "I can't believe you actually came."

"Well, if I recall, I didn't have much of a choice."

She giggles and I smile. I can't fucking help it. She's the perfect mix of cute and sexy and I'm certain I'm losing brain cells trying not to gawk at her.

"Milo, I'd like you to meet my friend Lena," she introduces and gestures toward the blond woman in a dress that reminds me of hippies and Woodstock.

"It's nice to finally meet you," I say, and her smile is knowing and secretive at the same time.

"Trust me, the feeling is mutual."

The douche in the Fedora holds out his hand and introduces himself. "I'm Canyon."

Canyon? His name is Canyon? God, I shouldn't be surprised.

"Milo," I say and shake his hand.

"Canyon is a photographer for *New York Weekly*," Lena offers up. "And for the last fifteen minutes, he's been trying to talk Maybe into modeling for an article showcasing this fall's most up-and-coming fashion."

I narrow my eyes at her words, and the sudden urge to have a word with the hipster bastard is so strong, I can taste it. I know how assholes like this work, and I'd have to be ten feet underground before I'd let him use a photo shoot as a pathetic guise to get into Maybe's panties.

Not that she's not beautiful.

But he doesn't give a shit about some article for *New York Weekly*. His true motives are written all over his slimy-fucking-face.

"He was kidding." Maybe rolls her eyes, and Canyon shakes his head.

"No, I wasn't."

"See?" Lena grins. "I told you he wasn't kidding."

"Well, he should be kidding," Maybe retorts, and before the photographer prick can respond with words I probably shouldn't hear, a big, boisterous voice grabs everyone's attention.

"Milo fucking Ives! You have got to be kidding me!"

I turn around to find the one and only Caplin Hawkins striding toward me with a big, shit-eating grin on his face.

"I'll be a son of a bitch," he crows. "Sometimes, Mr. Workaholic does come out to play!"

I roll my eyes, but I also grin when he slaps his arm around my back for his version of a bro-hug. "What are the damn odds I'd see you out and about in SoHo tonight? And at a fucking house party, at that."

But before I even get a chance to respond, Lena is stepping forward and shoving two hands into Cap's chest.

"Seriously, bro?" she mutters. "Can I go to one damn party without your big ass showing up?"

He laughs. "Aw, I love you too, little sis."

Little sis?

I glance back and forth between them, and it doesn't take a genius to recognize the resemblance.

Same eyes. Same chin. Same nose.

Maybe's new friend Lena is Cap's sister.

What are the damn odds?

Although, I can't deny Lena is far more feminine and better-looking than that already big-headed, good-looking bastard I call a friend. And if she is anything like her older brother, I'm slightly terrified that this is who Maybe has been palling around with for the past few weeks.

Maybe looks between us, obviously as surprised as I am that her friend is related to someone I know.

"Maybe, this is my brother, Cap," Lena introduces them, and her brother offers his infamous overly friendly smile.

But by the time he's offered his greeting and given her a hug, realization starts to show behind his eyes.

"Wait...your name is Maybe?"

She nods, and immediately, he looks at me.

"Evan's sister, Maybe?"

Oh shit, here we go.

"You know my brother?" she asks innocently, and Cap grins like the Cheshire cat.

"Yep. I know him and," he says and reaches out to wrap a strong arm around my shoulders, "this bozo right here."

Both girls miss the meaning behind his words, but I don't.

I know exactly what's running through his nosy-fucking-mind.

"So, let me guess," he continues and meets Maybe's eyes. "You're the reason Milo decided to pull his head out of his workaholic ass and come out for the night."

She shrugs. "Well, in his defense, I wasn't really taking no for an answer."

Cap just grins like he's got Willy Wonka's Golden Ticket in his pocket. "Man am I glad I decided to show up at this party tonight. *Lots going on.*"

The rat bastard doesn't have to utter another word for me to know exactly what he's saying.

You're here with Evan's off-limits sister, Maybe, and you can bet your ass I'm not going to let this one go until you spill-the-fucking-beans.

Son of a bitch.

"It *was* a great party until you showed up," Lena grumbles, but Cap just laughs it off and turns his attention to her.

"C'mon, little sis. I have someone I want you to meet."

Lena puts a defiant hand to her hip. "Who?"

"Does it really matter?" he questions with a grin.

"Yes, actually, it does."

Cap ignores her completely, and with an arm around her shoulders, he all but forces her to follow his lead.

"Girl, please excuse me for a minute while I go kick my stupid brother's ass!" she calls over her shoulder.

Maybe laughs, and it doesn't take long before they disappear into the throng of dancers in the center of the room and completely out of sight.

But Canyon, the moron, is still standing here, looking at Maybe like he's trying to come up with another pathetic excuse to get her on her own.

It takes all of two seconds for me to step in before he has a chance to utter a single word.

"You want to grab a drink?" I ask her, and she immediately nods.

"Yes, please."

I can't stop myself from reaching out and taking her hand into mine as we head toward the bar set up in the kitchen.

"Thank you," she whispers toward me, and I quirk a brow as I look down at her.

"For what?"

"For saving me from that creep."

"You had it handled. I was just trying to save us all from the scene I knew you'd make, kid." I smirk. "It's bad manners to turn into a little pit bull at a snobby socialite's party."

She giggles at that, and it's like music to my ears.

And just like that, I'm lost in her fucking cuteness.

Cap forgotten.

Canyon really long forgotten.

Maybe's hand in mine seared into my memories forever.

Chapter
TWENTY-FOUR

Maybe

"**G**irl," Lena whispers as we step inside one of the large bathrooms on the second floor of the penthouse. "Things are looking good from where I'm standing."

Two minutes ago, she interrupted my conversation with Milo on the balcony under the pretense of needing to talk to me for a minute and all but dragged my ass up the stairs and into this insanely ornate and ridiculously huge bathroom.

"Dang, how much money does this chick have?" I question as I peer around the expansive, all-marble space. "I mean, this bathroom is bigger than my damn apartment, and it's not even the master bathroom. It's a guest bedroom bathroom. Like how—"

"Forget about the damn bathroom, Mayb," Lena cuts me off and pulls herself up to take a seat on the large, double-sink countertop. "Shit is about to go down tonight."

I tilt my head to the side. "What?"

"It is going down, honey," she repeats. "We are going to make sure that Milo takes you home, and then, you are going to plant a big fat juicy kiss on his lips."

"What?" I watch my eyes go wide in the reflection of the giant mirror behind her. "You are insane."

The night has been going pretty much perfectly.

Milo actually showed up, and we've spent the last two hours just chatting and drinking out on the balcony.

I'm afraid to rock the boat by doing something crazy like kissing him.

"When are you going to learn that I'm aces at reading people?" She smirks like the devil. "Between the way he nearly went all cave-man on that idiot photographer and hasn't left your side for the past two hours, he's practically ordered a neon sign describing the way he feels about you and set it up over your head. It's time for you to make a move."

Make a move? On Milo?

Holy fried potatoes, I might start hyperventilating.

"I don't…I'm not… Fucking hell, Lena, this is freaking me out."

"Girl." She hops off the counter and places two steady hands on my shoulders. "Just take a breath."

I stare at her as I inhale some much-needed oxygen into my lungs and let it out slowly.

"Let's just look at the big picture here, okay?"

I nod.

"You like Milo."

I nod again. I do like Milo. I've *always* liked Milo. Now that I've gotten to know him as an adult, I'm borderline obsessed.

"And over the past few weeks, he's shown enough signs to prove that, although he wants to see you as just his best friend's little sis, he can't. The man is into you, whether or not either of you is ready to admit it to yourselves."

"I just don't know—" I start to refute, but she raises a hand in the air.

"Just think about everything that's gone down between you two."

I recount everything in my head.

His near-overzealous willingness to help me with my career.

Our constant supply of daily text and phone conversations over the past few weeks.

The sexting. Holy hell, the sexting.

Him being here tonight. At the exact kind of party he hates.

"So," Lena continues with a little cheeky grin. "You leave the whole *you catching a ride home from him tonight* to me, and just prepare yourself to put on your big-girl panties and do the one thing you've wanted to do for a long fucking time."

"Kiss him."

Her smile consumes her whole damn face. "Bingo."

Holy mother of mangoes, I hope I don't screw this up.

Somehow, some-insane-way, Yoda—*aka Lena*—pulled through.

With some expert finagling, she made her brother Cap drive her home and arranged for Milo to do the same for me.

I swear, she might be a witch or something.

And now, I sit inside Milo's fancy ride—some kind of sexy sports car that I don't know the name of—while he drives me to my apartment in Chelsea.

The normally bustling city streets are empty and bare at this hour of the morning, the clock on the dash shines with two a.m., and soft classical music plays from the speakers.

I feel like I'm flying.

High off the night.

High off the awesome time I had at the party.

High off Milo's blue eyes and his full lips and the way he looks when he's laughing.

High off *him.*

The man is like my own personal drug, one hit off his smile and I'm done for. Addicted. Desperate for more.

Our conversation hasn't waned since he showed up at the party this evening. We've talked about anything and everything. His business. His favorite places he's traveled to. My time at Stanford. Bands we want to see live. My favorite book recommendations. The best secret spots in New York that tourists don't know about.

You name it, and it's been discussed.

And the more we talk, the more time we spend together, the more I understand why I've always carried a torch for him.

Milo is the one guy who makes me realize why I've never dated or been in a long-term relationship, why no guy has ever held my interest for longer than a few weeks.

It's like I've been waiting for him or something.

Which feels downright insane and a bit terrifying, if I'm being honest.

What if this is only one-sided?

What if Lena is wrong about him?

What if I'm the only one who's starting to fall deeper into like?

Fuck. My brain feels like it might short-circuit if I keep circling around these racing thoughts.

For once in your life, just stop overthinking shit and live in the present.

Yes, that is exactly what I need to do. Live in the present. And right now, the present is enjoying the company of this intelligent, sexy, downright wonderful man.

"Do you think that photographer managed to dupe some girl into doing his pretend photo shoot?" I ask, and Milo smirks at me.

"So, you did know he was full of shit?"

"Of course I did." I snort. "When it comes to men and dating and relationships, I may be inexperienced in a lot of aspects, but I can smell a bullshitter from a mile away."

"I don't think you're as inexperienced as you think you are," he comments, and I tilt my head to the side.

"What do you mean by that?"

"You can hold your own, kid," he answers, and there is this genuine honesty highlighting his voice. "Behind that pretty, innocent face of yours resides a woman who seems to know what she wants. Truthfully, it's jarring. But in a good way."

"Jarring?" I question. "How is that jarring?"

"Because you may look like some delicate little flower, but you're not. You're feisty and sassy as hell when you want to be."

"I am not *that* sassy." I try to disagree, but Milo flashes a knowing look my way.

"Oh yes, you are," he retorts with a little smirk. "But you've been like that since I've known you. Honestly, it's one of my favorite things about you."

His words stun me into silence.

One of his favorite things?

So, he has more than one favorite thing? About me?

My heart threatens to find a way out of my chest.

Thankfully, Milo pulls up in front of my apartment building and double parks, and I grab my stuff to make a swift exit.

With his hand at the small of my back, guiding me toward my building, my head starts to feel lighter than my body, and I search for words of any kind—anything that will serve as a distraction.

"Is avoiding getting towed one of Billionaireman's superpowers too? A cloaking device perhaps?"

"Sure. It's called having enough money that you don't have to care."

"Ah," I sigh with a little laugh. "Must be the same thing that allows you to drive in New York City in the first place. Normal people don't pay to have cars here. Except Bruce," I amend. "But I'm pretty sure he sacrificed my wedding fund to pay for it."

"I had a lot of fun tonight," he says, changing the subject entirely, when we come to a stop just outside the entrance door. A smirk crinkles the left corner of his mouth. "Thanks for being such a pain in my ass and making me come to that party."

"You're welcome, old man." I giggle.

"Old man?" he questions in feigned outrage. "Really?"

I shrug, and a little smile touches my lips. A sarcastic retort sits at the tip of my tongue, but my phone chimes inside my purse. And then does it again. And again. And again.

"What the hell?" I mutter and pull it out to find my inbox finally decided to update from this morning. "I swear to God, sometimes

Gmail gets a thrill out of commandeering my emails for like twelve hours."

Milo just laughs, and I quickly scroll through the delayed emails to make sure I didn't miss anything important.

But my hand freezes and my eyes go wide when I spot the subject line of one particular email.

"What?" he asks, but I'm too dumbfounded to utter a word.

Instead, I tap one shaking finger to the screen and read the message.

To: MaybeWillis@gmail.com
From: Taylor.McHough@BeaconHouse.com
Subject: Interview Request

Good morning, Ms. Willis,
After reviewing your resume and seeing your lengthy list of credentials, we would like to schedule an in-person interview with you next week.
Does Friday, June 28th at 12:00 p.m. work for you?
I look forward to hearing from you.
Friendly regards,
Taylor McHough
Editor in Chief, Beacon House

"Oh my God," I whisper and look up to meet his curious eyes. "Oh. My. God."

"What?" Milo asks again. "What's going on?"

"Beacon House wants to interview me!" I practically shout into the otherwise quiet night air. "They want me to come in Friday for a freaking interview!"

Milo's smile beams. "I knew you could do it, kid."

The excitement and joy become overwhelming, and before I know it, I'm catapulting myself into his arms and wrapping my legs around his waist like a little monkey.

"Milo!" I exclaim. "Beacon House wants to interview me!"

He grins and looks down at me. "I heard."

"Friday, Milo! I have an interview this Friday!"

A soft chuckle leaves his lips. "Proud of you, kid."

"Holy macaroni salad at a barbecue! I can't believe it! God, Milo! Thank you so much for making this happen! I couldn't have done any of this without you!"

Those big blue eyes of his glisten and shine, and I can't stop myself from getting lost in them. From getting lost in him. Interview and excitement long forgotten, all I seem to be able to see is him.

And I'm still in his arms, his strong hands keeping me there by gripping my hips.

And then we're both quiet and just...looking at each other. Searching the other's eyes. My gaze flitters between his eyes and his lips, and I'm just so tempted.

So tempted to lean forward and find out if his lips are as soft as they look.

"Milo," I whisper his name, but he doesn't respond.

Instead, he fixates his gaze on my mouth.

He. Is. Staring. At. My. Lips.

Lena's advice plays inside my head, and I know I'd be an idiot if I let this moment pass me by.

So, I don't.

One inch, two inches, I move my mouth toward his until our lips are just barely brushing.

And right before I find the courage to finish the job, to actually kiss him, Milo takes me by surprise and presses his mouth to mine, stealing my fucking breath.

God, his lips are so soft. So full. So perfect.

A quiet moan escapes my throat when he slips his tongue inside my mouth to dance with mine.

Gently, slowly at first, until a barely there growl leaves his mouth and enters mine.

Our kiss turns fast and deep. My hands are in his hair, gripping the thick locks in fervor, and his strong hands caress my ass.

And we just keep kissing.

Lord Almighty, he tastes so good. Like mint and honey and heaven and Milo.

I dreamed about kissing him at least a thousand times, but not once did I ever anticipate it would be this good. Feel this good.

I never want it to end.

But at the same time, I know it needs to end.

And for some strange reason, I know that I need to be the one to end it.

When our kiss starts to slow, I ease myself from his perfect, lush mouth. But before I remove myself from his arms completely, I place one final, lingering kiss to his lips.

Silence fills the space between us, and it takes me a good thirty seconds before I can find my voice again.

"Thank you for bringing me home," I whisper and look up into the stunning blue of his eyes. "And thank you for coming to the party. I had fun with you."

"I had fun with you too."

The temptation to catapult myself into his arms and kiss his fucking face off is so strong, but I compose myself, swallowing down the urge, and focus on ending the night on the least awkward note possible.

"Good night, Milo."

He leans forward and presses one final kiss to my forehead. "Good night, kid."

And just like that, we part ways.

I walk into my building.

And Milo heads to his car.

But I can't deny that my heart is so full, it's damn near bursting.

I kissed Milo Ives.

And more than that, he kissed me right back.

Chapter
TWENTY-FIVE

Maybe

When the sun filters into my bedroom and the clock barely strikes eight, I am up and out of bed with the kind of energy even Red Bull and coffee can't provide.

If I didn't know last night actually happened, I would think it was a damn dream.

But it did happen. Oh boy, did it happen.

Not only did I get to spend an entire evening with Milo, I *kissed* him.

If it wasn't the best kiss of my life, I don't think I'll be able to survive the kiss that could top it.

Everything is coming up fucking roses.

After a quick pit stop in the bathroom to pee, brush my teeth, and wash my face, I head into the kitchen and set a fresh pot of Folgers to brew.

Mr. Coffee makes me proud, and it's not long before one of my favorite smells fills my apartment.

But, seriously. Is there anything better than the smell of fresh coffee in the morning?

Definitely not.

I fill my favorite pink mug to the brim, stir in a little sugar and milk, and plop down onto my sofa, fully prepared to fit in an hour of prerecorded *Project Runway* before I have to get ready for another boring Saturday shift at the shop.

But I'm barely five minutes into finding out what the next challenge is before my phone pings several times in a row with text message notifications.

What the…? Did somebody die?

I snag my phone off the coffee table and find five messages from Lena.

Lena: GIRL. Tell me everything.

Lena: Wake the fuck up right now before I die from anticipation.

Lena: MAYBE, WAKE UP.

Lena: Seriously, wake up. My nipples are all tingly and when my nipples tingle that means the seventh sun is in the house of fornication.

Lena: REALLY? No response to the house of fornication? That was clever as hell, and I'm disappointed in you.

Lena: Helloooooooooooooooooooo?

I grin and type out a response.

Me: Well, good morning to you, too. And for future reference, I track my behaviors on the SIXTH sun. The seventh was just one too many.

Lena: There's no time for your little jokes, friend. I need to know what happened last night.

My cheeks blush and my lips tingle just thinking about the perfect, almost unbelievable sensation of Milo Ives's lips on mine.

Me: Well…it was no house of fornication, but I did kiss him.

Lena: YES. YES. YES. I knew it! How was it?

Me: If I were less in control of my emotions, I'd probably cry every time I think about it.

Lena: Holy hell! You may be in control of your emotions, but I am NOT. I feel like a proud momma. I literally might start sobbing.

I laugh.

Me: No need to cry, Yoda. It was just...a really great kiss. No big deal.

Lena: NO BIG DEAL? C'mon, Mayb. You and I both know that wasn't JUST anything. We're talking you and MILO. That was a freaking milestone. It was something you've been waiting to happen for like a decade now.

More than a decade, actually. But no need to get lost into the logistics.

Me: I know. Honestly, I'm still having a hard time believing it happened.

Lena: It happened, girl. It mother-flipping-fucking-sucking happened. So...after the kiss, how did it end?

I'm still shocked I had the willpower to be the one to end it. It was like I somehow channeled the Hulk and forced myself not to turn into a bumbling, rambling weirdo.

Me: Well...I just kind of ended the kiss and told him good night.

Lena: You did what????

I grimace and bite my lip.

Me: Was that wrong?

Lena: Was that wrong??? Hell no. That was genius, my friend. Fucking genius. And it's official. I am a proud momma, and I'm going to cry.

Me: LOL. Slow your roll, momma. I need your sage advice on what I'm supposed to do next.

Lena: What do you want to do next?

What do I want to do next? I honestly have no fucking clue.

Me: I'm not really sure yet, but that reminds me of something I overheard when I was at Starbucks the other morning.

Lena: Excuse me? Did you just say Starbucks?

I grin.

Me: Chill out. It wasn't for me. It was a coffee run for my dad.

Lena: I'll let it slide. This time. But if I ever hear and/or see you type that name again, I reserve the right to smack you.

Me: HA. Noted.

Lena: So...don't leave me hanging here. What did you hear at that shitty, overpriced, terrible coffee establishment?

Me: These two girls were chatting about DP. They said it was the most intensely awesome sexual experience they've ever had. I think I want to try it...

Lena: Give me a second...currently trying to revive myself. This bout of laughter was officially too much.

Me: What? Why is this funny?

Lena: Do you know what DP is?

Me: No, not really.

But the way those chicks were quietly going on and on about it over Frappuccinos, I'm assuming whatever it is, it's *really* good.

Lena: Now I know what your next step with Milo is.

Me: ?

Lena: Text him and tell him exactly what you just told me.

Me: About DP?

Lena: Uh-huh.

Me: What in the hell do I say? "Oh hey, I want to try DP"?

Lena: Oh yes, honey. That's pretty much perfect.

I take a sip of my coffee and shrug to myself.

It's not like Lena's advice has ever steered me in the wrong direction.

Chapter
TWENTY-SIX

Milo

Although I planned to take Saturday off from work, when Emily—one of Fuse's top finance gurus—called me about a discrepancy that needed to be worked out, I found myself getting out of bed about three hours earlier than I planned and heading into the office.

Being in the back seat with nothing to do while Sam drove proved to be a test of my sanity.

I couldn't stop thinking about Maybe, that stupid party, and that really and truly *stupid* kiss.

Goddamn, I shouldn't have done that. I should have backed away instead of leaning in, held my ground in the name of self-preservation.

But I'm finding I'm powerless against her. Her sassy words and contagious giggle. Those big brown eyes and gorgeous smile. And the way those cheeks of hers blush when she's feeling embarrassed...

Fuck... She is apparently my kryptonite.

And even knowing that, I'd do it all over again. It's all too much—the sweet smell of her shampoo, the warmth of her body, the absolutely perfect sensation of her lips under mine—and when it comes to her, I fear I'd do just about anything, rational thought be damned.

Get it together, you bastard.

As Sam drops me at my building and I close myself into the solitude of my office, my neuroses over my best friend's little sister become acutely more obvious. For the love of God, if I'm going to get anything done today, I need to shut down that section of my brain completely.

I glance down at my semi-hard cock and scold him too. *Absolutely no more running through that kiss for the rest of the workday!* I wouldn't call his response compliant, but I push onward anyway.

Yes. I can do this. I can just think about work.

I glance at the clock on my desktop computer and see I have another thirty minutes before I need to be in the conference room to discuss the accounting discrepancy with Emily and ten other employees of the finance team.

I resign myself to my fate of catching up on late emails, but I only get through ten messages before my phone starts to ring. A FaceTime request from Cap.

Oh, here we go…

Normally, I might be surprised to hear from him so early on a Saturday. But after our encounter last night, I wouldn't expect anything less. Caplin Hawkins is a shitstirrer of epic proportions, and I know from way too much experience, he isn't going away if I ignore him.

Not after seeing me with Evan's sister.

On a sigh, I accept the call on my desktop, and his big ole fucking head fills the screen. He's looking down and tapping out something, and before I know it, Thatcher Kelly is there too, smiling back at me.

Fucking hell. It's the whole goon squad.

"Oh man! Is that the office I see behind you?" Cap exclaims. "And here I thought you might've come to your senses and learned that Saturdays are meant for relaxing."

"I told you he'd be in the office," Thatch chimes in. "Why don't you ever listen to me?"

"You two are so cute, bickering like an old married couple. Is your anniversary coming up? I'll have my assistant send a gift," I retort.

Cap gives me the finger, and Thatch, the crazy giant, smiles. "Like Cassie would share all of this—" He runs his hands down his body in a horrendous display of eroticism. "With just anyone. She needs a twelve-inch, trick-performing, light-saber-powerful cock to even consider it."

Cap laughs hysterically, and I cover my eyes. *Dear God*, "To what do I owe this horrible occasion of video-chatting with you?"

Cap's laugh turns to wolflike. "Well, I was having a nice Saturday chat with Thatch and telling him how I saw you last night at Daphne Ares's party…"

My pulse races in my throat as I gear up for the shit I *know* is coming.

"And needless to say, we both decided it was the perfect time to call and catch up with the devil himself."

Thatch nods. "And here we thought you'd all but given up on having a social life."

"Yeah, buddy," Cap adds with an annoying smirk. "What's going on? Mind clueing us in on what changed your old-man ways?"

Old man. That's the second time I've heard that in the past twenty-four hours, and of course, the sheer mention of it makes me think about Maybe and our kiss…*again.*

My chest tightens with the unease of a man who knows he's in the wrong, but Thatch keeps right on talking as though there isn't a vise closing in on me every second. "Is it the summer air? A new diet? Or, maybe, just *maybe*, the motherfluffing girl I *knew* you were already lusting after!"

"All right, you assholes. No need to spell it out any further," I respond on a heavy sigh. Having to deal with my conscience is bad enough. Being interrogated by Thing 1 and Thing 2 is just plain cruel. "I thought you'd shaken your *Gossip Girl* addiction, Cap."

No doubt he's spent the early part of his morning gabbing like a damn drama queen.

"Now, now, there's no need to bring *Gossip Girl* into this," he snaps. "If I hear you talking bad about my girls Blair and Serena, consider our friendship over."

I roll my eyes and Thatch chuckles.

"I'm a *Vampire Diaries* man myself," Thatch comments insanely. "But let's not stray from the important shit."

"You're right, dude." Cap nods. "And the important shit is that our good friend Milo here is playing with fucking fire."

"I am not playing with fire."

I am. I most certainly am. But sometimes denial is just a hell of a lot easier than facing reality head on.

"You're so full of shit, and we all know it." Cap eyes me shrewdly. "You, the man who loathes socialite parties, were at one. Last night. With a girl who just so happens to be our good buddy's little sister."

I start to open my mouth to try to explain, but apparently, he hasn't hit his fucking word count for the conversation yet.

"Wait. I forgot to add the most important detail of all," he rambles. "Our good buddy's *off-limits* little sister."

Son of a bitch. His words shouldn't bother me, but they do.

Guilt had already found its way into my veins this morning. Now, that infection feels so pungent, I fear I'll go septic.

"We're just friends," I deny with a thick tongue. "She asked me to go to that party with her last night, so I did what any good friend would do. I met her there."

"Oh, okay," Thatch responds. "You met her at the party. Nothing more. Nothing less, right?"

"Right."

Thatch snorts. "Yeah, okay. And Cassie's the Virgin Mary."

The word *virgin* lands in my head like an arrow. God, what a fucking mess I've gotten myself into.

"Don't forget that you spent the whole night standing out on the balcony with her, drinking and laughing it up like you were the only two lovebirds at the shindig."

"Lovebirds!" Thatch whoops wildly.

I might kill Cap. Surely, no one would miss him, right?

"*Or* that you drove her home," Cap continues. "Can't forget that either."

"It's nice to know that you were so invested in my whereabouts last night," I deflect. "I know you get upset when I don't give you all of my attention, sweetheart, but there's no need to stalk me."

Cap grins. "I can't deny I'm still pissed at you for not taking me to lunch, but that is not the subject at hand, brother. But, hey, two points for your efforts in deflection."

An annoyed laugh escapes my lungs. "What do you want me to say? Evan asked me to help Maybe get a few interviews with publishing houses in the city. Which I've been doing. And yes, I'm friends with her. I went to a party with her. I took her home. Pretty sure we've covered it all."

"Wait…" Thatch chimes in. "How long have you been helping her with the whole career thing?"

"I don't know." I shrug. "A few weeks."

"More like over a month," Cap kindly offers, the prick.

"Does it really matter?"

"I *knew* there was something different about you when I saw you at the gym!" Thatch smiles like a fucking loon. "Goddamn, I'm good."

"You saw him at the gym?" Cap asks, and Thatch nods.

"Damn right, I did. The Supercock could tell something was different. It was pinging all over the place."

"Not sure I like the thought of your dick having feelings about me."

Thatch ignores me and booms on. "And now, it's safe to say that Little Miss Maybe was the reason."

"Damn, you two could turn anything into something," I grumble. "It's a true talent."

They both laugh like what I said is the most ridiculous thing they've ever heard.

"All right, honey," Cap says. "It's pretty obvious you're not ready to dish the dirt, but just know, when you're ready, when you've officially lit yourself on fire and are up shit creek without a goddamn paddle because you've fallen for your best friend's little sister, we'll be here. Ready to listen."

Fallen for my best friend's little sister? Now they're really talking crazy.

Yeah, keep telling yourself that, you denying bastard.

I roll my eyes. "That's mighty generous of you, but I can already guarantee that's not going to happen."

Are you sure? You're already feeling things for her that are anything but friendly...or by Maybe's definition, very friendly.

I shake off my slightly terrifying thoughts and redirect the conversation. "So, is there any other reason you girls called me, or can I get back to work and try to get out of here before I waste my entire Saturday in the office?"

"You're really keeping it close to the vest, eh?" Thatch smirks. "Ah, well, can't say I blame you. Cap showed me a picture of Maybe, and I'd do the same thing if I were in your shoes."

I quirk a brow. "Do the same thing?"

"Yep." He nods. "I'd light myself on fucking fire too. I'm certain there isn't a single guy in New York who could resist those big, innocent brown eyes of hers."

"Thatcher Kelly!" a female's voice screeches in the background. "I can fluffing hear you!"

It takes exactly one second for me to know that voice belongs to his wife, Cassie.

"Ah, calm down, honey," he calls over his shoulder. "I'm just talking in hypotheticals. You know your glorious tits are the only tits I want in my big fucking hands."

"Tits! Tits!" a small child's voice chimes in behind him. "I like tits!"

"Gunnar don't repeat what Daddio says, little buddy."

"Fluffing hell, Thatcher!" Cassie exclaims. "I swear to God, if I find out he's walking around day care saying 'I like tits,' I'm going to kill you!"

The Kelly household, ladies and gentlemen.

"Ah, hell," Thatch sighs. "I better get off here before Cass loses her shit."

Both Cap and I grin at each other on the screen. Thatch's zoo means that for once in this conversation, I'm not the main attraction.

I don't wait for another opportunity to end the call and escape. This one is as good as it's going to get.

I hit the end button, and both of their big heads give way to blackness on the screen. The breath of relief that leaves my lungs is immediate.

Thank fuck.

Before I can let their disturbingly perceptive words sink in, I glance at the clock and see my time is up. I need to head into the conference room for the meeting with the finance team.

I head out of my office, and after a quick pit stop in the break room, I step into the conference room a few minutes later with a much-needed coffee in my hands.

"Good morning, everyone," I greet all eleven people sitting around the table. "Thanks for spending your Saturday trying to fix this issue. I appreciate the dedication."

"No problem, Mr. Ives." Emily nods. "Shall we get started?"

I gesture toward her and take a seat at the head of the table. "By all means, the sooner we get through this, the sooner all of you can get back to your families and actually enjoy your weekend."

Get back to your families. I don't know why those words make my chest ache, but I swallow it down and choose to revisit that a different time. It's more than apparent that my idiot friends have truly fucked with my head.

Thankfully, Emily dives right in, pulling up our current accounting numbers on her laptop and projecting them onto the big screen at the foot of the table. "Okay, so, initially, I wasn't sure where we went wrong. But, good news, after scouring the numbers for the past few hours, I think I've figured out the issue. If you all just give me about fifteen minutes to explain what I've found, I think we can get this sorted out quickly."

"Fantastic," I say, and she offers a grateful smile.

I'm not sure if she expected me to be on a tirade over the discrepancy, but if there's one thing I've learned about Emily Willow over the past three years, it's that she is thorough as fuck, and if there's an issue, her numbers-oriented brain and eagle eyes will locate it.

I have nothing but admiration and respect for her as an employee.

She continues to lead the meeting, showing the final numbers from last quarter and comparing them with the projected numbers of this quarter.

So far, so good. What she shows makes sense.

And, it's apparent by the nodding heads and reassuring comments, the rest of the table agrees.

Just as she directs a few questions toward her colleague Mark Wallace, my phone vibrates in my pocket.

I take a sip from my cup and discreetly pull my phone out to check my messages.

Maybe: I think I want to try DP.

I nearly choke on my coffee.

What in the hell?

In the middle of an important meeting or not, I think my brain will explode if I don't respond.

Me: Uh…no, you don't.

And, in true Maybe fashion, she doesn't hesitate to keep this insane conversation going.

Maybe: I've been told it's the most intense sexual experience a girl can have. Why wouldn't I want to try it?

Holy hell. Where is this coming from?

Me: You've been told? Where are you getting this advice, exactly?

Maybe: I heard two girls talking about it at Starbucks.

I bite my lip to prevent my laughter.
Cap's crazy sister Lena, I could understand. But Starbucks? Of all the fucking places.

Me: You heard people talking about DP and decided that's the next step for you, all while you were ordering coffee?

Maybe: Yes.

Me: You were at Starbucks, just picking up a cup a joe to start your day, and you decided right then, DP is the next thing you want to do?

Maybe: Yes! Why do you keep asking me things I've already told you?

I bite my lip and type again.

Me: Maybe, do you have any idea what DP is?

Maybe: Uh...an intense sexual experience. Duh.

I grin. *Jesus, why is she so adorable?*

Me: Let me rephrase. Do you know what DP stands for?

Maybe: Double Pleasure.

A laugh escapes my throat, and everyone sitting at the conference table turns their eyes toward me.

"Sorry," I mutter and nod toward Emily. "Please, continue."

She gets back to the meeting, and I discreetly type out another text message to Maybe.

Me: Double Penetration.

Maybe: Huh?

Me: That's what DP stands for. Double Penetration.

Maybe: I don't get it.

Me: In most cases, it requires three people, two of whom have dicks.

When she doesn't respond, I keep going.

Me: Two men.

Me: One woman.

Me: Two cocks.

It's not until that final text that she chimes back into the conversation.

Maybe: IT'S THAT???

Me: Yes, it's that.

Maybe: Oh my God. I thought it was like two orgasms or something! I've never been penetrated by one penis, much less two at the same time! Gah!

Me: Sounds like you're changing your tune on DP…

Maybe: Have you ever done it?

Jesus. This not at all where I want this conversation to go.
I'd much prefer to keep my wild and crazy past just that. In the damn past.
So, I do my best to change the subject.

Me: What are your plans tonight?

Maybe: OH MY GOD. YOU HAVE DONE IT

Me: How about Tuesday night? Do you want to grab some dinner Tuesday night?

Maybe: I CAN'T BELIEVE YOU'VE DONE IT.

Me: Personally, I'm in the mood for Mexican.

Maybe: Do you DP often???

Fucking hell. She's relentless.

Me: I'm not much of a threesome kind of guy, Maybe.

Maybe: What's that supposed to mean?

Me: It means, when I'm with a woman, I'm selfish. I like to have her all to myself. Plus, I'm not a twenty-one-year-old bastard anymore who looks at sex like it's some kind of challenge to try anything and every-thing. It was a one-time experience when I was a wild college kid. And not one I want to repeat. It's just not my style.

Maybe: OMG you did it in college. PLEASE GOD DO NOT TELL ME THE SECOND COCK WAS MY BROTHER'S

Me: That sentence is disturbing on so many levels. But no, Evan and I didn't make a porno version of Three's Company.

Maybe: THANK GOD. I thought I was going to have to give up food for the day.

Me: LOL You're safe.

Maybe: If threesomes aren't your style, then what is?

Back to the sex. Just when I thought I'd escaped at least somewhat unscathed. Still, I can't help but answer her honestly.

Me: Thorough. Sex for me isn't a sprint. It's a marathon. I like to take my time. Explore. Savor it. And I don't like to fucking share.

Maybe: Are you sexting me right now?

Me: HAHA. Nice one. And no, you asked, and I'm nothing if not honest.

Maybe: Well, your honesty is...well... Anyway... So, about that dinner?

Hmm...I'm far too intrigued by her sudden change in tune.

Me: Are you aroused right now, kid?

No response.

Me: Shall I change the subject to dinner?

Maybe: Yes.

But before I can respond and successfully steer our dangerous conversation to safer territories, she sends another one.

Maybe: Mexican takeout. Your place Tuesday night. And I have a surprise.

Me: What kind of surprise?

Maybe: If I tell you, it wouldn't be a surprise, silly. You get the food (I'm a crunchy taco and chips and salsa kind of gal) and I'll meet you at your place around seven.

Me: You drive a hard bargain. But fine. See you Tuesday at 7.

I send up a prayer that Maybe's surprise isn't showing me her wrong-day underwear. Because, fuck, I'm not sure if I'd be able to handle it.

Please God. If anything, send Maybe to my apartment Tuesday in a parka.

Chapter
TWENTY-SEVEN

Maybe

A little after seven, I make my way to Milo's apartment building. It's a large, sophisticated looking structure on Park Avenue, otherwise known as one of the richest streets in New York.

Part of me wanted to strangle Lena for not telling me what DP was and encouraging me to text Milo instead. Because holy balls, it's a little embarrassing I legit thought it meant some kind of double orgasm thing. But another part of me, the one that's about to have a quiet dinner with Milo, is damned thankful for it.

I can't deny it was one of the catalysts that brought me right here—*standing outside of his swanky apartment building.*

A doorman—*yes, a fucking doorman*—lets me inside.

Once I give him my name, he leads me toward an elevator off the beaten path of the marble encased lobby and escorts me to the sixteenth floor.

Per Gill's update, "Mr. Ives is expecting you."

The instant I reach Milo's floor, the elevator opens directly into his flipping apartment.

He greets me in the foyer in bare feet, a pair of jeans, and a gray T-shirt.

Hell's bells, bare feet on a man has never looked so damn sexy before.

"Exactly how rich are you?" It's the first question that pops out of my mouth, and Milo smirks.

"What makes you ask that?"

I look around his place dramatically.

Well, the entrance of his place. Which is damn near the size of my living room.

"Because your building, your apartment...well, these are some swanky digs, Mr. Ives."

He groans. "You can go ahead and drop the Mr. Ives unless you want me to feel like an old man again."

I giggle. "Well, you are, like, six years older than me so..."

He rolls his eyes. "Are we going to stand here and discuss my old age or head inside and eat some food?"

"Hmm..." I tap my chin, but he doesn't give me any time. Instead, he steps forward, tosses me over his strong shoulder and carries me through the foyer, down the hallway, and into the kitchen.

"You can put me down now!" I shout through a giggle.

Milo sets me on the expansive kitchen island and proceeds to grab some plates and cutlery for our food.

"Would you like a glass of wine, Ms. Willis?"

"Is it expensive wine?"

He furrows his brow.

"I mean, is it like a thousand-year-old wine that only rich people like you drink?"

"No." He snorts. "It's a fifteen-dollar bottle of white I got at Duane Reed."

A laugh escapes my lips. "No shit?"

"No. But it is somewhere in between the two. I have a lot of money, but I'm a pretty simple guy, Maybe."

"A simple guy with a driver and a doorman."

He laughs. "I never said I don't enjoy some of the luxuries money can buy. But I don't make a point to be extravagant in everything I do."

"I know." I smile at him. "And I admire that about you."

"Yeah?"

"Of course," I admit. "I read an interview with you in the *Times*, and I was pleasantly surprised with your responses about living off ramen noodles and Kraft Mac & Cheese for the first few years of your company."

"I've forgone the ramen, but," he says and opens the pantry, "I'll never quit the occasional Mac & Cheese."

I snicker when I see no fewer than ten blue and yellow boxes of Kraft sitting on the center shelf.

"Only a crazy person would quit Kraft."

"Exactly."

Together, we carry the wine, plates, and takeout bags into the living room and sit down beside each other on the couch.

Once we're both settled, and our plates are covered with delicious Mexican, he turns to me with a grin. "So...the surprise..."

"What surprise?" I question. "There's supposed to be surprise...?"

He laughs. "You're a terrible liar."

"Fine." I grin and set my plate on the coffee table. "But prepare to be excited. You are in for the most enlightening night of your life. Do you have Netflix?"

He nods and hands me the remote.

It doesn't take long before the opening credits of the *Gilmore Girls* are vibrating from the speakers of his flat screen hanging on the wall. I sing along to the song, and Milo glances at me in confusion.

"This is the surpri—" he starts to say but stops when the title of the show is revealed on the screen—*Gilmore Girls*. "Wait...it's a TV show?"

I snort. "Of course, it's a TV show."

"I thought you were talking about real fucking people."

"I wish I were talking about real people!" I exclaim and grab my plate. "Oh my God, if Stars Hollow were a real place, I'd move there quicker than you could say 'Where are you going?'"

When Lorelai and Rory start doing their Lorelai and Rory thing on the screen, Milo glances at me with a raise of his brow. "So, we're going full-on chick flick kind of vibes tonight?"

"You bet your sweet ass, we are." I nod and take a big bite of my taco. "I mean, we're not going to be able to watch all of the episodes tonight, but if we're lucky, we'll be able to get through the first half of season one."

"How long are the episodes?"

"An hour or so."

"And how many seasons?"

"Seven."

"And each season wouldn't happen to be one episode long?"

"Don't be silly. There're at least eight episodes per season."

Milo sighs and I giggle.

"You're such a Luke, it's not even funny."

"Who is Luke?"

I waggle my brows. "Oh, don't worry, Mr. Grumpy. You'll find out real soon."

I leave out the whole part that Luke Danes was my fictional man crush from the very first episode of the *Gilmore Girls*. Or the fact that Milo Ives was my real-life man crush from the time I was like ten years old.

Yeah, let's just leave out those minor details and enjoy the food and the company and the show.

Two episodes into the *Gilmore Girls* and Milo throws the white flag.

"All right," he says and picks up the remote from the coffee table to put episode three on pause. "I think I need a little Stars Follow break."

I laugh. "Stars *Hollow*."

"Yeah. That," he says and lies back on the couch like he's been forced to run a marathon. "My eyes and ears just need a break."

I giggle again. "You want me to head out so you can get some sleep?"

He shakes his head. "I fear if I go to bed now, I'll dream about the fucking *Gilmore Girls*."

"You're so Luke, it's not even funny."

Milo glares at me. "I am not Luke."

"Oh yes, you are," I retort and pick up a pillow from the couch to playfully smack against his chest. "You're surly and cranky and grumpy. Exactly like Luke."

"I am not."

"Trust me, Milo," I say with a little grin. "In your old age, you've grown into all of those things. Just face the facts, buddy. You're no longer bad boy Jess, you're Luke Danes now."

"Who the hell is Jess?"

"You'll find out in season three."

"I'll have to watch it from the grave because I don't think I can survive much more."

I giggle.

God, he's adorable.

And sexy.

And I can't stop my eyes from moving up the length of his body. Up the denim covering his firm legs, over his zipper, over the barely visible lines of his toned abdomen.

But my eyes take a detour and reroute themselves back to the zipper of his jeans.

Back to the visible bulge beneath it.

Back to the place that has me recalling the photo he sent me. Of him. In his boxer briefs.

I'd be a liar if I didn't admit I saved that photo *and* I've looked at that photo one too many times since he sent it to me. And I've fantasized about said photo even more.

I've daydreamed about what he looks beneath the boxer briefs. About how big and thick he is.

About what he would feel like hard between my hands. Heavy inside my mouth.

Holy Kraft macaroni… Would he even fit inside my mouth?

Pretty sure this is why deep-throating is a thing, Maybe…

I don't know anything about deep-throating—or blow jobs, for that matter. Never even done it before. But fuck, I'd want to give it a shot. With Milo.

"Having *Gilmore Girls* withdrawals already?" His voice pulls me from my thoughts, and I look away from the zipper of his jeans to his blue as the sky eyes.

"Huh?"

"I lost you for a minute there," he says with a small smile. "Where did you just go?"

Uh…to you and deep-throating and your penis and deep-throating your penis.

"Yeah…uh…" I pause and dig my teeth into my bottom lip. "I probably shouldn't say."

He tilts his head to the side. "What were you just thinking about?"

My cheeks flush red. I don't respond.

"Maybe?"

"How do you deep-throat?" I blurt out the question, and Milo's eyes go wide.

"What?"

Screw it. I mean, I asked him about DP the other day. What's the big deal about asking him about blow jobs too?

The big deal is probably because you weren't just thinking about blow jobs, you were fantasizing about giving him a blow job…

"Am I supposed to deep-throat?" I ask. "You know, like, when I'm giving a…you know…am I supposed to deep-throat? Do most guys expect that?"

His jaw goes unhinged for a brief moment, but he quickly recovers. "Well, I think that depends on the guy, Maybe."

"Do you like deep-throating?"

"I like whatever feels good to the woman," he responds without a second thought. "The only thing I don't like is for a woman to give me a blow job because she feels obligated or like she's supposed to. I want her to want to do it. I want her to enjoy it as much as I enjoy it."

"I've never given a blow job," I whisper, and his eyebrows rise. "Really?"

I shake my head. "I mean, I've touched a penis before with my hands." I gesture awkwardly in a showy jazz motion. "But I've never actually given a blow job."

"Is there a specific reason for that?"

"Not really." I shrug. "I guess it just never felt right. I never felt comfortable enough with the guy to do it."

"That's not a bad thing, Maybe," he says with a soft smile across his lips. "I really admire you for waiting until it feels right."

"Seriously?"

"I wouldn't lie to you, kid." He holds out his arms. "Come here," he says, and I lie down beside him on the couch.

Milo runs his fingers through my hair, and I rest my head against his chest.

And God, his strong body against mine feels so good.

Just so incredibly good.

Instantly, I start to throb between my legs.

Fuck. I'm attracted to him. I've always been attracted to him. Even when I was a teenager and didn't really understand what it was I was feeling whenever he was around.

I want him.

I want to explore his body with my fingers and lips and tongue.

I want to know if his cock feels silky and hard between my hands like I've imagined.

Or if he'll actually feel heavy inside my mouth.

Stop overthinking, then. Just do it. Find out the answers for yourself.

Before I can second-guess it, I slide my body down his and rest my face right beside his zipper. Hesitantly, I lift my hand and place it right over the bulge of his jeans.

"Maybe?" he asks, his voice quiet but undeniably raspy with arousal.

I ignore him and move my fingers to the button and zipper of his jeans. They're undone a few seconds later, and I can't stop myself from sliding my hand beneath the waistband of his boxer briefs until I can feel his cock against the palm of my hand.

He's hard and getting harder.

And he's big. And thick. And perfect.

And now I want to see him.

Taste him.

Wrap my mouth around him.

And I don't hold back.

Instead, I pull a Nike and *Just Do It*.

Chapter
TWENTY-EIGHT

Milo

My cock is in her hands.

Her petite fingers grip me at the base and move up and down in a gentle, hesitant motion.

I'm hard, so fucking hard, I'm certain my dick could hammer nails.

"Maybe?" I say her name again, but she doesn't respond.

Instead, she looks up at me from beneath her lashes and searches my eyes for a long moment. But her hands, well, they keep touching me, caressing me, stroking me.

"I want to know what it feels like," she whispers. "I want to know what it feels like to make a man feel good."

This is a bad idea, Milo. A bad fucking idea.

"I don't think this is a—" I start to say, but when she leans forward and wraps her perfect little mouth around the head of my cock, all rational thought flies out of the fucking room. Out the front door. Out of the damn city.

Her mouth is warm and soft and so insanely perfect, I have to bite back the groan that threatens to escape my throat.

"I've never done this before," she whispers, and uncertainty fills her brown eyes. "Tell me what makes you feel good."

"I can assure you, anything you do right now will feel good."

Because it's the truth.

It's a fucking certainty.

In my eyes, anything she does will be perfect. It's a fact when it comes to her.

She slides herself down my body so she's between my thighs, and all I can do is watch her as she wraps her mouth around me again. Her long locks create a veil around her face, and I reach forward to brush the rogue strands behind her ears.

With her hand gripped around my shaft, she moves her mouth up and down my length. But her tiny mouth can only take so much, and the mere idea of that only makes me harder.

"There is more cock than mouth, sweetheart." I reach forward to brush my fingers across her lips. She starts to hesitate, but I add, "It's fucking perfect. What you're doing is perfect."

You're perfect.

My words encourage her further, and the way her eyes glaze over with satisfaction and confidence has my heart beating harder and faster inside my chest.

I watch the way her legs fidget beneath her. Her thighs clenching, her hips moving from side to side. I take in the way her shirt falls forward, revealing the soft curves of her breasts. And I'm riveted by the way her pretty little lips look wrapped around me.

She is beautiful and timid yet assertive and seductive.

She is sex and innocence, a fucking goddess before my very eyes.

The tip of her tongue moves up and down my length, and my thighs tighten with pleasure. My eyes glaze over as I watch her explore me. Taste me. Suck me. Her fingers grip and stroke, and her fingertips caress me.

A moan escapes her throat, vibrating against me, and the movement of her hips becomes more apparent.

She's turned on. Craving. Wanton. Turning more aroused by the second.

Fuck, it's nearly too much for my brain to process.

And it's most definitely too much for my dick to handle.

My climax hits me hard, starting at the base of my cock and spreading throughout my whole damn body.

My heart pounds inside my ears and my breaths come out in erratic pants, and Maybe stays with me through the whole thing, her soft mouth wrapped around me, swallowing my orgasm through soft moans.

It's the best fucking orgasm I've ever had in my life.

And it's not because of what she did.

It's because it was her lips wrapped around me.

It was her eyes locked with mine.

It was her moans in my ears.

It was her hands on me.

It's because it was Maybe.

And you tried to say you weren't falling for her...

Chapter
TWENTY-NINE

Maybe

I step off the subway and head up the stairs and toward my fate.

Well, seeing as I still have another two hours before my interview with Taylor McHough at Beacon, not directly toward my fate, but that's minor semantics.

I'm two blocks away from the building where Beacon House headquarters reside, and I can't find the strength to finish the job.

I'm pacing. On the sidewalk. While fellow pedestrians bitch and moan and maneuver around me.

But I'm too lost in my own head to care.

In a few hours, I will be in the middle of what is the biggest interview of my life.

The pressure is suffocating.

God, what am I going to do until then?

I can't just stand here pacing like a lunatic. No doubt, someone will call NYPD with a complaint of a deranged woman if this goes on any longer.

With a sigh, I turn on my heels and head in the opposite direction, four blocks east and another two blocks south and don't stop until I'm standing directly in front of Fuse's office building.

If anyone can understand my current insane state of mind, it's Milo.

With my phone already white-knuckled in my hand, I pull up our ongoing text conversation and shoot him a message.

Me: I'm freaking the hell out.

Thankfully, he doesn't disappoint and responds in one minute flat.

How do I know this? Because I'm currently a lunatic obsessed with watching the time.

Milo: What's wrong?

Me: I have the interview, Milo. THE interview. With Beacon House.

Milo: Just take a breath. You're going to do just fine. I promise.

Me: Oh, trust me, I'm taking breaths. I'm practically panting with nervousness. Soon, my goddamn tongue will be hanging out of my mouth like a dog.

Milo: LOL. For the love of God, kid. Take slower breaths. What time is your interview?

Me: Noon.

Milo: So, two hours. That's plenty of time to go grab a coffee, take a walk, and try to relax your mind.

Me: That plan is shit, Milo. I've been up since five this morning. Trust me, I've tried everything. Anyway, I'm here.

Milo: Huh?

Me: Your office. I don't care if you're in the middle of some big billionaire meeting, I'm coming up.

Milo: Billionaire meeting. LOL. I'm in my office. Come on up.

Not even ten minutes later, I've ridden the elevator twenty flights and I'm stepping past his secretary and into his office.

Milo sits at the center of the room, behind a sleek desk, with large floor-to-ceiling windows framing the city behind him. He looks like some kind of sexy-fucking-dapper-business-suit-clad king. A man with glimmering blue eyes and sin-worthy lips running a billion-dollar empire.

If I weren't so riled up about this stupid interview, I might find myself drooling. Or, thinking about the one experience I haven't been able to get out of my head since I wrapped my lips around his cock.

Good God, his cock...

Shit. Focus, Maybe. There is no time for cock right now!

"Help me," I whine, and I shut the door to his office behind me.

"Well, hello to you too," he says with a grin.

But I don't have time to waste on pleasantries. I'm in DEFCON Red—or whichever the hell DEFCON means I'm shitting myself—the apocalypse-is-coming kind of panic mode, and it takes all of three seconds for me to dive headfirst into amped-up word vomit. "I'm freaking the hell out. I want this job so bad, Milo. So flipping bad. I feel like everything is resting on this interview, and it is completely mindfucking me."

The heels of my stilettos tip-tap across the marble floor as I pace in front of his desk.

"What am I going to do?" I nearly shout. "Am I good at interviews? Do I make good first impressions?" That question sends me into a tizzy. "Oh God. I bet I make horrible first impressions, don't I? I'm probably one of those people that you meet and immediately think, 'she's either crazy, weird, or too awkward to befriend.' Fucking hell, I'm socially inept! I don't—"

"Hey," he says calmly and stands up from his chair. "Just calm down. It's going to be okay."

"Calm down?" My eyes nearly bug out of my head. "How can I be calm in a moment like this? How can I be calm when I'm supposed to be interviewed by the editor in chief of one of the biggest publishing houses in the world! I can't be calm at a time like this!"

He doesn't respond.

Instead, he steps away from his desk and over to the windows that look out toward the inside of the office building. In a matter of seconds, the blinds are shut, and his secretary's back is hidden from my view.

"What are you doing?" I question. "Are you afraid I'm going to scare away your employees? Though, that's probably valid." I keep pacing. "For sure valid since I'm basically a ranting crazy lady in heels right now."

"Sit on the desk."

I stop mid-step. "Huh?"

"Sit on the desk, Maybe." He steps toward me and leans closer so his lips are just barely brushing my ear. "Slide your panties off from beneath your skirt, and sit your sexy little ass on my desk."

I'm frozen. Still as a fucking statue.

Did he just say what I think he said?

"Do it, Maybe," he whispers. "Take off your panties and sit on my desk."

Instantly, goose bumps pepper my arms, and a shiver rolls up my spine.

Holy maple-syrup-pancakes-on-a-Sunday.

The heat in his blue eyes says Milo ain't playing.

And my now-wet panties say my body is one-hundred-percent down with playing.

"Do you want me to do it for you?" he asks, and I nod.

At least, I think I nod. Hell, I don't know what's happening. I mean, I like it. I'm digging it. I'm so down for this panty-less cause, I'd sign a blood oath to go commando for the rest of my life, but I have no idea what is going on right now.

His fingertips graze the skin of my thighs as he reaches down with both hands and slides my skirt up toward my hips. Slowly, inch by inch, more of my legs are uncovered until my white pencil skirt is bunched at my waist, revealing the panties he apparently wants gone.

Go figure. Apparently, I did nod.

Those devious hands of his move to my lace boyshorts, and before I know it, they're making a deliciously slow path down my legs.

My skin tingles. My nipples harden. And all I can do is stand there, naked from the waist down, still in my heels, and watch him.

He rises to his feet and doesn't waste a second. A true man on a mission.

His big hands are beneath my bare ass, lifting me up, wrapping my legs around his waist as he carries me toward the desk.

He is thick and hard and aroused beneath his suit pants, and I'm damn near panting by the time he sets me on the desk.

"Right now," he says and stands between my spread thighs. "You have one responsibility." With a wicked gleam in his eyes, he licks his lips and reaches out with one long index finger to feel how wet I am. "You just focus on relaxing, and I'll do the rest."

The rest? The rest of what?

But I don't have to ask.

He sits down in his chair, flips his tie over his shoulder, grips my trembling legs with his strong hands, and moves his mouth to the apex of my thighs.

The instant I feel his tongue pressed against me, my back arches.

"Oh God," I moan, and Milo looks up at me from beneath his lashes with a devilish smirk etched across his perfect mouth.

"God's not here right now, sweetheart. This is all Milo."

Well, *fuck.*

I bite my bottom lip when he flicks his tongue against my clit.

And I have to grip the edge of the desk when he starts eating and licking and sucking at me like I'm his most favorite treat.

"*Ah...oh...ohmygod,* that feels good," I whisper through erratic breaths.

Because fucking hell, it does.

It feels so damn good, I start to lose sight of why I came to his office in the first place.

Pleasure rolls up my spine and my hips start to move of their own accord, trying to hurry his pace, and my body puts on its gym shoes and tries to race to a climax.

But he doesn't speed up.

And he doesn't slow down.

He just keeps going at the exact same pace, not too slow, not too fast, but goddamn, not quite enough to push me over the edge.

It's heaven. It's hell. It's painful-glorious-mind-blowing-bliss.

"Please," I start to beg, damn near desperate. "Please, Milo."

He ignores me completely, and I reach down with my hands to grip the lush locks of his dark hair.

"Please do it. Oh God. Oh please...fuck, fuck, fuck."

I don't even know what I'm saying at his point. I just know I want to come.

"Such a pretty girl. Such a dirty mouth," he whispers against me, and it only spurs my need for climax deeper. "How bad do you want to come against my tongue, Maybe?"

"Bad," I whimper. "S-so bad."

"But you taste so good," he says through a moan. "I don't want to stop."

"F-fuck, Milo. N-now isn't the time to be s-selfish."

His responding chuckle vibrates against my pussy, and the constant, incessant ache turns to an outright throb that is so hard, so relentless, I swear to everything, my heart has migrated its way to my clit.

"Okay, greedy girl," he whispers. "I guess we'll do this your way."

And then, I'm falling. Floating. Sailing. Losing my mind as waves of pleasure crash into my body like a freaking ecstasy hurricane.

I pant. I moan. I whimper. And every muscle in my body shakes.

My orgasm feels like it lasts forever, and the whole time, Milo keeps his tongue pressed to me as my hips ride it out against his mouth.

Holy fucking shit.

"Now," he says and leans back in his chair. "I think someone is relaxed enough to go to their interview."

Interview? Who has an interview?

It takes my brain a good fifteen seconds to compute the reality.

Oh, *that* interview. My interview. *Holy post-orgasm amnesia.*

"You did all of that so I would be relaxed for the interview?" I ask.

Milo smirks. "Well, that was part of the reason."

"And what was the other part?"

"Because I needed to."

THIRTY

Milo

One glance at the time and I see it's already nearing four o'clock, but this meeting with the marketing team is still going strong. They're talking about the logistics of doing a full-fledged international campaign—*all good things*—but my mind might as well be on the other side of the world.

I can't stop thinking about her.

It's only been a few hours since Maybe left my office to go to her interview, and I can still taste her on my tongue. I can still hear the way she sounded when she came against my mouth. I can still picture her sitting on my desk, legs spread, pussy wet and bared for me.

Son of a bitch.

I don't know what came over me.

One minute, she was pacing my office floor, and the next, I had my mouth on her, eating and sucking at her sweet-as-fuck pussy like a man starved.

And now, it's all I can think about.

Hell, I'd be lying to myself if I didn't admit that, lately, she is all I can think about. Morning, noon, and fucking night.

Before I know it, while Laura goes through her PowerPoint and discusses marketing goals for this quarter, I'm pulling my cell out of my pants pocket and discreetly typing out a text.

Me: How did the interview go?

It doesn't take long for her to respond.

Maybe: Honestly, I think it went really well. I wasn't a disaster like I feared I would be, I was able to speak in actual sentences and not ramble, and I left feeling like I actually gave a good first impression.

A sigh of relief leaves my lungs, and I grin.

Me: So, no My Little Pony references?

Maybe: HA. No. Thank Everything.

Me: I knew you'd kill it.

Maybe: Pretty sure you were the only one who knew that. LOL.

Me: Nah, you knew it too. You just needed a little help to calm down.

Maybe: If what you did to me on your desk is your go-to way of calming people down, then I hereby hire you as my Director of Calming Down.

Visuals of Maybe's spread thighs fill my head, and my cock starts to respond beneath my zipper. Shit, this girl, she might be the death of me.

Any response I have to her message is one thousand shades of dirty, and it takes me a good thirty seconds before I can come up with a response that doesn't revolve around taking her panties off with my teeth.

My cock, though? Well, he thinks that's the best idea we've ever had. But that horny bastard has been one-hundred-percent Team Maybe ever since she wrapped her pretty little lips around him.

He can't be trusted.

And the rational side of my brain? Well, it's urging me to hit the brakes.

This is Maybe Willis we're talking about here.

My best friend's little sister.

If anything, she should be off-limits, just like my best friend—her fucking brother—said to Cap.

Not the one and only star of my far-too-dirty fantasies.

Pretty sure it's way, way, way too late for that, dude. You've officially fallen, and you can't fucking get up.

I push my scattered thoughts to the back of my mind and attempt to change the subject.

Me: So, I take it plans of celebration are in order tonight?

Maybe: Slow your roll, Ives. I haven't gotten the job yet.

Me: But you will.

Maybe: Jesus. We don't know that yet! They still had three more candidates to interview after me.

Me: Trust me, Maybe. Come Monday, you'll get the "We'd like to offer you a position at Beacon House" call.

Maybe: Stop trying to get my hopes up, you nutcase.

I know Maybe will get the job.

She is brilliant, passionate, and deserves to be at a publishing house like Beacon.

A few weeks ago, when I first contacted their editor in chief, Taylor McHough, he was more than on board with bringing her in for an interview. Not to mention, he already told me, with her credentials, and the fact that their competitor wanted her badly, she was basically a shoo-in. The interview was just logistics.

Me: Just trust me, kid. You got the job.

Maybe: Well, I guess it's safe to say that, now that you've officially gotten my hopes up, you have to come out with me tonight.

Me: Come out with you?

Maybe: Yeah. Me, you, and Lena are going to go to a dance club in Tribeca.

Me: Pretty sure I haven't agreed to this...

Maybe: But you will. Trust me, kid. You will agree.

Me: Kid. That's cute.

Maybe: C'mon, Milo. Come out with me tonight.

Me: What club are you going to?

Maybe: Paul's Cocktail Lounge.

That's a rowdy fucking club. Fun, loud, and a place I frequented quite a bit in my twenties. But it's been years since I've done the night-club scene in NYC. Working seventy-plus hours a week tends to put a damper on going out.

Maybe: Pretty please... Lord knows, Lena will leave me on my own by ten because she pretty much knows everyone in the entire city. I need a dance partner...

That last text hits me straight in the chest.

Visuals of horny pricks looking for their next one-night stand grinding on Maybe fill my head, and I'm instantly on edge.

More like jealous...

Me: Fine.

Maybe: YOU'LL GO???

Me: Yeah. I'll go.

Maybe: FANTASTIC.

Her enthusiastic response makes me grin.

But once our conversation is done and I'm left to my own thoughts, the unsettling discomfort and the stark reality that I'm more than playing with fire—*aka just fucking pouring gasoline onto the flames at this point*—starts to sink in.

I'm into this girl.

More like, you're so far into her, it's too late to go back now.

Chapter
THIRTY-ONE

Maybe

"**S**top fidgeting with your hair." Lena grins at me in the reflection in my bathroom mirror. "You look gorgeous."

I can't help it. I'm on emotional overload. All hyped up like Jessie Spano that time she took caffeine pills. Nervous. Excited. *Freaking out. I am all the things.*

Between the interview with Beacon House today, and Evan and Sadie coming into town tomorrow for their wedding, so much is happening at once.

Yeah, but you can't forget the most important thing—knowing Milo is going to come celebrate with you tonight...

Holy Mother of Baloney, the more I think about seeing him tonight, the more nervous I get.

Fidgeting with my hair is simply a side effect.

Between my cute little dress and heels and the subtle but sexy makeup Lena applied to my eyes and lips and cheeks, I know I spruced up nicely.

I feel good. Confident, even.

It's just the whole Milo thing that's screwing with my head.

We've come a long way from the time he didn't recognize me at the floral shop.

He's helped me with my career.

We've spent an insane amount of time together.

We've hooked up...*more than once.* And a day doesn't go by

without us talking in some form or way. Texts, phone calls, you name it, and we're connected.

Truthfully, I'm having a hard time wrapping my head around it all. What used to be a crush has blossomed into something more.

Something that feels a lot like falling.

Pretty sure you've already fallen, girlfriend. Right off the cliff and plummeted straight to the rocky bottom o' love.

I sigh. Out loud. And Lena doesn't miss a beat.

"What's going on, honey?"

"Nothing." I run the brush through my locks one last time.

"You're freaking out." She eyes me knowingly in the mirror as she applies a fresh coat of lip gloss. "It's written all over your face."

She's right. I *am* freaking out.

I turn and rest my hip against the bathroom counter, and everything that's filling my head just kind of pours from my lips. "I'm falling for him, Lena. Like, hard kind of falling for him, and I'm starting to get really flipping scared about how this is all going to play out." I blow a heavy breath out of my lungs. "I mean, where do I go from here? What's the next step in the plan?"

"There isn't a next step," she says with ease and slides the tube of lip gloss back into her small, gold clutch.

What? No next step?

Anxiety fills up my chest like a balloon.

"What do you mean, there isn't a next step? You're supposed to be my dating Yoda! How can there not be a next step?"

"Maybe baby, relax." She sets her purse on the counter and places two steady hands on my shoulders. "I'm not sure if you've been paying close attention, but you're the one who's been running the show the whole time."

My face contorts into utter confusion.

"I might've put some ideas into your head, given a few hints on what I think you should do, but when it comes down to it, you've been the one in control, honey."

"Uh..." I blink once, twice, and three more times. "I'm not following."

"Girl," she says through a soft laugh. "All of my suggestions have always ended up with Maybe's spin on things... The sext messages... The TapNext dating advice... Hell, I'm certain I wasn't the one to suggest a night of *Gilmore Girls* and a blow job." She winks one smoky eye toward me. "You name it, and you've always done it your way. Not my way. But *your* way."

She searches my face for a long moment, but it's not long before she's laying it all out there for me.

"You need to let yourself accept that Milo has been more than a participant in this," she states without even the slightest hint of doubt in her voice. "As much as you've texted him or initiated *things* with him, he's more than reciprocated. Whether he's admitted that to himself yet or not, the man is invested. In you. What you're feeling isn't one-sided. No doubt, he's falling too."

I try to make sense of her words.

Milo is falling too?

Could Lena really be right about this? Or has all of my wishful thinking rubbed off on her?

"Okay...so...hypothetically... Say you're right. If you were me, what would you do now?"

"I think it's safe to say you've reached a point where rationality isn't really a thing. There is no planning at this juncture."

Lord Almighty, it would be nice if she'd stop speaking in riddles.

"What's that supposed to mean?"

"Girl, your heart is involved now. And, unfortunately for all of us, the heart does what it wants. She's a bit of a confusing bitch that way."

Ugh. For some strange reason, her words don't bring the relief I was hoping for.

I much preferred things when I felt like I had some kind of control. Like I had some form of guidance to follow.

To just be out on a fucking limb with my goddamn fingers and toes crossed and offering up hopeful prayers that Milo really does feel what I'm feeling is quite the opposite of reassuring. I might as well be tightrope walking two hundred feet in the air with Evan and Sadie's wedding cake in my hands.

It's pretty fucking terrifying, if I'm being honest.

What if Lena isn't right and everything comes crashing down?

And what if my dumb heart screws things up?

She's never really been the brightest crayon in the box when it comes to love. Until Milo, the little bitch hasn't done much besides remain apathetic toward any possible love interest that's come my way. Hell, I'm starting to wonder if she commandeered a TV back in my college days and was all Netflix and chill behind my rib cage.

And here I thought finding a man was going to be easy.

I seemed to have forgotten to calculate the whole "falling in love" aspect on my "Maybe Becomes an Adult" checklist.

Ugh. Now, what?

I look at my reflection in the mirror and then back at Lena.

"Do you think this is going to end in a disaster?" The words are almost too difficult to speak out loud, and my question comes out in a barely there whisper.

"You want my honest opinion?"

I swallow down the anxiety and insecurity sitting heavy against my throat and nod.

"No," she says. "There can't be a disaster when your auras mesh together like they do."

Auras. Good Lord. Sometimes, she is so out there, it makes me laugh.

I mean, right now, I'm not laughing, but that's par for the course when second-guessing and overthinking and anxiety show up to the party. That little trio sure has a way of sucking all the fun out of the room.

"You realize, I still have no idea what you're talking about, right?"

"Yeah, but that's what makes it fun." Lena snorts. "Listen, auras aside, I know what I see, and when I saw the two of you together the other night, I saw a man with genuine eyes looking at a girl like she was walking on water."

I stare at her like she has two heads.

"You might not believe it now, but sooner rather than later, you're going to completely let your guard down and allow yourself to pay close enough to attention to see, know, *and* feel what I'm saying."

God, I hope she's right.

But hope isn't a guarantee.

I guess all I can do is keep my heart open and pray like hell he accepts it with open arms.

"All right," Lena says and grabs her purse off the counter. "Now it's time to go dance our asses off and celebrate the fact that you had a fan-fucking-tastic interview today! Let's do the damn thing, honey!"

Am I ready? No, not really.

But hopefully, by the time we get to the club, and I've managed a glass of wine or two, I'll get there.

Paul's Cocktail Lounge in Tribeca is unlike any nightclub I've ever been to.

The bouncers' standards are insanely high—pretty much denying anyone who isn't famous or doesn't know a friend of a friend of a friend. Thankfully, Lena knows everyone, so the instant we stepped up to the entrance, a large, burly man by the name of Vito flashed a wink and a nod and opened up the red velvet rope to let us through.

I'm certain if I'd shown up here by myself, access would have been *denied*.

Once we step inside, my senses are hit from all angles. Pounding beats coming from the DJ at the center of the room. A hoard of people on the dance floor. Servers in cute dresses and a hip take on tuxedos rove around the club with silver drink trays. And bright floral wallpaper covers the walls, while the whole space is accented by reclaimed wood and dark leather.

This is *the* place to lose yourself to the music and dance.

And, after two glasses of wine and a round of dancing with Lena, I am *here* for it.

The DJ announces that we've officially hit the eleven o'clock hour, and I've yet to spot Milo anywhere. I discreetly check my phone just in case he tried to get ahold of me.

But no messages. No calls. *Nothing.*

Disappoint floods my belly, but I force myself to ignore it.

I came here to have a good time. To have a few drinks, dance, let loose, and celebrate that I'm possibly one step closer to getting the job of my dreams.

Not sit at the bar by myself and watch the time pass me by.

I spot Lena in the center of the dance floor, her long blond locks swaying across her back as she dances with an attractive-looking man in a white T-shirt and dark blue jeans. He grabs her by the waist and pulls her closer, and she grins up at him, never once stopping the rhythmic movement of her hips.

Within the five minutes I took to pee and grab a glass of water at the bar, she's managed to hook herself a dance partner. A good-looking one, at that.

I grin to myself, amused by the girl who has managed to insert herself into my life and become one of my closest friends. *Thank God for Lena.* I honestly don't know what I'd do without her at this point.

And then, I put on my big-girl panties and head to the dance floor.

It doesn't take long before I'm losing myself to the music, shaking my hips and raising my hands in the air and just letting go.

I don't care that I'm by myself.

I don't care that occasionally I get bumped by my fellow dancers.

I don't care about anything besides having fun.

Lena grins at me from the other side of the room, and I smile back.

She's having fun. Her new handsome friend is having fun. And I'm having fun.

Just one big fest o' fun right here.

By the second song, I've officially committed myself to my dancing queen cause.

But by the third song, I'm no longer by myself. Strong hands gently grip my hips from behind and pull me back toward a firm chest. Warm breath brushes my neck as the words, "I thought I'd never find you" fill my ear.

I turn on my heels to find my favorite blue eyes gazing down at me.

Milo.

My heart kicks up in speed, and a smile kisses my lips. "I didn't think you were going to come," I say toward him, and immediately, he shakes his head.

"Of course, I was going to come."

Like he'd never let me down.

Like he wants to be here. With me.

In that moment, with his ocean eyes gazing down at me and his hands pulling me closer, I know I'm in deep. This isn't just a crush. And I'm not merely falling for this man.

Nope. I've already fallen.

Right past infatuation. Barreling away from like. And directly into love.

The realization makes my chest tighten, but Milo doesn't give me any time to get lost in my thoughts. With a handsome little smirk on his lips, he takes me by the hand, twirls me away from his body, before bringing me right back into the strong embrace of his arms.

I giggle and he grins.

"Let's dance, kid."

So, we do.

For five full songs, we shake our asses and move our hips. We laugh and we smile and we dance. *Together.*

Through each pounding beat, we stay as close as two people can be while they are fully clothed and dancing in the middle of a crowded nightclub.

And God, it feels good.

Letting loose with him. Being with him. *Touching* him.

Which, I do. I never take my hands off of him.

His firm chest. His strong arms. His warm neck. There isn't a second that goes by when my fingers aren't playfully in contact with Milo.

And I'm not the only one.

Not once does he let me go. His hands are always guiding my hips or skimming the curve of my ass or gently running up and down the bare skin of my arms.

We can't seem to keep our hands off each other. *I fucking love it.*

"I feel like a bastard for not telling you earlier," he whispers into my ear. "But you look beautiful tonight."

I look up at him and search his eyes. For what, I don't know, but I can't deny there is something resting behind those blue orbs. Something that makes my heart stutter and has my breath getting all tangled up inside my lungs.

God, this man. I'm so in love with him, it's not even funny.

"Thank you for showing up tonight." I stand on my tippy-toes to press a soft kiss to his lips. "I'm glad you came."

"I didn't want to be anywhere else."

Me either.

A sexy, seductive beat starts to play from the speakers, and Milo reaches down to grip my hips and slowly guide my body to match his rhythm.

Rihanna. "Love on the Brain."

The lyrics speak to me.

And the beat only further fuels my need for him, to deeper, more intense depths.

He slides his thigh between my legs, and I wrap my arms around his neck, sliding my fingers into his hair. Our faces are mere inches from each other. His warm breath brushes my skin, and his eyes stay locked with mine.

He glances down at my lips, and my nipples harden.

He slides his hands up my hips, up the sides of my abdomen, until his fingers brush just below my breasts.

Goose bumps erupt on my skin, and my breaths come out in soft pants.

He slips his fingers into my hair, and it takes two blinks for his lips to move to mine.

Soft and teasing at first, just tiny kisses and licks against my mouth.

Until the kiss intensifies, and our tongues mingle and dance.

A tiny moan escapes my throat, and he swallows it down, kissing me deeper, *harder*.

It drives me crazy.

I ache and throb between my thighs, and now, I understand why people want to have sex. Now, I understand why sex is something that, when it's with the right person, you can't resist. You want it. You need it. You crave it.

Fuck, I want to know what Milo feels like inside me.

I want him to feel me. *All* of me.

I want to feel his climax.

I want to hear his moans.

And I want to see what his blue eyes look like when he is sliding inside me.

I want it all. And I want it with him.

"Do you want to get out of here?" he whispers into my ear.

It's like he's reading my mind.

And it takes me exactly zero seconds to agree.

"Yes, please."

Chapter THIRTY-TWO

Milo

I had to get us out of there.

Between the feel of her warm, tight, perfect little body against mine and those big brown eyes of hers staring up at me and the way she kissed me with the kind of fervor that had my cock hardening behind my zipper, I needed to get her out of that fucking club and somewhere that didn't have an audience.

Somewhere private. Quiet. That doesn't include anyone but us.

Once she told Lena we were leaving, we didn't waste any time grabbing a cab and heading straight to her apartment.

Evan's old bachelor pad.

Good God, I know this place too well.

Parties. Drunken bar nights. A lot of wild shit went down here.

I witnessed Ev meet his wife-to-be in this very space.

He was several beers deep, but once his drunken gaze fixated on the little redhead who stepped through his door, it was like he instinctually knew he had to be near her.

By the end of the night, they were practically glued to each other.

And the rest is pretty much history.

Tomorrow night, he'll be back in New York, and we'll celebrate his bachelor party. And two weeks after that, he'll commit himself to Sadie for the rest of his life.

The thought makes me smile and frown at the same time.

I'm happy for him. Of course, I'm happy for him.

But if I'm really being honest with myself, I'm also jealous.

Not of him, but of what he has with Sadie. Someone he loves so much, so deeply, that he's ready to say "I do" and commit to a forever with her.

At times, it's all so hard to believe and has me thinking a lot about my future.

I've mellowed out over the past few years, throwing in the towel on one-night stands and bars and all-night parties, and I'm just now starting to understand why.

It's not that I've grown tired of that kind of life. It's that I've grown out of it.

I've matured. I've changed. And I've become more aware of my reality. I'm ready for more. I'm ready to settle down and build a life with someone.

Good God, now isn't the time to have a fucking midlife crisis.

I shake off my thoughts and reinsert myself into the present.

And while Maybe is in the bathroom doing whatever it is girls do in bathrooms, I walk into her bedroom and sit down on the edge of the mattress. The room is so much Maybe, yet it still has remnants of her brother.

A few spots of the horrid forest-green paint he'd covered the walls with still speckle the ceiling.

The same cozy leather chair sits in the far corner of the room.

But mostly, it's Maybe. Her clothes. Her shoes. Her pictures and books.

Even the smell of her soft, flowery perfume is in the air.

A scent I've managed to memorize and one that never hesitates to put a smile on my face. It's soft and subtle yet unforgettable at the same time.

The bathroom door whines as it opens, and soft footsteps echo off the hardwood floors as Maybe makes her way down the hall.

"I'm in the bedroom," I call out toward her.

She doesn't respond, but I know she hears me when her footsteps move closer, until they stop just outside the bedroom.

My jaw damn near hits the floor when I see her.

She stands there like a fucking goddess, her long hair hanging past her shoulders and brushing her arms, and her glorious skin bare of any clothes.

Maybe is naked, wanton, and standing there staring back at me. It is a vision I will never forget for the rest of my life.

Hesitantly, she steps toward me, and I don't miss the way her soft, full breasts sway with each step. I don't miss the way she bites at her bottom lip when she stops right in front of me, her knees just barely brushing my knees. And I don't miss the way my heart speeds up inside my chest, damn near bouncing around inside my rib cage.

Fuck. She is hands down the most beautiful thing I've ever seen.

Slowly, I reach out and run my fingertips up the creamy, smooth skin of her thighs, and a little whimper escapes her throat.

I take her in with my eyes, gliding them up her body and memorizing every detail of her soft, lush curves. Drinking in every long and smooth line. Obsessing over every perfect little detail that is Maybe.

I can't stop myself from pulling her into my arms until her thighs are spread across mine. And I sure as hell can't stop myself from taking her mouth in a deep kiss, slipping my tongue past her lips and swallowing her moans.

Her hips move against me until my cock is hard and aching for her.

"Please," she whispers. "Please, Milo."

I don't know what she's asking or what she wants, but all I can do is pull her into my arms and lay her down on the bed.

Her hair fans out across the mattress, and my body hovers over her as I stare down at her. At this perfect fucking creature whose big brown eyes have the power to cut through all of my layers and grip on to my heart.

I know, with every cell inside my body, I have never looked at another woman the way I look at Maybe. I have never wanted or desired or adored another woman like I do her.

Before her, no one had the ability to affect me like she does.

I'd felt affection and like, and I've cared about another person.

But in this moment, with her beneath me, I know I have never actually felt the undeniable, emotional pull with someone until right now. Until her.

The realization steals my fucking breath, and all I can do is lean forward and take her mouth again, kissing her like a man starved.

More like a man in fucking love.

That single thought hits me straight in the gut, but when Maybe moans again and her fingers grip my shirt, that thought flies out the window and my need for her moves to the forefront of my mind.

God, I want her.

Her fingers move to my jeans, unbuttoning and unzipping with fumbling fingers until she reaches into my boxer briefs and pulls out my cock.

Fuck. I groan.

She grips me and strokes me, and I start to lose sight of everything but how goddamn good it all feels. How good she feels.

"I want you inside me," she whispers and inches my cock toward her entrance. "I don't want to be a virgin anymore, Milo. I want to know what sex feels like."

Her words hit me like a fucking truck.

She doesn't want to be a virgin anymore.

She wants to know what sex feels like.

Son of a bitch, I don't like it. Her first time shouldn't be because she merely wants to know what sex feels like or because she thinks she doesn't want to be a virgin anymore.

Her first time should be because she wants to give herself to someone. Because what she's feeling is too intense not to give in to the desire to connect with someone in the most intimate way.

It should be soft and slow and motivated by love.

No matter how badly I want her, I can't bring myself to do anything but put on the brakes. I can't bring myself to do anything but end this before it goes too far.

I want Maybe more than my next fucking breath, but I can't make her mine; I can't slide my cock inside her unless it's for the right reasons.

Unless real feelings are involved.

More like, unless she feels the way you feel...

Holy shit. I am in way deeper with her than I even realized...

Yeah, you bastard. You're pretty much in as deep as one person can go at this point.

Ah fuck. I shut my eyes briefly and look away from her, and when I open them, the very last thing I would ever want to see stares back at me from across the room.

A picture of Maybe *with* Evan.

My best friend. Her brother.

Shit. Shit. Shit.

Something that feels a lot like freaking out starts to take over, and I try to breathe through it. But when I move my eyes back to Maybe, I can't stop myself from feeling like the biggest asshole that's ever lived.

I am in love with her. My best friend's sister.

And I am the only one who knows it.

Even though it's the hardest thing I've ever done, I press one final kiss to Maybe's lips and stand up from the bed.

"W-what are you doing?" she asks, her eyes searching mine in confusion. "What's wrong?"

"I can't," I whisper back. "I just can't."

Immediately, I start to doubt myself. I start to wonder if it's all in my head.

"You can't what?" Maybe pushes herself up on her elbows. "You can't have s-sex with me? You can't fuck me?"

I cringe at her last question, and it solidifies my decision.

Her first time shouldn't involve the word fuck at all.

"I'm sorry." I shake my head, and I feel my lips turn down at the corners. "I can't."

You could never be a simple fuck. You mean too much to me for that.

I open my mouth to try to verbalize how I'm feeling, but I don't have a fucking clue what to say. How can I tell her how I'm feeling when I'm just now starting to understand it?

"Wow. Okay," she mutters. "Well, then, I guess you can just go."

Shit. Say something. "Maybe, it's not—" I start to say, but she cuts me off at the fucking legs.

"I'm not going to ask you again."

"Maybe—"

"I said, leave!"

Fuck, this isn't how I pictured this night ending.

Chapter THIRTY-THREE

Maybe

Something is ringing, and I hate it.

I groan and pull the comforter back over my head and shut my eyes tighter.

But it's no use. Someone is calling me, and they evidently don't know I've decided to spend the rest of my life in bed. Well, not the rest of my life, but more like until I have to wake up and head to Wendy's Bridal to meet my mom and Sadie and the rest of the bridesmaids for our final fittings.

Another stupid ring fills my ears, and I blink open my eyes and reach out from beneath my blankets to snag my phone from the nightstand.

Still under the covers, I squint to check the caller, but my vision is too damn blurry to make out what's on the screen. From what I can see, it's just a bunch of damn numbers.

I make a mental note to change my ring tone because it's quite possibly the most annoying sound that's ever existed and hit accept on the caller, fully expecting some asshole telemarketer to be on the other end of the line.

"Hello?" I grumble and shut my eyes again.

"Hi, is this Maybe Willis?"

"Yep. You got her." *And I guarantee I don't want whatever shit you're peddling.*

"Oh hello, Maybe," the man greets in a friendly voice. "This is Taylor McHough."

That name has me sitting straight up in my bed.

"Taylor McHough?" I question and blink my eyes several times. "With Beacon House?"

"That's me. Did I interrupt something?"

"Uh…no…no, not all," I stammer.

"Well, I apologize for calling you on a Saturday, but I didn't want to wait until Monday," he continues. "I really enjoyed our chat yesterday, and after speaking with a few of the editors on my team, we've all come to the conclusion that you would be a fantastic asset at Beacon House."

"I would?"

"You definitely would," he responds, and I can hear a hint of a smile in his voice. "So, Maybe Willis, consider this an official job offer."

"You're offering me the job?"

"I am," he answers.

"Holy sh—Oh God. I mean, wow. Okay. Wow."

"I take it you're a little surprised?"

"Uh…yeah, just a teensy bit." An embarrassed laugh leaves my throat. "I thought you still had more candidates to interview and that I wouldn't hear from you until next week…"

"After interviewing you, I decided it wasn't necessary. I know you'll be a perfect fit."

Holy. Fucking. Shit.

"I don't even know what to say." I lift my hand to cover my mouth.

"Well, I'm hoping you'll say you accept."

"Of course, I accept!" I exclaim a little too loudly, and I cringe. "Ugh. Sorry. I'm a little excited, but I promise I'll work on my volume control before my first day at the office."

He chuckles softly. "I don't consider that a bad thing, Ms. Willis. And let me be the first person to welcome you aboard. I have a feeling you're going to do great things here."

By the time we end the call, I know I'll be starting with the next round of orientees next month, and that a woman by the name of Ruth in HR will be sending a whole packet of information to my apartment in the next week or so.

I also know that I got the fucking job. *At Beacon House.*

Oh. My. Gawd!

I toss my phone down onto my mattress, jump off my bed, and dance around my bedroom in my underwear. Booty-shaking. Twerking. The robot. I'm doing all of the moves.

"Yes! Yes! Yes!" My voice bounces off the walls, and I throw myself back onto my bed and squeal. "I don't have to work with Bruce anymore!"

I feel exhilarated and insane and, hell, I need to tell someone!

I snag my phone back off the bed, and without even thinking, I find Milo's name in my text message inbox.

With one tap of my finger, I pull up our most recent conversation and, just as I start to type out a message to tell him the good news, the reality of our situation crashes down on my shoulders and ties a firm knot inside my chest.

Fuck.

I reread his message from earlier this morning, the one that asked me if he could come over and talk.

I reread my brush-off of a response.

And then, the memories of last night flood into my mind.

It was quite possibly the worst night of my life.

And, yeah, that's one of those things people tend to use in dramatic generalizations.

Flat tire on the way home from work? Worst night of my life.

My DVR didn't record the Project Runway *Finale? Worst night of my life.*

Those Taco Bell chalupas gave me the shits? Worst night of my life.

I can attest to experiencing at least two of the above.

But I can also guarantee that last night was, in fact, The. Worst. Night. Of. My. Life.

A girl doesn't get naked, throw herself at the man she's in love with, beg him to take her virginity, and then, have said man tell her he "can't do it" without it actually being an experience she wishes a lobotomy could cure.

I don't know where it all went wrong.

We danced. We kissed like teenagers. I got naked. We kissed some more. I touched Milo's penis. Then, *boom.* Things took a turn. One minute we were full throttle, and the next he was standing across the room, tucking his cock back into his jeans, and apologizing for not being able to have sex with me.

"I'm sorry" is the very last thing you want to hear when you're ready to turn in your V-card to the man of your dreams. *The man you are head over heels in love with.*

Apparently, my biggest fear was actually my reality.

What I'm feeling *is* one-sided. I'm both feet, all in, ready to take the next step, and Milo's had one foot out the door the entire time.

The mere thought of him and what happened and the awful realization that you can't just fall out of love with someone even if they don't love you back has tears filling my eyes.

Now, I remember why I wanted to stay in bed all the livelong day.

But when I spot the time on my phone, I realize I have to get it together. I have to swallow back all of my emotions and get ready to head to Wendy's Bridal.

Today isn't about me. Or my fucking feelings.

It's about Sadie. Evan's fiancée. My soon-to-be sister-in-law.

It's about watching her slip on her wedding dress one last time before her big day.

With a deep, cavernous breath, I force some much-needed oxygen in and out of my lungs and command myself to walk into the bathroom and hop in the shower.

I will not screw up this day for her.

I repeat that mantra during my shower and when I'm blow-drying my hair and even when I'm getting myself dressed.

I repeat it for the entire six blocks it takes me to reach the bridal shop.

And I repeat it two more times before I wrap my fingers around the chrome of the entrance doorknob and step inside.

"Maybe!" My mom greets me with a giant grin, wrapping her arms around me and squeezing me so tight, I fear she might crack a rib. Luckily, though, she lets go before internal damage sets in. "I can't believe the big day is almost here!" she squeals.

"It's hard to believe," I say, trying like hell to remove the sadness from my voice and end up sounding like I'm in a damn musical. "But so very ex-cit-ing!"

My mom tilts her head to the side. "Are you feeling okay?"

Whoops. Guess I overcompensated a bit there.

"Of course." I clear my throat. "I'm just so happy that Sadie is going to officially take Evan off our hands."

"Now, be careful what you say. There's still time for me to back out." Sadie's laughter fills my ears, and I turn to find her stepping out of one of the dressing rooms.

My amusement gets caught in my throat when I take in the beauty that is Sadie Cleary—*soon-to-be Sadie Willis*—in her wedding dress.

"Oh my gosh." I put a hand to my lips. "You look so beautiful that I literally might cry."

"Yeah?" she asks and steps up onto the elevated platform in front of the floor-to-ceiling mirrors.

"Yes. You are perfect," I say, and I sincerely mean it. "Evan is going to die when he sees you."

"Well, Lord Almighty, I hope that's not the case. It'd be awful to have to plan a funeral the day after my wedding." She grins and I giggle.

"You know what I mean."

"It's good to see you, Maybe."

I step past my mom and the bridesmaids and Sadie's mom and

the bridal shop attendants seeing to her train. Carefully, I wrap my arms around my future sister-in-law's shoulders and give her a gentle hug. "I've missed you."

"I've missed you too."

I lean back, keeping her hands locked in mine, and take another look at her dress.

Creamy white with lace and exquisite beading and the kind of ideal mermaid fit that shows off all of her fabulous curves, this dress couldn't be any more perfect if she'd dreamed it up.

"Beautiful," I whisper. "You truly make a stunning bride."

Tears fill her eyes and a smile lifts her lips. "Aw, Maybe, you're gonna make me cry!"

"Too late for that!" my mom says behind us. I turn to find her, along with three other women in our party, dabbing tissues beneath their eyes.

I shrug and smile, and for a little while, I actually forget about the emotional Milo baggage hanging heavy on my shoulders.

I laugh with my mom and Sadie's bridesmaids over embarrassing stories about Evan.

I tell Sadie how gorgeous she looks in her veil.

I try on my pale-pink bridesmaid's dress and pick out the perfect pair of nude heels to go with it.

I even hug and joke around with ole Bruce when he stops by to say hello.

But when the afternoon is done and I'm back in my apartment, my brain fixates back on Milo. Racing thoughts of rejection and confusion and the horrible realization that a broken heart is one of the most painful things I've ever felt consume me.

I can't even walk into my bedroom without remembering the look on his face when he backed away from me. Or the way he sounded when he said, "I can't."

I only manage to sit in my apartment for a whole hour before the walls close in on me and I need to step outside and get some fresh air.

I walk around my neighborhood, my mind a million miles away as I move past my fellow pedestrians and my favorite Chelsea shops.

It doesn't take long before I'm standing in front of Jovial Grinds. Desperate to talk to the one and only person who might be able to help me sort this whole mess out.

The instant I step inside the front doors, Lena looks up from a display of bagels and meets my eyes. Between one blink and the next, her face goes from carefree to concerned.

"What's wrong? Are you okay?" she asks, and the worry in her voice is the last emotional straw.

The dam breaks, and I just start sobbing right there, in the middle of the damn coffee shop.

Without hesitation, Lena moves around the counter, wraps me up in a giant hug, and gently guides me toward the back, far away from the customers.

Surely, no one can enjoy their coffee with a woman bawling her eyes out in the middle of the café.

Once we're behind a closed door, she sits me down in a chair, and I look around the room to find a fridge and a table and a few small lockers against the wall.

"Is this the break room?"

"Yep."

"This isn't at all how I pictured it."

"Girl, *focus*," she says on a sigh. "What is going on?"

"Well..." I pause and my lip trembles, but the emotion lodged in my throat doesn't stop me from word-vomiting pretty much everything that's inside my head. "Apparently, this virgin is still a virgin because no one wants to have sex with her. Oh, and I'm in love with Milo, but he doesn't love me back. Like, at all. Honestly, it's quite possible that the thought of me naked is repulsive to him."

Her mouth goes unhinged. "What?"

"Last night, after we left the club," I start to explain. "We went back to my apartment and things were getting kind of hot and heavy, and I decided to go for it, you know? I decided to just put myself out there. So, I got naked and I tried to seduce him into having sex with me, but when I asked him to, you know, *have sex with me*...he got all weird and got off the bed and then..." I pause as tears start to slip from behind my lids. "He said he couldn't do it. He couldn't have sex with me."

"Oh no."

"Oh yes."

"Well, *shit*," she mutters, and her face morphs into utter shock. "I didn't expect that to happen."

"Yeah." I half snort, half cry and bury my face into my hands. "Join the damn club."

She stays quiet for a long moment, and eventually, I lift my head and search her eyes.

"What?" I question through a sniffle. "What does that expression on your face mean?"

"I'm just trying to wrap my mind around it all," she says and reaches out to brush a lock of hair behind my ear.

"Well, there isn't anything to wrap your mind around," I grumble. "Milo isn't into me like you thought he was."

"That's bullshit."

"How is that bullshit?" I question with a little too much annoyance. "I basically threw myself at him last night, and he told me he couldn't do it. He left my apartment while I was still naked on my damn bed, Lena. It's not bullshit. It's reality."

"Did he leave because he wanted to, or did you ask him to leave?"

"What does it matter?" I spit. "He left. End of story."

"Actually, it matters a lot, honey." Her voice is soft and caressing, and it only enrages me more.

"I know you think you know *everything* there is to know about men, but I'm telling you, when it comes to Milo, you were dead wrong."

"I know you're upset—" she starts to say, but I cut her off.

"Upset?" I spit again. "I'm not just upset, Lena. I'm embarrassed. I'm mortified. I'm fucking heartbroken!"

When the word *heartbroken* leaves my lips, my chest tightens and the tears flow down my cheeks like a waterfall.

God, this is horrible.

And, not only is this horrible, but I'm now lashing out her. Lena. The one person who offered up her friendship on a silver platter and hasn't been anything but the best kind of friend to me.

"I'm sorry," I mutter through my tears, and she doesn't hesitate to wrap her arms around my shoulders. "I'm so sorry for being such a bitch. I know none of this is your fault."

"Girl, I get it," she whispers and rubs a gentle hand on my back. "And I wasn't exactly being a good friend just then. What happened last night was fucking terrible, and I think you just need a little time to process it. You don't need me analyzing something so vulnerable right now. You just need me to be here. To be a friend."

She lets me cry into her shoulder, and I fully take advantage.

Who knows how many minutes pass by, but I let all these damn emotions leave my body in the form of tears and sniffles and sobs. And Lena just stays there, with me, like a best fucking friend.

Once I finally manage to get my emotional ass together, I remove my snotty nose from her cute, bohemian blouse and take the tissue from her outstretched hand.

"Thank you." I blow my nose and it sounds like a damn trumpet, but I'm too much of a mess to care.

"You're welcome." A soft, slightly amused smile crests her lips. "So, your brother's big day is two weeks away, right?" she asks, and I nod. "How did the fitting go this morning?"

"Good," I say, and there's relief in talking about something that has nothing to do with Milo. "Sadie looks amazing in her dress, and thankfully, the bridesmaids' dresses she picked are actually really pretty."

"No peach taffeta or purple tulle?"

"No." A soft laugh escapes my throat. "Thank God."

Lena grins. "You know what I think you need?"

"Prozac?"

"No, you lunatic." She laughs. "A girls' night. Just me and you, some pizza from Vino's, and a *Gilmore Girls* marathon."

"Shut up, you're a GG fan too?"

"Girl, I'm an OG GG fan. My love for Lorelai was established *before* my love of coffee."

"I'm game as long as we avoid talking about anything that occurred last night and get way too much junk food to celebrate my new job."

Lena looks at me with wide, puzzled eyes. "New job?"

"Beacon House called me this morning."

"Seriously?"

I nod. "I start next month."

"Maybe!" she exclaims and quickly wraps me up into a hug. "Girl, I am so insanely happy for you! Holy hell! That's certainly the best news I've heard all week!"

A full smile covers my mouth for the first time in what feels like forever. "Thanks."

"And you have my word," she adds. "There will be a shit-ton of junk food and no talk of the man whose name we shall not mention until you're ready to talk about him. Sound good?"

"Sounds perfect."

For now, I am going to avoid all things Milo-related until I give my brain time to actually process what in the fuck happened.

Or, at least, until you have to face him at Evan's wedding…

Chapter
THIRTY-FOUR

Milo

I check my messages again. And still, no response from Maybe.

This morning when I woke up, I sent her a text asking if I could come over and talk to her.

I wanted to make things right. I wanted to tell her why I did what I did.

I just wanted to be honest with her. Well, as honest as I could be with her. Hell, I'm still trying to process it all.

Her response.

I can't. I already have plans. Sorry.

I can't. Sorry. It was all too reminiscent of the words that fell from my lips last night.

I wanted to text her back. Call her. Show up unannounced at her apartment.

But I knew that wasn't right. Or fair.

She asked me to leave last night. And it's pretty damn obvious, after her abnormally short and flippant message this morning, she wants space. From me.

Damn, it's a knife to the chest.

And several hours after that painfully brief text exchange, just before I left my place and headed to get things set up for Ev's party, I got a call from Taylor McHough.

A close acquaintance and the editor in chief at Beacon House.

The one who interviewed Maybe for her dream job.

He thanked me profusely for recommending her, and then proceeded to tell me he went ahead and offered her the job, *before* they finished interviewing the rest of the candidates.

Today. This morning, to be exact. Taylor McHough called Maybe and told her Beacon House wanted her to come aboard as their newest junior editor. Per Taylor, she accepted the position and will start with their next group of orientees in August.

Two days ago, I would've been the first person she called with that news.

She would've been a rambling, excited, adorable ball of energy, and I would've been the person who got to see her brown eyes shine and her full lips crest up into her cute-as-fuck grin.

But today, after the horrid way things ended last night, I'm the very last person she called—*aka she didn't call me.*

The realization makes my stomach turn.

How in the fuck did it all go so wrong?

Especially when everything about her felt so right...

Evan's big-ass grin catches my attention from the across the bar, and I force myself to stop thinking about the one person I most definitely shouldn't be thinking about tonight.

My best friend looks happy. A little drunk, but happy nonetheless.

It makes me feel guilty and relieved at the same damn time.

What a nightmare.

Thankfully, our good buddy Cap doesn't hesitate to step up to the plate and grab the attention of everyone in the room, including me.

"I'd like to propose a toast!" He stands up from his barstool and punctuates that statement with a wolf whistle.

If there is one person who is a guaranteed distraction in all things, it's Cap.

For once, I'm thankful for it.

"To the man who is about to give up his bachelorhood in less than fourteen days and commit himself to one pussy for the rest of his life." Cap grins. "We're all so happy for you, man. Well, terrified for you, but also happy. Or, at least, we're pretending we're happy..."

"You done?" Evan asks with a slightly annoyed, but mostly amused, smirk.

"Almost," Cap responds and raises his glass in the air. "To Evan, may your dick always be harder than the rest of your happily-wedded-life."

Evan rolls his eyes. I shake my head on a sigh. Thatch bursts into laughter. And the rest of the guys at Ev's bachelor party join in on the hilarity. Cheers and chuckles go around the room, until everyone has offered Evan their teasing condolences and downed their beers in his honor.

Tonight, we celebrate my best friend's last days of singledom.

And being the good best man that I am, I've rented out his favorite hole-in-the-wall bar in Brooklyn, invited fifty of his closest friends, and made damn sure the bar would stay open, flowing with booze, and all drinks would be put on my tab.

It's not even eleven o'clock, and already this crowd of idiots is rowdy.

Thatch and Cap act like they can break-dance in the center of the room, knocking over tables and barstools in the process, while five of our other buddies stand in the corner downing beers through a funnel.

Where they obtained a funnel is beyond me, but who am I to tell them no.

Fuck, it's going to be a long night.

You'd think the best man would be enjoying the hell out of the groom's bachelor party, but after what went down with Maybe last night, I can't stop thinking about her—the off-limits sister of the groom-to-be.

I've never felt more like a prick than I do right now.

I feel guilty for keeping this from Evan.

I feel guilty for telling him I would do a simple favor and help his sister out with her career in publishing, and instead of just doing that, I fucking do a whole lot of things I definitely shouldn't have done and wind up falling for her.

But what's killing me the most, what's making me feel like the biggest asshole on the planet, is the way things ended last night with Maybe.

When she asked me to have sex with her, to be the one who took her virginity, I just kind of freaked out. The realization of what I feel for her and what she is to me hit me like a goddamn bullet to the chest—*I am in love with her.*

In love with my best friend's little sister.

It all became too much.

Her. The fact that I love her. The fact that we were inside Ev's old apartment. The fact that she pretty much asked me to fuck her.

Not make love to her. But *fuck* her.

I had to ease off the fucking gas of this insane, addictive ride. I had to stop it before it went too far.

And now, I'm in the middle of Ev's bachelor party, and I can't stop thinking about her. I can't stop wondering if she's okay. Or what she's thinking. Or if she is ever going to speak to me again.

It's all fucked. I'm fucked.

Pretty sure you mean you're in love with Maybe and fucked.

Yeah. That too.

I order another beer from the bartender, and the instant he slides it my way, I lift the pint to my lips and down half the glass in two gulps.

"Well, well, well, someone is hitting it hard tonight."

I look beside me to find Cap grinning like a son of a bitch.

"Mind if I join you?"

I nod toward the bartender, and he slides a fresh beer to my obnoxious friend.

He drinks it down and proceeds to call Thatch over and order three shots of tequila.

"Ah hell, tequila?" I question, and Thatch claps his hand on my back.

"C'mon, Mindy," he teases. "Just open wide, relax your throat, and let the nectar of the gods flow into your belly."

"You dick." Cap frowns. "And here I thought I was special. Apparently, that's the line you use on all the girls."

Thatch smirks. "But only the girls I really like, bud."

Against my better judgment, I raise my tequila glass in the air, cheers the two bozos standing beside me, and down the hatch the liquor goes.

It burns the entire way, but I finish off the rest of my beer to soften the blow.

"Another round!" Cap exclaims, and internally, I groan.

Welp. Looks like I'm not getting out of this night without a shitload of booze and a Sunday morning hangover.

The clock on the dashboard of the cab shines bright and red with four a.m.

Cap sits in the passenger seat in the front, talking to our poor driver about who the hell knows what, and Thatch and I are stuffed into the back.

We closed the bar down around two, dropped an extremely drunk Evan off at his apartment on the Upper East Side, and now, the cabbie is in the process of getting the rest of us home.

First, me.

Then, Cap.

Before he has to make the long, thirty-minute trek to New Jersey to drop off Thatch.

I glance out the window and watch the streetlights pass us by on a blur, but my phone vibrating in my pocket grabs my attention.

Evan: DUDER. BESTIE NIGHT OF MY LIVES. I LOVE YOU.

I grin and shake my head.

Even though I had a hell of a time getting my head out of my emotional ass, it appears the groom didn't notice I was only partially present at his bachelor party.

Thank God.

The last thing I wanted to do was ruin his night with my fucking baggage.

Or worse, unload the kind of news that could literally ruin our friendship.

I sigh and run a hand through my hair. I have no idea what Evan will do when he finds out about what happened between Maybe and me. But I know I'm going to have to tell him eventually. Even if she never speaks to me again, I still need to be honest with him.

He deserves that from me.

I tap the screen of my phone and check my emails, but it doesn't take long before I'm back in my text inbox, scrolling through all of the exchanges between her and me.

Her sassy remarks. Our silly jokes. Our near-daily conversations over the past several weeks. Those dirty sext messages from what feels like forever ago. The **Deflower me, please?** text she sent me after my visit to the Willises' floral shop.

It's all there. A trail of how we evolved from friends to more than friends.

How I went from a man who simply adored her to a man who's in love with her.

God, it's hardly been twenty-four hours since I saw her, and already, I miss her.

I know I'm a little drunk and I'm probably not in the right state of mind, but fuck, I just want to talk to her. I just want to see how she's doing.

My drunken brain in charge, I hit the text box and start to type out a message.

How are you?
How in the fuck do you think she is?
Delete.

I miss you. I wish you'd talk to me.
You sound ridiculous.
Delete.

I'm in love with you.
No way I'm telling her that via a drunken text message.
Delete.

"Whatcha doing, bud?" Thatch's voice fills my ears, and I glance beside me to find him staring down at my phone, clearly reading what's on the screen.

"What the hell, dude," I mutter and quickly slide my phone back into my pocket. "Nosy, much?"

"Wait a minute..." He pauses for a moment. "Did I just see you doing what I think you were doing?"

Cap's ears perk up, and he turns around to look into the back seat. "What was he doing?"

"Texting little Miss Maybe Willis." Thatch smirks like a real asshole, and Cap's eyebrows practically touch his hairline.

"No shit?"

Thatch nods. "Yep. That's exactly what he was doing. And you wouldn't believe the things I saw him typing—"

I cut him off with a groan. "Can you just drop it?"

"Nope," they say simultaneously.

"Drop the shit, bro," Cap adds. "And for once, tell us the truth when it comes to her."

Well, fuck. I mean, it's a little too late to act like nothing is going on.

I might be drunk, and I might regret it in the morning, but I can't find a reason *not* to tell them. If anything, I just want to tell *someone*.

"Fine." I fold like a deck of cards. "But before you bastards start chiming in with your usual sarcasm bullshit, you need to know things aren't good between me and Maybe. They're pretty fucking horrible, actually."

Both of their faces fall.

"What? Why?" Thatch questions, and for once in his life, even drunk, he manages to appear serious.

Even Cap joins in and flashes concerned eyes my way. "You okay?"

"I've been better." I shrug. "Yeah, I've definitely been better."

It only takes a few more questions from two of my best friends to break the dam.

And before I know it, I just kind of unload it all on them.

I tell them how it all started.

I tell them how shit just kept happening between us.

I tell them about last night.

And I tell them the most important part of it all—I'm in love with her, and she wants nothing to do with me.

By the end, Cap is staring at me with wide, slightly drunk eyes, and Thatch appears to have something in his eye.

"Are you crying, T?" Cap questions.

"Fucking right, I'm crying," Thatch answers through a sniffle. "Shit like that makes me emotional. I feel like I'm watching *The Notebook*, but only it's not *The Notebook*. It's Milo's fluffing life."

"It's going to be okay, dude." I reach out to put a comforting hand on his shoulder, but he still has more to say.

"Goddammit, Noah." He sighs and rubs at his eyes some more. "You should be with Allie, for fuck's sake. You two belong together. You fluffing belong together!"

And here I thought I was the emotional one.

I want to laugh, but I figure it's probably better if I let the big giant process his feelings.

So, for the rest of the ride to my place, I find myself comforting

Thatch while Cap watches on with a slightly confused look in his eyes.

Thankfully, though, when the cabbie pulls in front of my building, Cap climbs into the back seat to sit with Fiona Feelings so she doesn't have to process her emotions all by herself.

I tell them goodnight and toss the driver more than enough money to cover not only his full night of driving a bunch of drunken fools around, but also a generous tip.

"Thank you," the cabbie says.

"It's the least I can do," I say. "Mind getting these two home safely?"

"You have my word."

When they pull away from my building, I offer up a silent prayer that after the cabbie drops off Cap, he doesn't have to pull over to console Thatch.

And just before I step inside my building, I pull my phone out of my jeans pocket and type out a text that I need to send.

Me: I heard you got the job at Beacon. I'm proud of you, kid. You deserve it. You deserve everything you want and more.

And I don't send it because I want a response from her. I send it because, even though she refuses to talk to me, I want her to know I'm genuinely happy for her.

Chapter THIRTY-FIVE

Maybe

Sadie, being the kick-ass, laid-back gal she is, insisted we start her bachelorette party at Applebee's in Times Square.

While I loathe Times Square, I love me some apps from Applebee's, so I can excuse the tourist madness and focus on the priorities—potato skins, mozzarella sticks, chicken wings...I'm talking all the greasy goodness.

The wedding countdown is officially on, and in just under six days, Sadie will walk down the aisle and commit herself to my brother for the rest of her life.

I'm both excited and petrified for her.

Ha. Okay, I'm just excited, but I can pretend to be horrified at the expense of my annoying big bro.

"If I could have everyone's attention." Jessica, Sadie's best friend and maid of honor, stands up from her seat, taps a fork against her wineglass and raises it toward the bride. "As we get this night started, I want to propose a toast to our girl, Sadie. Otherwise known as the soon-to-be Mrs. Willis."

All ten bridesmaids—including me—along with Lena, raise our drinks into the air.

"I can still remember that fateful night when Evan spotted the woman who would someday be his wife," she continues. "After a night of bar-hopping, we ended up in Chelsea, at some random dude's apartment with a group of people we'd just met not even two hours before."

"Not our smartest moment." Sadie cringes and Jessica grins.

"Yeah, but instead of ending up on the eleven o'clock news, you met your future husband."

"Thank God." The bride's face turns up in a smile.

"And," her maid of honor continues, "while you spent the night wooing Evan Willis with your fiery red hair and drunken charm, I spent the night hoping his sexy-as-hell best friend would go home with me."

Evan's best friend? Oh God. Please don't say Milo. Please don't say you slept with Milo.

"You tried to take Milo home that night?" Sadie bursts into laughter, and it takes me a Hulk-sized effort to keep a straight face.

"You bet your ass, I did." Jessica shrugs and my chest tightens. "Well, tried and failed, but I tried nonetheless."

My shoulders sag, and a breath of air I didn't realize I was holding releases from my lungs.

Why in the hell am I so relieved by that?

And why do I get the sense that I no longer like Jessica now?

Lena offers a gentle, reassuring squeeze of my thigh beneath the table.

"Anyway," the chick rambles the fuck on. "I just wanted to say that I love you dearly. I am so damn happy for you. And I can't wait to see the look on Evan's face when you walk down that aisle Saturday. Happy bachelorette party! Cheers, Sadie!"

Everyone clinks their glasses, and I find myself thirstier than I thought.

In four quick gulps, I down the rest of my wine, and I instruct the passing-by waiter to bring another one at his earliest convenience.

Lord knows, if Sadie's stupid maid of honor keeps talking about Milo, I'm going to need plenty of alcohol in my system to get through this night.

Jessica sits her flirty ass down and proceeds to ask Sadie a question I'd rather not hear.

"So, speaking of Milo Ives, is he still looking as good as ever?"

Sadie grins. "If you're wondering if he's going to be at the wedding Saturday, I can confirm that he is Evan's best man."

Jessica's stupid eyes light up like a Christmas tree. "Which means I get to walk down the aisle with him?"

"Nice try, sweetie," Sadie answers. "He'll be walking down the aisle with Maybe."

Hold the phone.

"I'm walking down the aisle with Milo?"

Sadie meets my eyes and nods. "Yep. That's how Ev wanted it."

Can you add your brother to your shit list? Like, is that an okay thing?

Because I just did.

"Oh, look!" Lena announces a little too loudly. "I think our apps are coming this way!"

For a woman who bitched about having to eat at Applebee's, she sure is losing her shit over food she was complaining about not even two hours ago...

Three servers fill our table with enough greasy food to feed an army, and all of a sudden, my appetite is nowhere to be found.

My stomach twists and turns, and this annoying ache forms on the right side of my abdomen.

Fucking Milo. Even the mention of his stupid perfect name causes me discomfort.

I finish off another glass of wine and tell the waiter to keep 'em coming.

He smirks and heads to the bar.

And a few minutes later, while the bridesmaids stuff their faces with chicken wings, my new best friend—*Kevin, the Applebee's server*—sets a fresh glass of Riesling in front of me.

"I love you, Kev," I say to him with a smile I can't quite get under control. "You da best, bud."

Kevin grins, and Lena laughs softly beside me.

"What?" I ask, meeting her eyes and taking another hearty swig of wine.

"Hot damn, momma," she says quietly, but amusement rests around the edge of her words. "The potato skins just got here, and you're already blitzed."

I shrug and take another sip. "It's a party."

"A pity party," she adds, but I have enough booze in my veins to remain unfazed.

"Fine. It's two parties. One to celebrate the drowning of sorrows, and one to celebrate my future sister-in-law."

Lena eyes me knowingly. "You do realize that if you keep up this pace all night, I'm going to have to find a wheelchair and wheel your ass home, right?"

"Sounds like a good plan." I shrug and focus my attention on *Jess-i-ca*. God, I hate that name so much right now. "So, Jessi-licious, you planning to put the moves on Milo Saturday night?"

I hear he's always up for a new fuck buddy.

Unless you're me. Then he can't.

Jessica flashes a flirty smile on her stupid face and pops a French fry into her mouth. "If that man still looks as good as he did way back when, consider me game."

"That's all well and good, but I'm pretty sure Milo is seeing someone," Sadie chimes in.

Jessica's face falls like a rock, and I furrow my brow in confusion. "He's seeing someone?" I ask and Sadie nods.

"At least, Evan is pretty sure he's seeing someone."

"W-what's her name?"

Sadie shrugs. "Heck if I know. Apparently, he's keeping it all pretty tight-lipped. You know how Milo is, always keeps shit close to the vest."

What in the ever-loving-fuck?

"Do not read into that," Lena whispers toward me. "Actually, it's best if you act like it was never said."

"Pretty sure it's too late for that."

"But it's hearsay, and for all you know, Evan's suspicions are related to *you*," she adds quietly, and I scrunch up my nose. "Girl, before shit went down last week, Milo was spending a whole lot of time with you. I find it hard to believe that workaholic even had the time to fit in another woman. *Or* that he even wanted to."

"But there is yet to be a confirmed girlfriend, right?" Jessica beats a dead horse with her horny, Milo-craving vagina.

Sadie just laughs. "All I'm saying is don't get your hopes up, sweetie. Evan is pretty damn certain something is up. Hell, when he was on the phone with Ev the other night, Cap even mentioned he actually saw Milo out a few weeks ago at a party. A *socialite's* party, at that."

"So?" Jessica questions. *Pow-pow, the horse is dead again.* "That doesn't mean anything."

"If you know Milo, you'd know he'd never be caught dead at something like that. Hell, when he found out Page Six named him one of New York's Most Eligible Bachelors, he was the opposite of happy. He's, like, averse to that kind of attention *and* the people who draw it."

At that point, the conversation becomes too much. The constant ache in my abdomen turns to a throb, and I excuse myself from the table to head to the bathroom.

And once I step inside the cold, red-and-green décor of the restroom, I lock myself in one of the stalls and try to catch my breath.

Jesus. I'm so confused.

Before I can stop myself, I pull out my phone and look at the last text Milo sent.

One week ago.

Milo: I heard you got the job at Beacon. I'm proud of you, kid. You deserve it. You deserve everything you want and more.

I never responded.

I wanted to respond so many times, but I just couldn't bring myself to do it.

Not after how things ended that night at my apartment.

Is there more to this than I realized?

God, don't be stupid, Maybe. Don't be some stupid, hopeful romantic who can't distinguish reality from fantasy

Just because I'm still in love with him doesn't mean I should put myself through any more pain. And it sure as shit doesn't mean I should talk myself into being hopeful when there is literally no hope to be found.

All of that hope was already snuffed out with two fucking words—*I can't.*

Chapter
THIRTY-SIX

Milo

I t is July 13th. Evan and Sadie's wedding day.

The day my best friend will say "I do."

The morning was spent fitting in a round of golf with Ev and the rest of the groomsmen. And the afternoon flew by as we checked in to the W Hotel in Union Square and got ready in the rooms we booked for the afternoon.

We're wearing black, fitted tuxes with white dress shirts and black bow ties; Sadie has chosen a simple yet classic style to signify her wedding. Personally, I'm thankful and not opposed in the slightest.

And once the clock strikes five, all of us men offer Evan good luck and early congratulations and head downstairs for the six o'clock ceremony.

I ride in the elevator with the rest of the group, but I take a quick detour once we reach the first floor. Stopping in the lobby, I say hello to my cousin Emory—*my date for the evening*. She's all smiles and chatting up a storm, alternating between thanking me for letting her crash the wedding and letting me know how much she needed this night out.

"Seriously, Milo," she says. "This wedding is a godsend."

Just over two months after having her daughter, Hudson, it's more than apparent that a night to herself was in dire demand for my favorite cousin. Even her husband Quince was on board with the plan, going above and beyond to make sure Em didn't have to worry about anything besides enjoying herself.

"I'm glad you came," I respond with a smile. "Well, let me re-phrase, I'm glad you made me invite you and that you went ahead and accepted the forced invite."

"Shut up." She smacks me on the shoulder on a laugh. "And you're welcome."

All is going well until I spot the bride and her wedding party fil-ing into the hotel lobby.

To be specific, all is going well until I spot Maybe.

Her long locks are up in a sleek and sophisticated bun, elongating the beautiful lines of her neck. Her dress is a pale pink and only seems to flatter and accentuate her curves. And a pretty bouquet of white flowers sits inside the grasp of her fingers.

She looks...stunning. But, to me, she always looks stunning.

She meets my eyes from across the expansive lobby, and it takes no time at all before she averts her gaze and looks at anything and everything but me.

I don't know what's worse. Whether she can't look at me, or that she just refuses to.

Both options make me cringe.

"Well, I guess I better get inside so you can go back with the bridal party," Emory says, pulling my attention back to her. "See you after the ceremony?"

"Definitely." I nod and step forward to give her a gentle hug. "And thanks again for coming."

She grins up at me. "See, I knew you'd eventually be grateful I invited myself."

A soft chuckle leaves my lips. "Whatever makes you feel better, cuz."

Em discreetly flips me the bird before turning on her heels and heading into the main entrance of the ballroom where the ceremony is being held.

And I resign myself to my fate. Walking Maybe down the aisle at my best friend's—*her brother's*—wedding.

Talk about a fucking mouthful.

When I reach the rest of the wedding party in a hidden corridor away from the main entrance, Margo—the wedding planner—waves me toward her. "I need the best man right here!" she exclaims and just kind of bounces around on her heels. "Two minutes, people! I repeat, we have two minutes before we begin!"

Damn, this woman is either incredibly excitable or mainlined Red Bull before she started her day.

In an attempt to not excite her further, I follow her instructions and stand where she tells me,

behind the rest of the bridesmaids and groomsmen, and right beside Maybe.

The very same Maybe who refuses even to glance in my direction.

It's misery served straight up, without a chaser. And it's as if the universe is saying *"Fuck you, Milo"* for being such a bastard. Between not telling Evan what was really going on between Maybe and me and handling that night at her apartment all wrong, I can't deny I deserve it.

Of course, the stunning woman beside me continues to ignore my existence, staring down at her shoes as if they have the power to teleport her somewhere far away from me.

Margo starts pacing, and the sounds of soft, rhythmic, and very familiar wedding music starts to seep out through the closed doors. "Okay! Okay!" she exclaims and waves her clipboard in the air. "It's time, people! I repeat, it's time!"

I'm starting to fear that the wedding planner might not make it through the evening without succumbing to a mental breakdown.

The doors open, and two-by-two, each pair of the wedding party begins their walk down the aisle.

Of course, Margo is there, giving each member of the wedding party one last once-over before she lets them go through the doors. She is the mother hen of weddings, adjusting ties, fixing bouquets, doing anything and everything she can to make sure the event is perfection.

When there's only one couple ahead of us, I don't hesitate to reach out and gently lock Maybe's arm within mine.

She startles at first, but I don't miss the way her eyes glance down at where we're connected. A little crinkle forms between her brows, and it takes everything inside me not to tell her everything that's on my mind.

I miss you, kid. Goddammit, I miss you.

Her big brown eyes look up at me, and my heart migrates into my throat.

She doesn't say anything, but I get the sense she wants to.

You can tell me anything. Say anything. For fuck's sake, just tell me something.

Her mouth opens and closes once, twice, and a third time, but before words ever come out, crazy Margo gives us the cue to start walking.

We make it halfway down the aisle, and I can't stop myself from telling Maybe the one thing I've wanted to say since I saw her in the lobby. "You look beautiful, kid. So damn beautiful."

To anyone else, my words can't be heard over the music, but I know she heard them.

Maybe doesn't respond, but out of the corner of my eye, I don't miss the way her throat bobs as she swallows hard against whatever emotion is inside her throat.

When we reach the end of the aisle, I have to let her go.

Without looking back, she moves away from me to stand near the other bridesmaids.

It stings like a bitch.

But I force a smile to my lips as I stand beside Evan and the rest of the groomsmen.

When the "Bridal Chorus" begins to play and everyone rises to their feet, all eyes move to the beautiful bride walking down the aisle.

All eyes except for mine.

Mine stay on Maybe the entire time.

Fuck. I wish I could know what she was thinking.

I wish I could take back that night and have a do-over.

But mostly, I just wish she were mine.

THIRTY-SEVEN

Maybe

My favorite David Gray song, "Sail Away," plays from the speakers inside the ballroom. I stand a few feet from the dance floor, a barely touched glass of wine in my hand, and watch as my brother smiles down at his wife, swaying gently with her to the music.

That's right. Evan is officially married.

And damn, I've never seen my brother look so happy. So in love.

My heart is confused as I watch them. It wants to soar, but at the same time, it twists and turns inside my chest. Discomfort still there. A stark, unavoidable reminder of *him*.

I can't stop my eyes from searching the room, taking inventory of all the familiar faces.

Until they stop on the one person they were looking for the entire time.

Milo.

He is on the other side of the dance floor, a gorgeous woman standing beside him. Together, they watch the happy couple enjoy their first dance as husband and wife.

He brought a fucking date.

He brought a beautiful woman to my brother's wedding, and I get to play the part of the solo bridesmaid with a broken heart.

Thanks a lot, you asshole.

The pain in my chest moves to my stomach and seems to set up shop on the right side of my abdomen again, throbbing and aching and annoying the hell out of me.

I attempt to wash it away with a drink of wine, but when I lift the glass to my lips and the first tiny drop hits my tongue, nausea decides to join the party.

I roll my eyes and set my glass of wine down on an empty table.

Jesus. Can't anything go right tonight?

The DJ encourages everyone to join the bride and groom on the dance floor, to share in the end of their first dance, and just before I can go back to my seat, a hand gently touches my shoulder.

I turn to find one of Evan's friends, Caplin Hawkins, standing there and grinning down at me.

"Can I interest you in a dance?"

"Uh...yeah...sure." *I mean, why the fuck not? It's not like I'm here with anyone.*

He leads me out onto the dance floor, and despite his reputation for being a bit of a playboy, he appears content with keeping things *very* PG between us. A chaste number of inches separates our chests, and his hands never veer away from my waist.

"You doing okay, sweetheart?"

"Uh...yeah." I furrow my brow and lift my eyes to his. "It's a happy day. I mean, I have every reason to be nothing but okay."

"You sure about that?"

What in the hell is he getting at here?

Uncertain, I half nod. "Pretty sure."

"I know you probably don't know this about me, but I'm a damn good listener," he says quietly, and I don't miss the way he flits his gaze across the dance floor and pauses for a few seconds too long on Milo. "So, if you need to unload some shit that's on your mind, consider Ol' Cap more than willing to lend an ear."

It's pretty apparent he knows something, and I'm just about to open my mouth and tell him to drop the bullshit, but an all-too-familiar voice fills my ears.

"Mind if I cut in?"

I glance over my shoulder to find the devil himself.

Milo. Standing there. Wanting to dance with me.

You have got to be kidding.

But Cap, the rat bastard, doesn't hesitate to agree, and I mentally curse him as he walks away, leaving me committed to a dance I didn't agree to.

Milo doesn't hesitate to pull me gently into his arms, and I hate how easily I let him lead me.

He sways us to the music, and I notice that he doesn't keep things as PG as Cap. Our chests touch, and his strong hands brush against my skin as he keeps me inside the safety of his embrace.

Goose bumps pebble my bare arms, and tears threaten to flood my eyes.

And when Ray LaMontagne's voice filters in from the speakers and he starts singing the lyrics of "Hold You in My Arms," one lone tear makes its escape and slips down my cheek.

Discreetly, I avert my eyes and wipe it away with my fingers.

God, I hate how good this feels. How good he feels.

I both hate it and love it, and I hate that I love it.

And I miss him…so bad. I miss being able to smell the soft hints of his cologne. I miss hearing his laugh and his voice and seeing his smile.

I miss it all, and I loathe the fact that I miss it all.

He is the one who said I can't.

He is the one who brought a damn date to this wedding.

But why can't I drop my torch for him and move on?

Because love is a motherfucker.

Milo pulls me tighter into his embrace, and I tremble.

"I've missed you," he whispers into my ear. "I've missed you like crazy, kid."

More tears threaten to fill my eyes, and I don't even know what to say.

Scratch that, whatever I want to say, I know I shouldn't say it.

But he doesn't hesitate to speak for the both of us. More crazy-romantic things that make my head swim and my heart clench.

"I know I said all the wrong things to you that night," he says softly, and his warm breath brushes my ear. "But just know, I didn't stop because I didn't want to be with you. I stopped because I wanted to be with you too much."

What is that supposed to mean?

I lift my eyes and search his gaze.

But I don't find any red flags. Or hints of dishonesty. Or anything but a genuineness inside the depths of gorgeous blue.

"I d-don't know what to say to that," I whisper back.

"You don't have to say anything," he says, and for the briefest of moments, I let myself rest my head on his shoulder.

And I let myself enjoy the way I feel inside his arms.

And I let myself shut my eyes and just savor the way he makes me feel.

But it doesn't take long before the bubble is popped.

"Milo." My father's voice is behind me. "I think it's high time I get a dance with my favorite daughter."

"Of course." He clears his throat, steps back, and lets my dad take his place.

Bruce doesn't hesitate to step in, taking my hands into his, and I watch as Milo offers one last look in my direction before he leaves the dance floor.

To go where, I don't know, but I can only assume it's wherever his beautiful date is located.

That's right, you idiot. You nearly forgot about that. He is here with another woman. A woman who is not you.

As Bruce sways us around the dance floor, stupid emotions tighten my throat, and I act like I'm just giving him a gentle hug, but in reality, I'm burying my face into his chest and trying like hell to hide my tears.

"Love you, Maybe," he says, and the smile in his voice only makes it worse.

"Love you too," I croak out.

He keeps guiding us around the room, and I focus all of my energy on getting my shit together.

But Bruce, being the Chatty Cathy he is, doesn't give his mouth one moment's rest.

"Beautiful wedding, huh, Maybe?"

"Definitely."

"You having a nice time?"

No. "Yep."

"Me too," he agrees. "Did you get a chance to say hello to your aunt Ethel?"

"Not yet."

"You need to."

I sigh and smile at the same time. Leave it to Bruce to ask enough questions to completely distract me. "I know, Dad."

"What about your uncle Joe?"

"He's on my list."

"Good, good," he responds. "Just make sure you make the rounds. Everyone is excited to see you."

"I will, Dad. Promise."

"I had a real nice chat with Milo's cousin," he adds, and it's that comment that has me lifting my head off his shoulder and looking him straight in the eyes. "She showed me pictures of her little daughter. My God, Maybe, that little baby is actually cute. Doesn't look at all like Wallace Shawn, like most other babies. I hope your brother doesn't wait too long to give your mom and me some grandkids."

"Wait…who are you talking about?"

"Milo's cousin Emory."

I scrunch up my nose. "Should I know who that is?"

He nods toward the other end of the room, where Milo stands by his stupidly beautiful date.

"She's right there."

What in the hell?

"She's his cousin?"

"Yep." Bruce nods, completely oblivious as to why my jaw has all of a sudden become unhinged. "She's a real ballbuster. Sweet and sassy. And apparently, quite good at finagling a way to get herself a night out without the old ball and chain. Reminds me a lot of your mom right after we had Evan."

That pain in my abdomen makes itself known again, but I breathe through it and force myself to finish this dance with my dad.

But I can't force my mind to slow down. It's already off at a sprint, racing with an overwhelming number of questions.

That woman, Milo's date, is his cousin?

Not some love interest or fuck buddy?

But an actual family member?

I'm officially confused.

Chapter
THIRTY-EIGHT

Milo

The clock is nearing one in the morning, and the bride and groom are still whooping it up on the dance floor. Evan twirls his wife around, and the biggest grin I've ever seen has become a permanent fixture on his face.

My best friend is the happiest he's ever been.

Married to the woman of his dreams. The apple of his fucking eye.

And I'm a miserable bastard who can't stop sneaking glances at his little sister.

Right now, she stands beside her dad while he talks animatedly to Sadie's father, John.

Beers clutched in their hands and with rosy, alcohol-tinted cheeks, the two men are laughing like hyenas, but Maybe is just... kind of standing there, her lips locked in a firm line.

I get the sense that something is wrong, but fuck, it's not my place to go ask her.

She's made it pretty damn clear she wants space from me.

And more than that, this is Evan's big day. This is the last place I should make some kind of scene and let him in on the secret that I'm in love with Maybe.

Pretty sure the happiest day of his life would take a drastic turn from bliss to red-hot anger.

That's the last thing I want to do.

Emory sits down beside me and sets two fresh slices of cake in front of us.

"I have to say," she says with a soft smile. "I was thankful for a night out without my little baby Hudson. It's been fun, honestly, but I'm getting the vibe that all is not well in your world, cuz."

"I'm fine." I shrug and lift a fork to take a bite of vanilla and chocolate.

"Seriously," she continues and locks her eyes with mine. "What's going on?" she asks and quickly glances across the room at the one woman I've managed to keep track of the entire evening. "I know something is up, and call me crazy, but I'm pretty sure it has everything to do with that beautiful brunette over there."

What can I say to that?

And fuck, am I that damn obvious?

For a man who's built a goddamn tech empire and prided himself on his poker face during important business meetings, I apparently can't hide the way I look at her.

She is the exception in all things for me.

"Well…" I pause on a sigh. "It's safe to say I got myself into the kind of situation I have no solution to."

"That's bullshit, Milo. There's *always* a solution."

I shake my head. "Not in this case."

"God, you really are a pathetic sack of sadness, huh?" she teases. "Do I need to get some tissues while you cry on my shoulder?"

"You've always had a knack for being a sarcastic little brat, you know that?" I toss back. "Even when we were kids, you were nothing but trouble."

Emory smiles. "My husband wouldn't hesitate to agree with you."

"No doubt, Quince deserves a medal of honor if you give him even half the shit you gave me when we were teenagers."

"It's more, actually."

I laugh for the first time this night. "A Purple Heart, then."

"You're such a dick." Emory's lips curl up as she finishes the last bite of her cake.

"What do you say we head out of here?" I ask, and she quirks a brow. "I'm sure you're ready to get back home to your family. No use spending the rest of the night with, what did you call me, a *pathetic sack of sadness?*"

"Yep. Pretty sure that hits the nail on the head." A soft laugh escapes her throat. "But are you sure you're ready to leave? I have no problem hanging around for another hour or two. I mean, it's been, like, a year since I've been able to drink alcohol. Surely, I can busy myself with another glass of wine and go make fun of Cap's twerking skills for a bit."

I glance toward the dance floor to find Caplin Hawkins doing exactly that, and I shake my head on a laugh. "Yeah, let's head out before he starts scaring Ev's Grandma Lucille with hip thrusts."

Twerking always leads to hip thrusts where Cap's concerned.

I help Emory out of her chair, and once we say our goodbyes to Sadie the dancing queen and her swoony-eyed groom, we head out of the main reception room and into the lobby area. Emory takes our tickets to the coat check to grab her purse and my suit jacket, and I take a quick glance at my phone to find a missed text message from my mom.

Mom: God, I hate that your father and I missed Evan's wedding today, but please give him our congratulations and tell him we'll make it up to him with a visit to Austin soon.

With the last-minute date finalization, my parents weren't able to cancel the Alaskan cruise they booked over a year ago. If Evan has reassured my mom once, he's done it a hundred times since he and Sadie set the date. Thankfully, he eased her guilt enough that she didn't do something drastic like cancel the non-refundable, "it's been on our bucket list forever" trip.

Just as I lift my fingers to send a quick message back, something catches my eye, and I look up to see Maybe moving quickly out of the main reception room doors, and her hand is over her mouth.

"Maybe? What's wrong?" I call toward her, but she doesn't stop. Instead, she damn near sprints toward the bathroom.

Emory meets my eyes and doesn't hesitate to toss her purse and my suit jacket my way and follow Maybe's path at a jog. "I'll go see if she's okay."

I follow their lead and wait outside the bathroom doors.

Not even two minutes later, Emory shoves open the door with wide, panicked eyes, and my stomach falls.

"Is she okay?"

"I don't know."

"What do you mean, you don't know?"

"I don't fucking know, Milo!" My cousin gestures me toward her, and I don't think twice about walking inside the women's restroom.

I find Maybe in the fetal position by one of the stalls, and my heart falls to my feet.

Sweat-drenched and clammy-skinned, she looks terrible. Her eyes are closed tight in discomfort, and she groans as she keeps her arm firmly across to her stomach.

"God, Maybe." I kneel down beside her and brush the wet locks of hair out of her eyes. "Are you sick? What's going on?"

"It hurts so bad," she barely mutters above a whisper. "S-something doesn't feel right."

She tries to move from her current position, but the instant she slides her arm away from her belly and lifts her head, she squeaks out in pain and proceeds to curl back up into a ball.

"I'm really worried, Milo," Emory whispers and leans down toward Maybe to brush a reassuring hand over her damp hair. "She doesn't look good at all."

Panic and adrenaline race through my veins.

"We need to get her to the emergency room."

It takes me all of two seconds to reach down and pull her into my arms. She groans with the movement but curls herself tighter into my body. And I swallow down my fear and focus on the one woman who is and always will be my priority.

With a soft kiss to her forehead, I carry her out of the bathroom while Emory holds the door for us.

"I got you, kid."

When I carry her into St. Luke's emergency room, the nurse behind the reception desk takes one look at a groaning Maybe in my arms and dives straight into action, leading us back to a room and calling for the doctor.

I lay Maybe down on the gurney, and three nurses turn into a blur of checking her vitals, removing her dress, putting her into a hospital gown, starting an IV, and drawing blood.

And my girl just lies there, curled up in a sweaty little ball, completely oblivious to what is happening around her.

She barely has the strength to answer their questions.

"Where were you tonight?"

"My brother's wedding reception."

"Did you consume alcohol?"

"One glass of wine."

"Are you pregnant? Or is there a chance you could be pregnant?"

"I'm a virgin."

"How long have you had this pain?"

"A week or so."

She's had this pain for a week and didn't tell anyone about it?

If I weren't so damn worried about her, I might be tempted to spank her stubborn ass.

"Milo," she whispers, and I step toward her and grasp her petite hand in mine.

"I'm right here, kid."

"I'm scared," she says softly, and I reach out to gently brush my fingers through her hair.

"I promise it's going to be okay. You're in good hands."

Fuck, it better be okay. I couldn't survive if something happened to you.

"S-stay with me?" she asks, and those big brown eyes of hers latch on to mine.

My heart clenches and I have the sudden urge to lean down and kiss her lips, but I swallow it back and find my comforting voice. "I'm here. I'm not going anywhere."

A man steps into the room and introduces himself as Dr. Scott Shepard.

"I'm just going to take a look, okay?" he softly instructs, and Maybe nods. "But I need you to lie flat on your back. I know it's not going to be comfortable, but it's important."

Maybe groans but does as she's told, turning onto her back.

More pain contorts her face, but she forces herself to breathe through it.

And Dr. Shepard gently feels around on her abdomen until he apparently finds what he needs.

"Carrie." He grabs the attention of the nurse standing at the foot of Maybe's bed. "Go ahead and let the OR team know we're probably going to need a room and get an ultrasound machine in here."

The OR team?

"What's going on?" I ask the doctor as Carrie moves out of the room.

"I can't be sure without an ultrasound, but I'm hoping we're just dealing with a bad case of appendicitis."

"You're hoping it's that?" I question. "And what exactly are you not hoping for?"

"A ruptured appendix."

The ultrasound machine is pushed into the room, and Dr. Shepard makes quick work of pulling up the bedsheets to cover Maybe's waist while sliding her hospital gown up to reveal her abdomen.

A nurse squirts gel on her belly and hands the doc a small device that he places on her skin.

Two minutes later, whatever he sees has him moving into action.

"Tell the OR team we're heading their way," he says and slides off his white lab coat. "Are you her husband?"

"Uh…" *I wish.* For some strange reason, I respond with, "I'm her boyfriend."

"Well, I am going to take her back for emergency surgery. It's definitely appendicitis, but there is so much swelling in her abdomen, I can't be sure if it's ruptured or just very damn close to rupturing. I won't know until I get inside."

"Go ahead and start the protocol, Sandy," he instructs the nurse holding Maybe's chart. "I want a dose of antibiotics in before we start."

My heart drops into my damn shoes.

"And if it has ruptured?"

"Let's just wait and see what we find, okay?" he responds. "I'm going to have Carrie take you back to the waiting room, and as soon as we know what's going on, I'll have someone come out and update you."

I barely have the chance to kiss her forehead before they wheel her out of the room and down the hall.

Fuck.

By the time I step back into the waiting room, I'm a mess. Pacing the floor and running my hands through my hair, I've never felt so helpless in my entire goddamn life.

I don't know how much time has passed before I spot a bride and groom rushing through the emergency room doors. *Evan and Sadie.*

When we left the reception venue in a rush, Emory helped me get Maybe into my SUV, and she volunteered to stay back and let the Willises know we were heading to St. Luke's ER.

"Is she okay?" Evan shouts the instant he spots me across the room. With long strides and Sadie's hand locked in his, he closes the distance between us. "Where is she? Can I see her?"

I shake my head. "They've taken her back to surgery."

"Surgery?" His eyes go wide, and panic takes over his voice. "What the fuck?"

"It's definitely her appendix, but the doctor isn't sure if it's ruptured or not. He said he won't know until he gets in there to remove it."

"Fuck!" Evan runs two frustrated hands through his hair, and his wife reaches out with a gentle hand to rub his arm.

"Just take a breath," Sadie says quietly. "It's going to be okay."

"She's in good hands," I try to reassure him even though I can barely reassure myself. "The doctor was quick and precise and seemed to have control of the situation."

Evan just sighs and takes a seat in one of the waiting room chairs. His wife sits down beside him.

I just keep on pacing. I can't help it. The sheer thought of something happening to Maybe has me straddling the line of barely keeping it together and completely losing my shit.

It feels like an eternity goes by before we hear anything.

"Uh...Maybe Willis's boyfriend?" the nurse behind the reception desk calls out into the waiting room.

Without even thinking, I respond, "That's me."

She waves me over and provides a quick update. "Dr. Shepard wanted me to let you know they've started the surgery, and she is doing great."

"Okay. Thanks. Will you let me know as soon as you hear anything else?"

She offers a kind smile. "Of course."

A hint of relief fills my veins, but it's not enough to completely remove the fear that's become front and center. And I'm pretty much lost in my own head as I walk back toward Evan and Sadie.

It's not until I lift my eyes to meet his that I notice the confused, albeit slightly irritated look on his face.

"Did she just call you Maybe's boyfriend?"

Ah fuck.

"Uh…" I pause, completely unsure of what to say. I mean, I'm not her boyfriend. But shit, that's what I want to be. And I can't exactly act like I'm just friends with her at this point.

Not when I've realized I'm in fucking love with her.

Evan stands up from his seat.

"Ev," Sadie mutters and pulls on his arm, but he ignores her.

"What the fuck is going on, Ives?"

Shit. The only time Evan ever drops last names is when he's fucking pissed.

"It's not exactly what you think."

He narrows his eyes. "So, you're not her boyfriend?"

"No, I'm not," I say, and I know I can't avoid this conversation any longer. I have to be honest with him. He deserves that much from me. I just didn't think I'd have to do it on the night of his wedding in the middle of an ER waiting room while Maybe is in the midst of surgery.

Call me crazy, but I never quite pictured those circumstances.

"But I am in love with her." I let the words fall past my lips, and between one blink in the next, Evan's fist moves from clenched at his side to straight into my face.

"Ah shit," I mutter and shake off the pain.

"Evan!" Sadie exclaims, but he's far too worked up at this point to heed her warning.

"I asked you to help her with her career, not fuck her!" he shouts. "Jesus! I fucking knew something was going on with you, but not in a million years did I think it was my baby sister!"

I cringe. "Whoa there, buddy. That's taking it a little too far."

He laughs in outrage. "Like you're one to talk. You apparently went a little above and beyond on doing me a favor, don't you think?"

"I'm sorry," I say, and I truly mean it. "I can tell you this is not what I planned on happening, but it happened. I can't help how I feel about her. Your sister is an incredible woman who gives me something to look forward to every day. I thought I could be happy to have her as a friend, but over the past few months, our relationship has turned into something neither one of us expected."

"So, you're, like, together?" he questions. "You're dating my fucking sister?"

"No." I shake my head. "I can assure you…" My voice is haunted. "We are *not* dating."

His face morphs into confusion. "Then what the fuck?"

"I *want* to be with her," I admit. "More than fucking anything. But right now, she doesn't want to be with me."

His brow furrows again, and his face gets hard. "What did you do to her?"

"When I realized I was in love with her, I couldn't…" I pause because how in the hell do I explain this?

"You couldn't…?"

I sigh. "Just know I couldn't take things to the place she wanted them to go."

He shakes his head back and forth, he closes his eyes, and he brings his hand up to cover his clearly uncomfortable face. "Yeah, okay. I don't want to know any more."

A long moment of silence passes between us.

But eventually, Evan finds his words again.

"You should've been honest with me from the start."

"I know. You're right. And I'm sorry."

"It's going to take me a while to get over this, you know?"

I nod. "Understandable."

"And it doesn't mean I have to like it at first."

I nod again. "I wouldn't expect that."

He sighs and runs a hand through his hair before lowering his voice to a grumble. "Sorry I punched you."

I shrug and smirk. "I deserved it."

"Yeah, you definitely did." A half smile lifts one corner of his mouth. "Thanks for being there for her tonight."

"I'll always be there for her," I say with conviction.

Evan laughs, just one startled bark before shaking his head. "Fucking hell, I guess I should be glad it's you and not Cap, huh?"

I smirk. "Silver lining?"

That half smile turns to a full smile, and I'm a bit surprised when he steps forward to clap a hand around my back. "You bastard," he says. "I love you, but you're a real fuck."

"Love you too, bud."

Still in need of some distance from me, Evan sits back down beside his relieved wife, and I head over to the vending machine to grab fresh coffee for all three of us.

By the time I walk back, Evan's parents are standing in the waiting room, getting the rundown on Maybe from their son.

Bruce turns to look at me, and immediately, he lifts a brow. "What in the fettuccine happened to your face?"

"Just got acquainted with a fist is all," I reply, and Evan grins before adding, "A minor disagreement."

Thankfully, before Bruce has time to ask more questions, Dr. Shepard comes through the emergency room doors. He stops right in front of our group, and once brief introductions are made between the Willises and the good doctor, he gives us an update.

"I have good news."

Relief fills my chest.

"She did great. Her appendix wasn't ruptured. Just extremely swollen. I removed it without any issues, and she is currently stable and resting in the recovery room."

Thank God.

I'd let Evan punch me a thousand more times if it meant this was the outcome every time.

Chapter
THIRTY-NINE

Milo

Once Maybe's family spent some time with her in the recovery room, I told them they could go home and get some rest and that I would stay with her tonight.

Surprisingly, no one refuted my suggestion.

It appears Bruce knows a hell of a lot more than he lets on, and Evan is coming to terms with the whole Maybe and me situation. Well, either that or he wanted to enjoy part of his wedding night outside of the emergency room.

I'm hoping for the former but know it's most likely the latter.

Baby steps.

Not to mention, it's still quite possible there isn't even a situation when it comes to Maybe and me. I mean, prior to her medical ordeal, she was doing everything in her power to keep distance between us.

I can only hope she'll give me another chance.

That she'll let me explain what really happened that night and actually listen to what I have to say.

But now isn't the time to get into all of that.

My girl needs to rest and heal.

Once I grab another fresh cup of coffee from the vending machine, I head back up to the fifth floor, where Maybe has been admitted overnight. A medical-surgical unit that Dr. Shepard assured me would take good care of her.

I step inside her room and find her bed adjusted to a slightly sitting position and her brown eyes open but foggy. She watches lazily as her nurse takes her vitals.

"How are you feeling?" I ask and close the distance between the doorway and her bed.

She moves her unsteady gaze to mine and just kind of looks at me with a half-dazed expression I can't quite decipher.

Worry starts to set up shop in my stomach, and I look to the nurse.

The gray-haired woman is quick to offer a soft smile. "She's still a little out of it from the anesthesia, but otherwise is doing just fine. Her vitals are stable, and the four tiny incisions in her abdomen look really good."

I let out a breath. "Okay, good."

But Maybe just keeps looking at me, and I tilt my head to the side as I reach out to run my fingers through her now-tangled locks.

"You should try to get some rest," I say softly, but she shakes her head.

"No sirree, Bob. That is not what I need." Her voice is a little slurred and sluggish, but mostly, just fucking cute. I bite my lip to fight my grin.

"You don't want to sleep?"

"Nope." She slowly shakes her head again. "I want to give you a piece of my mind."

"Is that right?"

"You betcha."

"All right," I respond, and even the nurse hears the amusement in my voice. Her little grin flashed in my direction is proof. "Let me hear it, kid."

"Welp…" She reaches out to scrub a lazy hand down her face. "I don't like how things went that night in my bed. I don't like it one bit."

"That makes two of us."

She ignores me completely. "And I didn't like when I got that job that I wanted and I couldn't even call you. I definitely didn't like that."

I smile. "Ditto, kid."

"And I pretty much hated that you were with that woman at the wedding. I mean, she's beautiful..." She pauses and tries to find her words. "She's sofa-cation...? A vacation...? An education...? *Meh.* You know what I'm saying. When I saw her, I thought, *she looks like the kind of lady he should be with.* She's probably deflowered and knows how to send out sext messages... She probably wears Tuesday underwear on Tuesdays...

"Who am I kidding?" She snorts. "Her underwear don't have days on them. She's the kind of lady who wears Victory's Secretive. I went into that store once and got overwhelmed. Too many choices, you know?" Maybe glances at the nurse, and the kind, older woman fights her grin by nodding.

"See?" Maybe points an index finger toward her nurse. "She knows. You know."

The nurse nods again, but this time, she's full-on smiling. "Yes, honey, I know."

And Maybe keeps going. "That place, Victory's Secret, they have bras with boobs already in them. *Water* boobs. I don't want water boobs, ya know? I want normal boobs. And I actually love my boobs. I have nice boobs." She turns that index finger in my direction. "And I love your boobs. Your pecs. Your man chesticles. I love them too. I love everything about you.

"You probs don't know this, but I've been in love with you since I was, like, eleven or something. Wait..." She pauses. "No. I wasn't. Well, I was crushing on you. But I didn't really start loving you, crashing into love with you, until now. Well, not now, *now,* but you know what I'm saying. I love you. I'm in love with you. And I was so happy when I found out that Victory's Secret model with the pretty face and the water boobs in her dress wasn't your date. That she was your cousin. Not, like, your cousin that you're dating, but just your cousin. I was so happy about that. Because I lover you so much."

Goddamn. This girl.

"Yep," she mutters as her eyes start to close a bit. "I lover you, you bastard."

"Maybe?" I say her name, but she doesn't open her eyes again.

"She's still pretty heavily sedated." The nurse's soft voice fills my ears, and I move my gaze to her.

"Are you sure she's going to be okay?" I question. "I mean, I know she had to go under general anesthesia, but is this normal?"

She nods. "Dr. Shepard is confident she'll make a full recovery. She'll probably be able to be discharged either tomorrow night or the following morning."

"Really? That soon?"

"Yep," she answers and connects a new IV bag to Maybe's line. "She just needs to sleep off the anesthesia a bit, but in a few hours, she'll be herself again."

I nod and look at a now-snoring Maybe.

"Can I ask you a question that's completely none of my business, but I'm just too curious not to ask?"

I look back at the nurse. "Sure."

"Do you love her back?"

I don't even have to think about my answer. "More than anything."

"Damn," she says on a dreamy sigh. "I sure do love the hell out of real-life romance."

Real-life romance. Yeah. I don't mind the sound of that.

FORTY

Maybe

I blink my eyes open, and as my foggy vision clears, I find myself in a hospital bed.

Holy cannoli. Shit really went down last night.

I'm in a hospital gown. An IV is stuck into my arm and connects to a line that has some kind of clear fluids going into my veins. And a cup of watered-down ice chips and a remote control that's connected to my bed sit on a side table to my left.

My mouth is drier than the damn Sahara, and I reach out with an unsteady hand to pop a piece of ice past my lips. It's cold and refreshing and gone in no time at all and, immediately, I toss a few more pieces into my mouth.

I grab the remote and turn on the TV and mindlessly watch the morning news as I try to recount last night's events in my head.

Evan's wedding.

Walking down the aisle with Milo.

Dancing with Milo.

Trying to drown my Milo sorrows in a glass of wine but stopping after a sip when my stomach started to hurt again.

And the pain getting so intense I thought I might puke.

Milo being there and taking me to the hospital.

Lying on the surgical table with the bright light in my face as the doctor told me he needed to remove my appendix.

Someone putting a mask over my nose and mouth and telling me to take a few deep breaths.

And then...nothing.

Good Lord, I really know how to go out with a damn bang.

"Well, lookie who is awake," Evan greets with a big smile as he steps into my room. "If it isn't Ms. Drama Queen herself."

I cringe. "God, I'm sorry."

"I'm kidding, Mayb." He shakes his head and sits in the chair beside my bed. "I'm relieved that you're okay. I was pretty worried about you. We all were, actually."

"Sounds like I created quite the scene at your reception."

"Don't worry about it." He waves me off with a nonchalant hand. "Plus, it was nice that you waited to have a medical emergency until after we cut the cake."

I laugh, but the movement causes discomfort in my stomach. "Ow, don't make me laugh, you jerk."

He grins. "Sorry, sis."

"Liar."

He shrugs.

I'm just about to open my mouth with another apology when realization hits me square in the nose. "Oh no!" I exclaim. "You're supposed to be at the airport right now. Headed to flipping Hawaii! What the hell?"

"Calm down." He reaches out to put a reassuring hand on mine. "We were able to adjust our flights, and we'll be heading out tomorrow afternoon."

I frown. "Shit, Ev. I'm so sorry."

"You have nothing to apologize for. Both Sadie and I are just happy you're okay."

All I can do is nod. Because what else can I say? I mean, hell's bells, I really screwed up their wedding night.

"So...do you have anything else you want to say to me...?" Evan pauses, and I narrow my eyes.

294

"Shit, Ev. How long do you want my apology to be? I mean, if you're expecting me to get on my knees and grovel, you've got another thing coming, buddy."

A soft chuckle leaves his lungs. "That's not what I'm talking about, sis."

I tilt my head to the side.

"I had a nice long chat with Milo last night..."

Oh boy.

"And...he really unloaded some quite shocking news on me."

Ah *fuck*. Nothing makes you forget how to form words faster than your big brother finding out you've been very *friendly* with his best friend...

"You mind telling me what's going on between you two?"

"Well..." I cringe. "I'm not sure you want me to tell you *too* much..."

It all feels very NSFW to me. Or is it NSFB in this situation? Whatever it is, I'm not feeling too keen on giving him any of the gory details.

"Pretty sure I can take it." Evan grins. "I mean, I already had a chance to take my anger out on Milo and had a night to sleep on it, so consider me cool as a cucumber at this point."

"Take your anger out on Milo?" I question. "What are you talking about?"

"I might have punched him."

"Might have punched him, or you did punch him?"

He shrugs. "Minor details."

"Jesus, Ev! You're a lunatic!"

"Calm down, I didn't punch him *that* hard. And you're going to have to cut me a little slack here," he retorts. "It's not every day a guy finds out his best friend is in love with his little sister."

My jaw falls into my lap. "What did you just say?"

"You heard me."

"No," I refute. "I'm pretty sure you have the details all wrong, Ev."

He shakes his head. "How long have you known me?"

I roll my eyes. "As long as I've been alive."

"Do you *really* think I have the details wrong?"

I start to disagree with him again, even though I know he's the most detail oriented person I've ever met, but he doesn't give me any time.

"He's been here all night, you know," he continues. "Worried sick about you. Practically pacing the linoleum off the waiting room floor."

Milo is here? At the hospital? *Still?*

"And just so we're clear, I got the details, *the facts*, from him," he adds with the slightest hint of a smile. "He's the one who told me how he feels about you. I guess if there's any friend of mine I'd want to take care of my little sister, it'd be that fucking bastard," Evan mutters, but I'm too lost in my own thoughts to even hear what he's saying.

Milo is in love with me?

Chapter
FORTY-ONE

Milo

At a little after nine, I see Evan and Sadie off in the hospital lobby, wish them a safe flight and happy honeymoon, and head back up to the fifth floor to see Maybe.

While Evan chatted with her in her room, I went down to the cafeteria to grab a coffee and a donut. My neck and back are stiff and I slept like shit last night in the crappy chair beside Maybe's bed, but if I could do it all over again, I wouldn't change a damn thing.

There was no way I was going to leave her side.

By the time I reach her room, I gently push open the closed door and step inside to find a sight that has me both grinning and holding back laughter.

Maybe stands beside her hospital bed, one hand on her IV pole, the other hand reaching across the mattress to grab something off the bedside table. Her hospital gown is pushed forward toward her belly, and her cute little ass is bare and completely visible to my amused eyes.

She turns around and, instantly, her cheeks turn red.

"Shit," she mutters and tries like hell to grip the hospital gown to hide what's already been seen.

"It's too late for that," I tease and step toward her to offer a helping hand. "Also, I can't deny I quite enjoyed the view."

She huffs out a sigh as I hand her the cell phone.

"Thank you."

"You're welcome."

It takes her a minute to get adjusted back on the bed, her ass firmly and purposefully planted right on the mattress, and I take a seat in the chair beside her bed.

"You good now?"

"About as good and as awkward as I'm going to get." She snorts, but then her face falls when she looks directly at me. "Oh my God, Milo! Your eye."

Yeah. It's red and already bruised around the edges; my buddy Evan definitely delivered with that punch. Directly into my left eye, that is. No doubt, I'll have this shiner for a good week.

"It's fine." I wave it off and focus the conversation on the most important thing—*her*. "How are you feeling?"

"Better," she says, and her voice drops to a near whisper. "Thank you for taking care of me last night. For getting me here. For staying here. Just...thank you."

"I didn't want to be anywhere else."

Those chocolate eyes of hers search my gaze, but she doesn't say anything.

And that's fine by me. I have enough to say for the both of us.

"We have a lot to talk about."

"We do?"

Like she doesn't know we have a lot to talk about...

"You said you loved me," I say, and her eyes go wide.

"What?"

"Last night. In this very room. You said you loved me."

"I...uh..." She stumbles over her words, but I willingly let her off the hook.

"I love you too, Maybe."

She bites her teeth into her bottom lip. "You do?"

"I do."

A smile kisses her lips, but as fast as it appears, it's gone. "Oh God." She groans. "This isn't how it's supposed to go."

"How what's supposed to go?"

"The big romantic ending," she explains. "Like in movies. It's supposed to be this big thing with, like, rain and shit. Not bad appendixes and surgery and IV tubing."

I want to laugh. "Does it really matter?"

"No. I guess not." She shrugs one annoyed shoulder. "I mean, I would've preferred the rain or like a rainbow or something, but I guess the Jell-O is at least multicolored."

I actually laugh this time.

But then I lean forward, gently lift her into my lap, and press my lips to hers.

She wraps her arms around my neck, smiles against my mouth, and I don't hesitate to deepen the kiss a bit, slipping my tongue past her lips and letting her know I mean every fucking word I've said.

"I love you, kid," I say again, staring deep into her eyes and putting a hand to the side of her face. "That night at your apartment, I didn't stop things because I didn't want to be with you. I *more* than wanted to be with you. I am in love with you. I didn't want to have sex. I wanted to make love, and that couldn't happen until we both had our feelings for each other sorted out."

"You handled it terribly," she says and then adds, "But I did too."

"We both did."

"You really love me?"

"I definitely love you."

"I love you too." She presses a kiss to my mouth. "I just have one final question."

I smirk. "And what's that?"

"Deflower me, please?"

A cheeky little smirk lifts the corners of her mouth, and I laugh.

I'm going to do more than that. One day, I'm going to marry you, kid.

Epilogue

Maybe
Four weeks later...

Between my mom and Milo fussing over me after my surgery, my first official day at Beacon House, and more of Milo and Betty fussing, four weeks have flown by like the damn wind.

But stitches and pain meds and an appendectomy aside, it's been the best month of my life.

Milo and I are official. An us. A we. A *sure-fucking-thing*.

And my first day at Beacon House was more than I could have imagined.

I am Maybe Willis, junior editor at one of the biggest publishing houses in the industry.

I have my own office. My own desk. My own flipping stapler.

Hell, I even have a sign on my door *with my freaking name on it*.

I am legit. The real deal.

And Bruce was worried my degree in books wouldn't get me anywhere. As if.

I spot an open seat on the subway and plop my ass down. Eight hours in these brand-new heels proved to be a test in real strength and my feet complained the whole damn day, but I wouldn't change a thing.

There was no way I was going to show up for my first official day on the job and look anything but fabulous. I'll deal with the blisters later.

The subway jolts and whines as it heads up the tracks, and I pull my phone out of my purse to find a text message from Milo.

Instantly, I smile like the lovesick idiot I am.

Goddamn, everything really came up roses.

Milo: Where in the hell are you, kid? I have three bags of Mexican takeout sitting here waiting for you.

When I left his apartment this morning, he made me promise to come back home—*yes, he said home*—to his place after work so I could tell him all about my day and he could feed me takeout from my favorite restaurant.

Me: If there aren't crunchy tacos and chips and salsa, I'm not coming.

Milo: That's cute, smartass. What's your ETA?

I glance up to see his apartment is now only one stop away.

Me: Ten minutes, tops. Your stop is the next stop.

Milo: Pretty sure you mean YOUR stop is the next stop.

I furrow my brow in confusion.

Me: But I'm coming to YOUR place...

Milo: Exactly. And by the end of the night, I'm going to convince you to move out of Evan's old apartment and become my permanent roommate.

Me: Is this your clever way of asking me to move in with you?

Milo: If I say yes, is it working?

The subway begins to slow down, and I glance up to see we've arrived at my stop.

Me: Hold that thought. I'm getting off the subway now.

Off the train, through the evening rush of people, I head up the stairs and onto the sidewalk.

And when I catch my reflection in the window of an expensive chocolate shop, I don't miss the stupid grin that is apparently permanently tattooed on my face now.

Holy moly. I'm a loon. A happy, in-love, fucking loon.

I wave to Gill when he opens the lobby door of Milo's building and briefly chat with him about his wife and kids while I wait for the elevator.

"Have a good night, Ms. Willis," he says as I step onto the waiting cart.

"You too, Gill." I smile, and he taps in the code for the penthouse level. "Oh, and next time you see Milo, don't forget to give him shit for the Yankees losing last night."

"Will do." His responding chuckles follow me several floors up.

When the doors open, Milo is standing there, bare feet, jeans, and a simple white T-shirt.

God, he's handsome.

"Took you long enough, kid," he teases, and I drop my bags and stride right out of the elevator and jump up into his arms.

"Well, hello there," he says through a shocked laugh as I wrap my legs around his waist. "What do I—"

With my mouth to his, I cut him off completely.

It takes a second or two for him to understand what I'm putting down here, but eventually, he does. He deepens the kiss, slipping his tongue into my mouth, and before I know it, he turns on his bare feet and has my back pressed up against the wall.

302

Oh yes, please.

I moan against his lips, and he doesn't disappoint.

His hands grip my ass, and I can feel his growing arousal against me.

Yes. Yes. Yes.

I'm desperate for him. My body damn near shaking with need. And I try like hell to convince him we need to relocate so I can remove all of his stupid clothes.

"To the bedroom," I say through a moan. "Take us to the bedroom."

"Always in such a rush." He smiles against my mouth. "And I think you've forgotten about the food."

"Fuck the food."

He laughs. "Fuck the food?"

"Yes." The impatience in my voice is more than obvious. "Forget about the food and take me to your bedroom."

He presses his arousal against me. "And what exactly are we going to do in *our* bedroom?"

"Get naked. Get..." I pause and lean back to meet his eyes. "Hold up. Did you just say *our* bedroom?"

"That's exactly what I said."

"So, you were serious?" I question. "You really want me to move in with you?"

"Maybe..." His blue eyes search mine. "I'm in love with you, kid. And when I see my future, I see you and me, *together*. I see us waking up together. And I see us going to bed together at night. I want and need you to move in with me."

If my heart grew any bigger inside my chest, it might start cracking ribs.

"I'm in love with you too," I whisper, and emotion starts to clog my throat. "And I want that future too."

Literally the future I've always dreamed of...

"Well then, what are we waiting for?" he questions and leans forward to kiss my lips softly. "Let's start our future right now. Tonight."

"Wait...does this mean you're finally going to deflower me?"

"No, kid." His lips crest up into a giant fucking smile. "This means I'm going to marry you."

He's going to marry me? Holy wedding bells, I'm so in.

"You are?"

He nods. "I am."

I tilt my head to the side, narrowing my eyes and using the opportunity to tease him a bit. "Don't I get a say in this? It's not the eighteenth century, you know," I say and rub my nose against his. "Arranged marriages aren't a thing anymore. Ole Bruce isn't going to sell me off for some kind of bridal dowry. And I sure as shit don't want to lose my virginity on my wedding night."

He quirks a teasing brow. "Is that right?"

"That's a certainty."

"Well, then I guess we have some things to accomplish before I get down on one knee, huh?"

I snort. "You bet your tight ass, we do."

He laughs the whole way toward the bedroom, and once we step inside the master, he tosses me onto the mattress. My ass bounces softly against the plush material, and Milo stares down at me like I'm his favorite fucking meal.

Oh, hell yes.

"Before I have my wicked way with you," he says and takes off his T-shirt. "You're moving in with me?"

"Yes."

He grins and removes his jeans and boxer briefs.

Then it's my turn to grin. I also lick my lips because...Milo's cock is *right there.* Bared for my greedy eyes.

"And you're going to deflower me," I state.

"Uh-huh." He crawls onto the bed, and I watch in rapt fascination as he removes my stilettos and my skirt and my panties.

By the time he starts to unbutton my blouse, my nipples are hard and I'm clenching my thighs.

"But not right now," he adds, moving the rest of the way up my body.

Wait...*what?*

"Not right now?" I question. "What in the hell does that mean?"

He smirks and leans forward to suck one pert nipple into his mouth. I moan when he circles his tongue around it. *Boy oh boy, can this man play me like I'm his own personal instrument.*

He releases it with a soft pop and moves the rest of the way up my body until we're completely skin-on-skin, our eyes locked and our lips just inches from each other. "It means soon. But not right now."

I frown. I can't help it. I'm ready for the deflowering.

Milo, put your P in my V kind of all in.

"There's no need to pout, kid. I can guarantee you're going to love what's in store for you."

I start to ask him what that means, but by the time the words are on the tip of my tongue, Milo's moved down my body until his face is between my now-spread thighs.

Oh. So, that's what he means...

"Double pleasure?" he asks with a cheeky grin, and I roll my eyes.

"You're never going to let me live that down, are you?"

He shakes his head and reaches out to place one long lick against me.

Holy moly.

"But I'm sure you don't mind since I'm planning on spending a lot of time down here. Taking my time. Tasting and savoring this perfect pussy."

Well, who can get upset after that?

Not this girl.

"By all means, proceed."

And he does. Milo pro-fucking-ceeds to give me all the damn pleasure I can handle.

Milo

After I played with Maybe all night, making her moan and tremble and come against my tongue and around my fingers, she fell into a deep sleep on our bed. Naked, a teeny smile on her lips, and her chest softly rising and falling as cute little snores escaped her nose. I watched for a good hour before I finally left her to sleep in peace and headed into my home office to finish up some work that was too important to let go another day.

And I'm not talking Fuse kind of work.

But something else. Something even more important.

Something that is one-hundred-percent related to that beautiful sleeping goddess in my bed.

Well, *our* bed, actually. Mine and Maybe's.

As of tonight, I've convinced her to move in with me.

And next month, I'm going to take it one step further.

I'm going to ask her to marry me.

It might seem a little fast to some, but to me, it's not fast enough.

That woman is my world, the rest of my life, and I'll be damned if I'm going to waste any more time diving straight into our forever. Marriage. Babies. The whole-fucking-shebang. I want it all, and I want it with Maybe.

Hell, I'll even move to the suburbs, get the white picket fence, and strap our future kid in one of those Baby Bjorns around my chest if that's what will make her happy.

I grin at the mental image that conjures as I click to open the one email I've been waiting on.

To: Milo Ives
From: Dave Wilson
Milo,

The ring will be ready by Monday.
Your design turned out damned beautiful.
I've attached a photo below for you to see for yourself.
Don't hesitate to call my cell if you need anything.
Sincerely,
Dave Wilson
Infinity Diamonds
New York, New York

I click to open the photo, and the sight of it has me mentally patting myself on the back and grinning like a lovesick son of a bitch.

In the center of the photo sits a twisted pavé rose-gold band with the most exquisite pale pink diamond in the center. *Goddamn.* Dave was right. It's beautiful.

That pink is Maybe's favorite color, *and* per Lena's discreet advice, it's the exact color of my girl's aura—*whatever the fuck that means.*

The instant Dave showed me that diamond, I knew it was the one.

And once I secured Bruce Willis's approval, I set the wheels of my proposal into motion.

Next month, we're going to head to Austin for a four-day weekend, and I've already convinced Taylor McHough to give Maybe the time off.

She's going to think it's a last-minute Fuse business trip.

But I know better.

And so does Evan.

Less than thirty days and she'll be my fiancée.

And then, she'll be my wife.

I shoot Dave a quick email, thanking him for his help, and let him know I'll see him Monday.

Just before I dive into the next order of business, making sure my assistant Clara finalized all of our Austin trip plans, the sounds of footsteps moving down the hall give me pause.

I look up from my laptop to find Maybe standing in the doorway, completely bare, and on primal fucking instinct, my eyes turn hungry. Greedy. Damn ravenous for her.

I can't help it. When it comes to Maybe, I'm certain I'll never stop craving her.

She tiptoes into my office, walks around my desk, and I turn my chair to meet her.

She stops when her knees barely brush mine.

Her long brown locks hang past her full, pert breasts, and her eyes are so damn sweet and doe-like, they might as well be a live wire to my cock.

Fuck. She is sexy.

"Milo," she whispers my name, and I don't miss the way her teeth bite into her bottom lip or the way her thighs tremble as she fidgets underneath my gaze.

"What do you need, kid?" I ask her, but she doesn't respond.

She just looks at me with those big brown eyes of hers and traps me in their never-ending depths.

"Maybe?" I prompt again. "What do you need?"

"You." One word. Three letters. And powerful enough to make my cock harden and twitch beneath my boxer briefs. "Right now."

Déjà vu hits me like a fucking freight train, and it's like my fantasies have come to life.

And just like my dreams, I don't hesitate to give her what she wants.

Between one breath and the next, I'm on my feet and she's in my arms with her legs wrapped my waist.

My lips to hers, I kiss her deep as I walk out of my office, down the hall, and into our bedroom.

"I need you, Milo," she whispers into my ear. "I can't wait any longer. I need you inside me."

Fuck.

Before I know it, we're on my bed, Maybe beneath me and my boxer briefs a distant fucking memory on the floor.

My cock is at her entrance, the tip sliding through her wetness, and I groan at the painfully delicious feel of it.

God, I love her. I want her. I fucking *need* her too.

"Please," she begs. "Please make love to me." Her hips gyrate from side to side, and that movement pushes the head of my cock inside her.

She is so soft. So warm. So wet. So tight. So *perfect.*

She moans, and a deep guttural groan escapes my lungs.

The urge to push my cock in deeper is so strong, it makes my thighs shake, but I force a breath into my lungs instead. This is her first time. This needs to be slow. She needs time to adjust to my size.

"Yes. More. Please," she pleads, and her fingers slide into my hair, tugging on the strands with frustration. "I can't wait any longer to know what it feels like to have you inside me. Please, please, *please,* Milo. Make love to me."

Fuck. I'm done for. Powerless against her.

"I need to put on a condom," I whisper against her lips, but she starts shaking her head.

"No," she refutes and gently bites her teeth into my bottom lip. "No condom. Just you. Just you and me with nothing in between us."

My cock twitches at her words, but that bastard needs to wait.

I search the depths of her eyes. "Baby, are you sure?"

"I'm on birth control." She nods and wraps her legs tighter around my waist as her hips start up a rhythm again. "Please, Milo. Slide inside me."

I can't resist her anymore. Not for even a second longer.

I'm going to slide inside her and make her mine.

I'm going to *make love to her.*

Slowly, so slowly, I had no idea I had it in me, I slide my cock inside the perfect heat of her tight pussy. Inch by inch, stopping every so often to let her adjust to me.

When my cock is halfway inside her, a little whimper leaves her lips and a wrinkle forms between her brows. *Fuck. I don't want to hurt her.*

I start to pull back out, but she refuses, wrapping her legs around my waist again.

"More," she whispers, and her tongue sneaks out to lick across her bottom lip. "It's so intense, but God, it feels so good, Milo. Because it's you. It feels so good, so perfect, because it's you and me together."

Fuck.

I keep going, slowly sliding more of my cock inside her, and she just keeps begging, pleading for more.

If she's in pain, she doesn't show it. She is still staring deep into my eyes and telling me she wants more, that she needs more.

When I'm all the way inside her, as deep as I can go, I stop and let myself *feel* her.

And I never move my gaze away from hers.

I savor the moment. Imprint it onto my memory.

This is the moment I made her mine.

The first time I made love to Maybe.

I will never, for the rest of my life, forget this moment.

Not the way she feels. Or the way her brown eyes deepen with need.

Not the words she says or the way her thighs tremble.

And certainly not the way I feel.

I will *always* remember this.

"I love you," I whisper and brush my lips against hers. "More than anything in this world."

"I love you too," she whispers, and one small tear escapes her lids. "And I love making love with you."

In this moment, I'm more certain than I've ever been.

More in love than I've ever been.

My heart is hers, and I'm going to marry this girl.

I'm going to marry her and spend the rest of my life making love to her.

THE END

A (unauthorized) Note from Caplin Hawkins:
Well, ladies...
This is it. The time we've all been waiting for.
I, Caplin Hawkins, man of female dreams and lawyer extraordinaire, am getting a book.
A book all about me.
Sure, Trent Turner and Milo Ives have charm and swoon-factor and a whole bunch of other boring shit, but I think we can all agree I'm the main event, right?
I have so many surprises up my sleeves, so many ways to entertain you that you can't even fathom. I've trained and hydrated, and I'm ready.
It's time to show Max and Monroe that I can't be tamed.
I can't wait for us to get to know one another better.

But, in the meantime, if you have some time to kill and you haven't read anything about Trent Turner in the first stand-alone book in the *Billionaire Collection*, you need to get on that shit.
While the main plot of **The Billionaire Boss Next Door** is about my buddy Trent and his wildly funny leading lady, Greer Hudson, it's also—and most importantly—about me.
Max and Monroe didn't really give me enough stage time to fully spread my wings, but I think you'll agree my role in their love story gives a substantial glimpse into my star potential.
I mean, you be the judge. Give it a read to decide.
But if you've already read about Trent, don't despair. There are a few more mediocre substitutes for me out there.
If you want to start at the beginning, grab the first book in the *Billionaire Bad Boys Series* and see for yourself if you can understand what all the hype is about. If nothing else, it'll be really clear how right you were to love me most when you read my book.

Anyway, I promise it's finally time for us to really spend some time together.

Get all kinds of up close and personal, if you know what I'm sayin'.

Yeah. Come September 12th, my beautiful ladies, we're going to be, as little Miss Maybe would put it, *friendly*.

Sincerely,
The Cap-i-tain of your heart,
Cap

Love Milo and Maybe and ready for more from Max Monroe?

Well, we've got news for you!

More *stand-alone* romantic comedies are coming this year as a part of our new Billionaire Collection!

You WILL NOT believe the laughs you have coming for you!

Like that bastard Cap said, our next release is September 12th, and he has it all wrong.

Mark your calendar so you don't miss the taming of his wild ways. ;)

Want more from Max Monroe RIGHT NOW but have already read about ALL the billionaires?

Don't worry, girl, we've got you covered!

If you're in the mood for some sweet, sexy, swoony, downright hilarious Rom Com and Sports Romance, we know just the books for you!

Our *Mavericks Tackle Love Series*! Trust us, you don't want to miss meeting these sexy football studs if you haven't met them already.

Mavericks Tackle Love Series **Reading Order:**
Wildcat
Pick Six
Trick Play
4th & Girl

Stay up-to-date with our characters and us by signing up for our newsletter: www.authormaxmonroe.com/newsletter

You may live to regret much, but we promise it won't be this.

Seriously, we make it fun!

Character conversations about royal babies, parenting woes, embarrassing moments, and shitty horoscopes are just the beginning!

If you're already signed up, consider sending us a message to tell us how much you love us. We really like that. ;)

Follow us online:
Facebook: www.facebook.com/authormaxmonroe
Reader Group: www.facebook.com/groups/1561640154166388
Twitter: www.twitter.com/authormaxmonroe
Instagram: www.instagram.com/authormaxmonroe
Goodreads: https://goo.gl/8VUIz2

Acknowledgments

First of all, THANK YOU for reading. That goes for anyone who's bought a copy, read an ARC, helped us beta, edited, or found time in their busy schedule just to make sure we didn't completely drop the ball by being late and for tolerating all of our awkward and hilarious Maybe-style commentary inside our emails and Google Docs. Thank you for supporting us, for talking about our books, and for just being so unbelievably loving and supportive of our characters. You've made this our MOST favorite adventure thus far.

THANK YOU to each other. Monroe is thanking Max. Max is thanking Monroe. *Blah, blah, blah.* We do this in every book, but we don't care. We are so grateful for each other and this awesome journey that is writing together. Cheers to many more hilarious books!

THANK YOU, Lisa, our editor. Our main squeeze. Our number one lady. You're reading *and* editing this right now, and for that, we are thankful. It boggles the mind that two girls can still send you a manuscript with the word blond spelled two different ways (but seriously, which is right? Blond or blonde?) AND have the word fuck in it over 350 times. But here's to hoping by the time we hit publish, all those fucks are a little less, and we understand which blond is the right blonde.

THANK YOU, Stacey, for making the insides of our book look so much prettier than organs. And for acting like you don't hate us when we email you with a formatting date that is only a few weeks away. ☺

THANK YOU, JoAnna & Sandra, for being superior Counselor Feathers. You ladies amaze us on a daily basis, and you are the reason

Camp Love Yourself is the coolest place to be. I think we can all agree you do a better job at running it than we do. ;)

THANK YOU, Banana, for rocking our covers. And for spending lots of time covering nipples and enhancing crotches when we ask you to. It's a tough job, but somebody's got to do it.

THANK YOU, Social Butterfly PR, for doing So. Many. Things. *All* the damn things. We simply adore you, and we're not sure if you have figured this out yet, but Jenn, you're never allowed to break up with us. We're basically married now. Welcome to our forever.

THANK YOU to every blogger who has read, reviewed, posted, shared, and supported us. Your enthusiasm, support, and hard work do not go unnoticed.

THANK YOU to the people who love us—our family. They support us, motivate us, and most importantly, tolerate us. Sometimes we're not the easiest people to live with, especially when there is a deadline looming. We honestly don't know what we'd do without you guys. PS: You don't know what you'd do without us either, so suck it.

THANK YOU to our Camp members! You guys make us smile every day! Especially when we pop into Camp when we're supposed to be doing something else like finishing a book. We can't help it. We just love y'all so much.

As always, all our love.
XOXO,
Max Monroe